A most
IMPROPER
DUCHESS

ALIVIA FLEUR

SPENCER & CO
PUBLISHING

A catalogue record for this work is available from the National Library of Australia.

Cover design by Evelynne Labelle at Carpe Librum Book Design
www.carpelibrumbookdesign.com

For Sidekick Sophie
I could write something profound,
about how much teachers learn from their students,
and how one of the greatest joys of my career has been
watching you evolve from being my mentee to my colleague.
But that might sound a bit sappy and corny.
So instead, I'll say,
I've got a bottle of prosecco in the fridge. Come round on the
weekend. I'll bung on a roast, and we'll cheers the new book.
PS bring a salad.

Welcome to Honeysuckle street

In a quiet corner of London, on the north side of the river, is a little street called Honeysuckle Street.

Don't bother looking for it now—you won't find it on any map. But once, before progress was the catchword of the day, Honeysuckle Street cut a treelined path between two main thoroughfares. The street itself could comfortably accommodate two carriages passing by one another. The residents spent their days in each other's company, or spotted one another on walks, or attended balls and gatherings together. A few errant children played games, and the odd elderly neighbour watched from behind twitching curtains, muttering about *young people these days*.

An enterprising developer had purchased the entire row on the north side of the street, cleared it and erected in its place five terrace townhouses. Five stories high, modelled on the Belgrave style and as similar on the outside as they were on the inside, which is to say, apart from the inhabitants, they were identical.

Five villas, each four or five stories high lined the opposite side of the street, mostly built at some stage during the reigns of the past kings named George.

And king of it all was a grey cat with a white-tipped tail named Spencer.

Spencer lived at number 6, the house in the middle of the street on the south side. It was rumoured that the old lady who occupied the house had been a lover of the Russian Tsar. Others said she had made and lost several fortunes in the American West. Others said that she had scrimped every penny she earned as a washerwoman and made a sensible investment during the last financial downturn. No one knew for sure. She didn't receive callers. She didn't make house calls.

She passed her time in the company of her beloved cats. At the end of each day, she stood on the porch and called them in. 'Mittens! Georgiana! Jimmy! Spencer! And no matter if they were curled up in the last ray of sun, or stalking along a limb, the little cats would run at the sound of her voice.

All except Spencer.

When he didn't return home, the old lady would wander the streets, calling and calling, 'Spencer! Spencer! Time for tea!' Later, when her hearing faded, she took to banging a pot with a spoon. When it suited him, Spencer would emerge, saunter his way to the house in the middle of the street, where the old lady would scald him but later, when sat by the fire, Spencer was still allowed to curl up and sleep on her lap.

When the old lady died, and unable to locate an heir, the authorities boarded up the old house. The furniture was pilfered. And after applying at kitchen doors, the kittens found new homes.

All except Spencer.

Spencer continued to patrol his street, hunting mice and chasing away noisier, bossier toms who might encroach on his territory. In return, the residents of Honeysuckle Street would find a scrap for him. Miss Delaney's cook left him the joint from the roast on Sunday. Miss Hartright put out a saucer of cream each night after her aunt had turned in. Mr Babbage put out a slice of cold ham, and not to be outdone, Mr Hempel left out two. The Caplin care-taker snuck him a biscuit, and in the evening, Miss Abberton left the downstairs window ajar so that he could squeeze himself inside and curl up by the furnace, even though he always managed to get by cook and took the best chair in the parlour instead.

Each morning and evening, Spencer sat on the decaying porch of the house in the middle of the street, silently surveying his charges. He kept watch on their comings and goings, their petty feuds and their longing looks over fences. He knew them all, sometimes better than they knew themselves.

Welcome to Honeysuckle Street.

Who lives on Honeysuckle Street?

February 1876
Number 1
Phineas Babbage, Bank Clerk
Number 2
Odette Delaney, Soprano
Number 3
Lawrence and Wilhelmina Hempel, Hotel Magnates
and their children:
Rosanna
Johannes
Elliot
Beatrice
Garnett (deceased)
Amadeus
Nova
Ottile
Thaddeus
Number 4
Albert Abberton, retired
Lord Hamish Dalton, heir to Earl Caplin
Lady Iris Dalton, Director of Spencer and Co Travel

Number 5
Mrs Crofts, President of the Society for the Promotion of Civic Morality and the Adherence to Proper Values
Number 6
Vacant block mostly inhabited by Spencer, King of Honeysuckle Street
Number 7
Petunia Hartright, choir leader
Elise Hartright, assistant to Lady Iris Dalton
Number 8
Dalton family town residence, currently being renovated for Spencer and Co Travel
Number 9
Benton Hunter, Diplomat, currently abroad
Number 10
His Grace Arley West, Duke Osborne

CHAPTER ONE

8 March 1876

Meetings at Lords were never like this.

Fundraiser committees weren't like this.

The Ilex Rowing Club Annual General Meeting wasn't like this.

Arley didn't think there were *any* meetings in all of London quite like those held for Spencer and Co Travel.

'Phineas and Lawrence. If we could please focus on the agenda.' Lady Iris Dalton tapped at the list on the table before her. Her voice held her crisp, no-nonsense timbre, but Arley could feel her stamina waning. Or maybe that was just himself.

Further down the table, Phineas Babbage leaned back in his chair, arms crossed, a slightly smug grin tugging at one corner of his mouth. Lawrence Hempel, sitting opposite, had half stood and leaned in as if about to give Phineas a well-deserved wallop.

'He started it,' Lawrence snapped, sounding as petulant as one of his many children.

Arley tried to shoot Phineas a look to say, *must you*, but Phineas determinedly avoided his glare.

'You have five minutes. I have rehearsal,' Odette Delaney, soprano, announced. Arley shot a look at the clock. The meeting was meant to have finished over half an hour ago.

He gritted his teeth, then forced his jaw to relax. Last summer, he'd become an investor in the travel company formed by Iris. She'd worked secretly with her adoptive father, Albert, at his trading company for years, even taking over when he became ill and his memory began to fade. But when her father's decline had become known, the board of Abberton and Co had unceremoniously removed them both from the company. For Iris, her work was like air, and in a show of neighbourly comradery, the street had bound together to invest in Spencer and Co, her idea for a travel company providing bespoke and boutique tours for the middle classes. At the time, he had rather liked the idea, and Iris was more than competent enough to see it through. But he hadn't envisaged regular meetings, and he hadn't expected them to be so chaotic. Having to undertake the actual work, the affability of that afternoon had faded as quickly as the plate of biscuits that had been set before Iris's husband Hamish.

'Iris!'

Iris shuffled her papers and cleared her throat. 'As I was saying, the current list of itineraries covers short samplers to appeal to couples, but we'd like to offer—'

'Iris!' Closer now, the voice of Albert Abberton bounced down the hall. Iris looked down, blinking fast.

'Hamish, would you take over?' She pushed back her chair and darted from the room. Hamish had been staring out the window. He shook himself to alertness and shuffled the papers in front of him.

'As Iris was saying...' His eyes skated the page. 'Errrr...'

Arley internalised a frustrated breath. Hamish was many admirable things, but astute businessperson was not one of them. That moniker belonged to his wife, who had also taken the remaining shreds of calm with her when she left.

'The park is looking fresh already.' Phineas half turned to Odette. 'Don't you agree, Miss Delaney?'

'No one is interested in your view of the park,' Lawrence snapped.

'I wasn't speaking to you,' Phineas drawled.

Young Elise Hartright, Iris's assistant, tapped her fingers together. 'We really must continue with the agenda.'

Lawrence's daughter Rosanna toyed with a bracelet on her wrist.

'Two minutes,' Odette said, half standing. 'Covent Garden does not wait.'

Chatter, barbs and excuses. All of them swirled around the room, each one echoing louder than the one before. The grey tom with the white tipped tail leapt onto the table and skidded across the polished wood. The teapot rattled, milk spilled and splashed onto the floor. Sugar cubes scattered, and everyone gathered up their papers to stop them from becoming soaked. The cat lapped at the milk.

There was only one thing for it. Arley inhaled, broadened his shoulders, and found the necessary tone, the one he had started working on when he turned 6 and had mastered by the time he was twelve. His *duke* tone.

'Can we please focus on the task at hand?' His voice cut the raucousness, and the settling silence formed into a bubble that surrounded him, always, in everything he did.

Never raise your voice, but don't be meek. Never lower your gaze, but eschew condescension. Fill the space. Don't impose. Always, always remember who you are.

Dukes led, they commanded, they directed. Even here, around the table where Iris had insisted all votes and opinions were of equal weight, being a duke inspired a special type of respect.

Odette pushed back her chair with a look at the clock. Arley frowned. She settled. No one was going anywhere until this was done.

'Elise, the last item please?' he said.

'It's an idea for a tour,' Elise stammered. 'We're calling it a mini-grand tour.'

Phineas snuffled a laugh. 'Do you hear the contradiction?'

'It's an excellent idea,' Lawrence said.

'You haven't even heard what it is,' Phineas snapped.

'If you think it rubbish, it's likely excellent.'

'I never said—'

'Gentleman!' Iris, eyes weary, shoulders sagging, leaned against the door frame. Hamish pushed himself from the table and drew her against his side for just a little longer than was appropriate, before helping her settle into her seat at the head of the table. 'It's intended as a microcosm of the tour,' Iris said, her words drawn. 'A week in Paris, for the family who wishes to give a son or daughter a taste of the culture of the continent but cannot stretch to multiple locations or years of gallivanting around. A concert or two, rather than a year in Austria. A few famous paintings, rather than every masterpiece. Enough French to get by, over fluency. A taste of music, art, language, food... and whatever else you gents get up to when you go abroad to *culture* yourselves.'

It seemed unfair that she narrowed her gaze on him. Like everything he did, his tour had been very measured. How could it not have been, when he'd been accompanied by a minder and his itinerary had been packed with meetings with city officials?

'I was hoping someone would travel to Paris and put together a list of places. When I was there last year, parts of the city were still rubble as buildings were destroyed during the war and the Siege. Construction was only just getting underway. But every newspaper report I read speaks of a city reborn. There are likely new sights. I want to know what they are so that we can stay ahead of our competitors.'

Phineas looked at Arley. Odette looked at him, too.

'Perhaps someone with experience in what a grand tour is would be an excellent candidate. Then they could make comparisons to inform the advertising and even be a spokesperson for it. They could reassure potential clients that it's a sensible investment in their child's education,' Iris continued.

Lawrence. Elise. Rosanna. Even the blasted cat, sat on the window ledge, seemed to shift his attention from the milk jug to Arley.

'There is no time to co-ordinate such a trip,' Arley said.

'I've already planned it!' Elise leapt from her seat and pushed a folder before him. 'If you leave the day after tomorrow, you can get the train to Dover, then a steamer. You'll connect at Calais...'

Arley looked at the ceiling as Elise ran through the itinerary. 'The House returns in a little over a month. I need to prepare. I really cannot—'

'Please, your grace,' Iris said, her eyes damp with tears. 'Phineas cannot obtain leave from the bank, and Lawrence and Rosanna will not leave Wilhelmina so close to her confinement.'

'What about—'

'Odette has rehearsals.'

'And—'

'Elise is far too young, and she keeps so much together. And before you suggest it,' Iris continued, 'I cannot go. Papa remembers less each day.' All her assertion faded, and instead, was replaced with quiet grief. 'He barely recognises Mr Rogers, and even sometimes forgets Gena, who has been with us the longest. I'm the only one who can keep him calm. If I go, and he forgets me, he'll have no one. I would send Hamish, but I need him. I feel selfish, but I would crumble if he left. If I could split myself into multiple pieces, I would, but I am just one woman. Would you take this on? I know Spencer and Co is one of many interests you have, but it means so much to us.'

'One problem. Paris is a little different when you're a duke.' He tried to keep his voice soft. He'd always liked Abberton. His deterioration was hard to witness, but harder still was its weight on Iris.

'You could go incognito,' Phineas drawled. 'At least try not telling people you're a duke all the time. Then you could experience the city like our clients might.'

Arley felt a sudden affinity with Lawrence, in that he could easily have leaned across the table and thumped Phineas. He didn't tell people he was a duke *all the time*. He didn't have to. They simply *knew*.

This is what happened from stepping out of his circle. From having associates.

'I'll give you one week,' he said as he closed the folder.

'I've booked two—'

'One!'

'Very well,' Elise said as she took back the papers. 'I'll change all your tickets. How exciting. One day, I'd love to go to Paris!'

Arley stood, buttoning his coat. 'It's highly overrated.'

Two days later, Arley stood in the foyer of his home at Number 10 Honeysuckle Street, waiting for his trunk to be loaded onto the carriage. He flipped through the stack of envelopes and cards piled on the sideboard. Cecil, his butler, had already dispensed with the silver tray that held his correspondence over the winter, and had replaced it with a low wooden box to better contain the pile and stop it from spilling onto the floor. Lady Harrington, Earl Brimford, Sir Stuart, Mr Fenway, the businessman... Men and women he barely knew. Who knew nothing of him, except for his first name... *duke*.

Arley extracted two letters—one from his estate manager and stepfather Tillman, the other, likely a request for funds from his bastard half-brother Winton—and tucked them into his pocket. He scooped up the rest of the stack as best he could and handed them to Cecil.

'Burn these,' he said.

Cecil wrung his hands. 'Your mother will be upset if you don't at least open them.'

'Then don't tell her.'

Cecil produced the same shocked expression he always did when Arley suggested he withhold information from Arley's mother. 'Your grace, I could never lie. Especially not to the duchess...' His hand wringing increased. With a huff, Arley tossed the stack of envelopes back into the box.

Of all the staff he could have brought with him from the estate to London, for reasons he could no longer remember, Arley had brought Cecil. Cecil served with devotion. He could not fault him that. It had even been from Cecil that he had learnt of his father's death. Arley, then five, had been in the nursery with the governess. In what he assumed was a melding of grief and duty, Cecil had announced, his voice heavy with emotion, 'Your grace, your mother requests you see her in her rooms.'

Arley shook his head to loosen the memory. Outside, the horses snickered. He was due at the station in a little over an hour. One of the staff opened the door and began hauling his trunk onto the boards.

He leafed through the letters again. 'Has Miss Hartright sent over the amended travel documents?'

'Not yet, your grace. I will go over there immediately.' Cecil made for the front door, but as he reached for the long brass handle, he half bent, rubbed at his lower back with an embarrassed smile, then continued forward at a hobble. 'Perhaps I shall send young Timothy?'

Arley checked his pocket watch. He kept a light staff—after all, it was only himself in the house—and if Timothy went, his case would still need to be loaded onto the carriage, and he'd be later than he already was. Trains waited for no man, not even dukes. 'I'll go. Tell him to bring the carriage round to Number 7. I'll leave from there.'

Cecil bowed as Arley left. '*Bon voyage*, your grace. Is that what the French say?'

A weak February sun strained against the grey clouds, and as Arley crossed the street, a cool gust bit his ankles. Despite his obstinance of a few days ago, a thrill dared to vibrate through him. What would Paris be like, as a mister?

The wall of five stucco clad townhouses shone bright against the overcast sky. The row had been constructed six or seven years before, and each house was built to an identical plan. Five stories high, the facade of the long row alternated between bay window and doorway, with a low fence delineating each connected residence. Elise lived with her Aunt Petunia in Number 7 and had done so since her older sister's scandal. Their bright pink front door gleamed like peach glace. They were forever changing its colour and altering the décor inside. Every decorator in London must have done work for them at some stage.

Arley ascended the short set of stairs and rapped the knocker.

'Pardon me, your grace, but I fear you have the wrong door.'

Arley sucked in a breath and looked across, past the window and to the landing of the neighbouring house. 'Good morning, Mrs Crofts. How are you today?'

'Much improved for having you attend one of our meetings. My ladies will be ever so thrilled to meet with you. They would love the opportunity to discuss matters of morality with our society's patron.'

He couldn't even blame alcohol, for it had been eleven in the morning, on his first day after relocating to London. Mrs Crofts had accosted him on his walk, introduced herself as the moral beacon of the street and asked him to be patron of her society. In a moment of confusion, 21-year-old Arley had stammered his agreement, and although he had never attended a meeting of the Society for the Promotion of Civic Morality and the Adherence to Proper Values, his name was still blazoned beneath their crest on the header of the newsletter she hand delivered each month.

Arley rapped on the door again. 'I am at the correct door, Mrs Crofts. Following up a matter with your neighbour.'

If he didn't know her to be such a nosey old biddy, he would have felt ashamed of himself for her visible disappointment. But as she had spread a rumour last summer that he would soon be engaged to her niece, despite having never met the woman, he instead felt a perverse burst of glee.

'Can we expect you at a meeting at Number 5 sometime soon?' she called.

At his feet, Spencer the cat sniffed his cuffs, and before Arley could shoo him away, he arched and smooched against his leg with one smooth movement, leaving a trail of grey fur in his wake. The door opened. Melody spilled out as the cat shot inside.

'Bloody feline.' He slapped at his leg before glancing up. Mrs Crofts' expression had gone from disappointed simpering to wide-eyed horror. Was she really so easily offended? 'I am a tad busy at this time. Perhaps after the season.' He looked at the man who had opened the door. 'Miss Hartright was going to send over some travel documents. Are they ready?'

'No idea,' replied the man.

With an awkward nod at a slightly flummoxed Mrs Crofts, Arley stepped into Number 7, relief exhaling from between his lips as the door closed behind him.

Arley didn't much need to call on the Misses Hartright, so didn't recognise the butler who had opened the door. Completely lacking in decorum, although groomed to the point of fastidiousness, he had a thin twisted moustache, slicked back black hair, dark sparkling eyes and wore the most horrendous coloured waistcoat Arley had ever seen.

'That woman could do with a right royal—'

'I'm looking for Elise,' Arley interrupted. He didn't need to imagine Mrs Crofts receiving a right royal anything. 'Is she here?'

'The Misses Hartright are organising a performance for their singing troupe. I have been asked to step in as baritone. They are in the sitting room, picking costumes. Follow me.'

A riot of pastel pink, with prints hung frame to frame, mismatched lampshades, and floral wallpaper flanked him as he walked down the hall. Trill laughter and light chatter served as an accompaniment to the visual onslaught, and while light, colour and cheer surrounded him, a warning twist in his stomach slowed his step. He willed his feet to stop, but somehow, Arley still found himself framed in the archway in full view of a very crowded sitting room.

Ladies. At least a dozen of them. Some fawning over bolts of cotton, others twirling a length of ribbon in the air.

Young ladies. With their hair pinned up.

Debuted ladies.

And their mothers.

'Miss Hartright!' The man's booming voice cut clear over the gabble. 'His Grace would like a word.'

Silence didn't so much settle as smother the room. Even the clock seemed to hold its tick. All eyes turned.

Elise shot to her feet, then picked her way through the group. 'Just a moment,' she called as she slipped by him and raced up the stairway behind them. 'Apologies, your grace. Everything is ready on my desk.'

The ladies, the staff, himself, all of them paused in a surreal tableau. They watched him, eyes blinking. He tried to avoid settling his gaze. One mother leapt off the chaise and wove her way across the room.

'Your grace! We met two years ago, at the opera. Do you remember? May I introduce my daughter?'

'Lovely to see you again... ahh...' He scraped his memory but found no recollection of the woman's face. What was taking Elise so long?

'Your grace, we sat together at the hospital charity benefit.' Another of them, this one a little more forthright, bumped in from the side. Like blackbirds on the lawn, a few more piqued, heads jerking, knees bending in anticipation. One squawked, then a few others called out in unison.

'Your grace—'

'Duke Osborne—'

The clock chimed to signify the hour, just one full throated, heavy bong, but it worked like a starter's pistol. Every daughter, every mother, discarded the fabric they had been inspecting, lunged from their seats and jostled across the room, their skirts pressing and voices rising in a cacophony of greeting.

Arley tried to locate his duke's voice to excuse himself, but could not trawl quick enough to find it. He took a quick step back, only to knock into Miss Hartright. Papers spilled from a folder she had been clutching and cascaded across the floor. Notes, tickets, travel papers. She bent to scoop them up. Arley crouched to help.

'What is it?' someone said.

'Travel documents.'

'Where is he going?'

'Paris, he's going to Paris,' someone else said, the murmur rippling.

Elise passed the stack of papers to him. Her eyes widened with confusion as she looked from the group to the papers in his hand, then to him. Arley's chest caught. The room swam. Their faces crowded as whispers passed between them. So many of them. And they *knew*.

Like the hand of a protector, the man who had opened the door tapped him on the shoulder. 'Down the stairs, then through the kitchen,' he said in a low voice. 'I sent your carriage around the back. Let us get you a speedy departure, shall we?'

Arley didn't question. He simply dashed beneath the man's outstretched arm and clattered down the stairs and through the kitchen, shouting 'pardon' and 'apologies,' as he raced. He took the stairs into the courtyard two at a time, before emerging into the weak spring light. Through the carriage house arch, he caught sight of the heavy wooden wheel of his carriage. He ran now, chest heaving, flung open the door and clambered inside before he fell back against the squabs. Behind him, someone shouted, and as the vehicle rolled forward, in climbed the man who had come to his rescue. He pulled the door closed behind him.

'Well, I'll pluck a goose. Does that happen often?'

'It's not usually so... intense.' Arley slumped back against the seat and stared up at the wood panelling. Each clip-clop from the horses sounded in his ear like the gossip telegraph that would no doubt already be humming through the city as news of his travel plans leaked. The wealthier families would be hurriedly organising steamer passages. Those with connections over the Channel would be writing, perhaps taking on the hefty expense of a telegram to deliver the information. At every turn, there would be someone wishing to make an introduction. To push forward a debutante. To ask a favour. Book a meeting. Any thoughts of moving through the city with semi-obscurity faded. He leafed through the papers Elise had given him. Tickets, accommodation, his travel itinerary. How much had they seen?

Everything. They had seen everything.

The man leant forward and presented his hand. 'Algernon Pascoe. I'm a friend of Hamish's. For a man about to embark on a journey to the most delicious city on the continent, you look awfully downcast, your grace.'

Arley gave the man's hand a firm shake. Hamish had never mentioned an Algernon before, but then, it wasn't as if they spent much time together. 'I was meant to be travelling incognito. I didn't realise how much I was looking forward to it. A week away from...' He waved his hand in the vague direction of the street. '*That.*'

'You were planning on moving quietly. Not making a fuss. And soon, everyone will know that the most eligible duke in England is traveling to Paris. That is most unfortunate.'

The streets writhed with people jostling against one another. A man driving a wagon stood and shouted at a person on the sidewalk and the two of them gestured obscenities at one another. A train whistle cut the air. Rain slapped against the glass.

'When were you last in Paris?' Algernon asked.

'A little over ten years. Not since I was 20.'

'Any old friends you were planning on reacquainting yourself with? Any spurned lovers who might recognise you? Leave behind any bad debts?'

Arley huffed. 'Nothing so exciting. I was with a minder the entire time. I imagine most of the men I met with would have fled the city in the revolution.'

'So, the chances of anyone recognising you are low.' Algernon swayed with the carriage, but as his lips curled into a devious smile, the movement almost looked as if he was swaggering. 'A duke is expected to arrive in Paris. What say we give them one?'

Chapter Two

Vivianne had not wanted to start the biggest day of her career running through the streets of Paris and arriving at the Palais Garnier puffed and dishevelled, but here she was, leaping over a stale puddle and dodging a stray dog as she raced down the rue Auber. Prima ballerina or not, the director Monsieur Sarcay would not tolerate tardiness.

Despite her puffing, as she skirted down the side street and slipped in through the dancers' entrance to make her way backstage, her body thrummed.

All the work at the bar. The endless rehearsals and failed auditions. The lecherous groping and propositions from wealthy subscribers, the so-called noblemen whose tickets gave them special access to the Foyer de la Danse and to the dancers' dressing rooms. The empty liaisons agreed to hoping one of them would have the clout to recommend her for a lead role.

All of it. *Fini*.

One man, and a Prussian noble to boot, who was only in town a few months a year, had promised her an apartment, and an allowance, and above all, the desire of her heart:

to speak to the administrators, and recommend she be the prima ballerina.

He was not an attractive man. Not especially bright. And, in their very brief session in his hotel, not skilled in the *boudoir*, either. For three months she had scorned the advances of other men, even though his small gifts and meagre allowance barely kept her in barley and broth, because unlike others, Archduke Baasch had the ear of the director, and recommendations from men like him saw ordinary members of the ballet corps catapulted to stardom. For Vivianne, dreams of love or marriage or even satisfaction in a partnership were out of reach. But to find a man willing to be her protector? To give her stability? That was what all the dancers sought. But to find one who could give her the chance to dance alone on the stage as Coppelia or Giselle, that was what she hungered for. And, finally, it was hers.

'Vivianne!' came a call from above as she clapped up the stairs.

'Not now, Nicole, I am late!'

Vivianne pushed her way down the hallway, jostling against the flow of dancers making their way up to the stage for rehearsals. She opened the door to the private dressing room before pulling off her satchel and plucking at her bodice buttons. One snagged on a loose thread, and she cursed.

'Vivianne!'

'I know, I know, I am late, but only a little...'

It took a moment for Vivianne to register the voice. Not unfamiliar, but not exactly a friend. She looked up.

'Adele? Archduke?' There was no reason to ask what they were doing in her dressing room. Adele's dishevelled hair, her downcast eyes, and the archduke's smug expression explained everything. A bunch of bright pink roses wrapped in brown paper and tied with white ribbon lay on the dressing table. Emblazoned on a card beside it was the name of the young dancer. Vivianne looked to the Archduke. 'You said you would recommend me.'

'I was going to,' he said as he hitched his trousers. 'But yesterday, I met the charming Adele...' He tilted Adele's chin upwards and pressed his lips against hers, his body tense with lust, but Vivianne saw the slight flinch in Adele, and the tenseness in her neck. She was barely seventeen. He pulled back, his lips smacking. 'And her talent is...' His gaze moved down Adele's face, caressed her neck, before pausing at the small swell of her bosom, easily twice the size of Vivianne's almost non-existent cleavage. 'Breathtaking.' He snapped back to her. 'You were fabulous, Vivianne, but the stage belongs to the young. Adele is the future.'

'Future? What do you know about the future?' A coil of anger, hot as iron, glowed deep in her stomach. 'You are a relic from a dead past. A symbol of the old, not the new. You come to Paris to indulge and eat and play and fuck, like we are a carcass for your feasting.' Grappling at the side table, she picked up a small bottle of perfume and flung it across the room. He flinched, barring his arms in defence. 'But the people will come for you, Archduke. Like in Paris. Their feet will march.' She flung another bottle, and another. Adele squealed and pressed herself against the window, while the archduke blustered as he tried to shield himself. Out of bottles, Vivianne grasped the tray they had been collected on and flung it across the room. It hit the wall above his head with a clang. 'They will come for you, and they will use your bones to flick the carnage from between their teeth.'

'Vivianne!' Regret pooled in her stomach as Vivianne stalled, still gripping a vase she had been about to volley across the room. She spun on her heel to find the director, Monsieur Sarcay. His mouth was a drawn line, his dark bushy brows knitted, his face was impassive apart from the fury in his eyes. A small group of dancers clustered behind him, some shocked, others hiding grins behind their hands. Nicole gave her a sad smile. Vivianne swallowed the hard knot in her throat as her anger turned to cold dread.

'Out,' he snapped, his nostrils flaring.

'Monsieur, please, he promised, and I...'

Sarcay only gave a slight, barely imperceptible shake of his head. He wouldn't repeat himself. Vivianne tugged at her satchel, and head bent, made her way to the door.

During the Siege of Paris, *les Jardins du Luxembourg* had been filled with ambulances. They had lined the lawn outside the Luxembourg Palace, which had been converted to a hospital. And after the Siege, after the revolution failed, it was the same place where the Communards had been lined up and executed by the government. The rubble had been swept away. Verdant green leaves concealed the scars left by bullets on the walls and balustrades. The garden was grown over with lush grass, so rich that no one would guess how much blood the soil had drunk.

Vivianne perched herself on the wall that ran alongside the pool of the Grand Bassin. *l'Année Terrible*, the Terrible Year, had shattered their world the year she turned seventeen, only ten months after she had arrived in the capital with dreams of silk slippers and tutus. In those days, the unfinished Palais Garnier had been a hospital, too. With no music to dance to, she had run water to the sick, wound bandages and made soup. Many gave up hope that dancing would ever be possible again, but not Vivianne. Even at the end of those days, when her muscles ached, her stomach growled and her heart was fatigued with loss, she had worked on her steps, kept her posture, and made time for the bar. She had never stopped believing that one day, Garnier would be finished, and that music would return to Paris. Like the swans that lumbered around the gardens stealing bread and cakes from distracted children, she too would fly.

Now, her career was scuttled, and by her own impetuousness.

Her reflection in the water silently screamed the truth. It had been over before she threw the first bottle. Before she opened the door to the dressing room. She was not a novice dancer with slightly fuller cheeks and an innocent smile. Hers were the cheekbones of a woman, her blonde hair plaited and pinned with an experienced hand, her eyes not bright like fresh dew, but dark with knowledge and cynicism. Of necessity, and at times, calculation, her arms had held too many. Her body had grown hard and lean with work and commitment. While her childhood had been happy, she had not always been well fed, so she had never grown tall and her silhouette remained thin.

She wanted to be angry at Adele, but she couldn't. Like Nicole, Adele had been a *petit rat* who spent years scrubbing floors and cleaning the opera between rehearsals and classes. She couldn't even bring herself to hate the Archduke. Her body was too relieved at the thought of being free of his attentions. Her anger, not fierce, just raw and aching, narrowed on herself. Why had she been so petulant, and so determined to defy her mother and leave their simple life to seek the brilliance of Paris?

A hand thrust a small bread roll wrapped in brown paper before her.

'Sarcay says you don't deserve it, but you can stay in the ballet corps for the next show.' Nicole sat down beside her on the wall, her pointed toes just skimming the path.

'I don't want to go back,' Vivianne said, her voice sad and sullen.

'What do you want, then?' Nicole said with her steady pragmatism. 'To starve? You want to sew again, with the *grisettes*? Because that is the choice, and you know it. You cannot eat your pride. We cannot all be the prima ballerina.'

A cool breeze, still laced with winter ice, gusted and Vivianne crouched into her pelisse, thin from too many winters. The water rippled, and the woman looking up from the crenelations sat hunched, her skin wrinkled. If she had still been young, a fresh ballerina with a temper and a jealous streak, her tantrum would have made her desirable.

'The war, the siege, the communards... they took my best years.' Vivianne let her voice drop to a whisper. 'And now I am old. And Paris dances like she was never on fire and like the streets never ran with blood.'

'Old. Pfft! You are being melodramatic again.' Nicole stood. 'Come back to rehearsal. Tonight, we'll go to the brasseries. And depending on who is there, maybe dancing. Vertical or horizontal.' Nicole wiggled her hips with her sensual, suggestive charm, the movement that sent so many men wild.

Vivianne huffed. 'I do not feel like dancing. Either type.'

'There is a rumour that a duke is coming to town, from London. Richer than your archduke. And you know what the English are like.'

'Stiff and uptight?'

'Obsessed with duty, but also with what others think. They like a sophisticated woman they can pet and preen, even for affairs. They have entire books written about it, you know.'

'I don't think they have books on how to manage an indiscretion,' Vivianne said.

'Maybe he is looking for a mistress,' Nicole continued, unperturbed. 'Maybe you will charm him.'

'And maybe I will return to Garnier and Sarcay will make me the director.' Despite the shadow on her heart, Vivianne laughed. '*D'accord, d'accord*, I will come to the brasserie with you. But I do not want to even think about another nobleman. I am done with dukes.'

Chapter Three

Algernon leapt from the train carriage and onto the platform with the grace of a tiger. He strode through the steam, swinging his cane and clipping it against the stone with each step. He emerged from the fog like an unholy spectre rising from the brimstone of hell—cock-sure and with a wicked glint in his eye.

Along the platform of Gare du Nord station, all heads turned as he passed. Hands raised to cover whispers and eyes widened, all of them firmly focused on Algernon.

'*C'est ce duc*,' someone whispered. Arley failed to suppress a smile. *It's that duke.*

How simple it had been. On the overnight passage from Dover to Calais, they'd talked phrasing, family, and ducal behaviours. Algernon was extraordinarily well versed in the manners and ways of the aristocracy already, and while not fluent like Arley, his French was passable. An exchange of jackets, waistcoats and a flat cap purchased from a store in Calais, and the illusion was complete.

Anyone in Paris who had heard news that a duke was arriving would surely be fooled. And while it was possible that the society hopefuls and their parents would follow, and know immediately that the much older, moustached man wasn't himself, he would, at least, have had a few days. He would have a small window of time to undertake the research for Iris and the others without having to fend off requests for introductions and favours. He inhaled a lungful of steam tainted, coal stained, congestion-streaked air. It was the most suffocatingly convoluted breath he had ever taken in his life. A city had never smelt so free.

Arley adjusted his coat cuffs. He wasn't used to tailoring that didn't mould to his body, and the puce and gold trimmed waistcoat sat a little snug across his chest, broad from rowing on the Thames, even over winter. He'd kept his own shirt and trousers, of course. No need to be too intimate with the man. He fingers rubbed at his signet ring, and he slipped it off and tucked it inside his coat. He'd need to hide it too.

Heads turned, ladies raised fans, scamps raced, no doubt off to inform whatever reporter or fortune seeker had paid for eyes and information. Arley tugged down his cap and watched the rumour mill leak and spread. After a few more steps, he dispensed with concealment. Not a person in all the station, possibly not in all Paris, bothered with him. He stretched into the commonness of his clothes, and despite their gaudiness, he felt absolutely, completely, invisible.

Algernon swung his cane in a full circle, then doffed his hat at a beautiful young woman, immediately causing her to flush, then winked at the much older man she was draped over. He growled at a lady's companion. '*Bonjour, bonsoir, ca va?*' he crooned. All the ladies tittered.

Arley increased his step to match Algernon's pace. He leaned in a little as they walked.

'Remember the rules,' Arley said in his duke tone. 'No running up bad debts. You will sign nothing, not a receipt, not a bill, not even a scrap of paper in my name. And you will do nothing—and I mean, *nothing*—that is likely to make its way back to England and cause my mother to give me grief.'

Algernon laughed. 'You dukes and your mothers. Browbeaten the lot of you.'

'Have you met her?'

Algernon frowned in thought. 'Duchess Osborne... I believe not. Although, I have met Dowager Outbridge, and my goodness...' A smirk tugged at one corner of his mouth, and his eyes creased with mischief. 'I understand why her poor husband's heart failed. *Ferocious*.'

Arley stifled an unwelcome image of the woman he had occasionally met at political dinners and lectures.

'Rooms at the Hotel du Louvre, yes? And surely a duke needs a little coin to grease his way through a city?'

Arley unclipped his purse. He retrieved a few coins and stuffed them into his pocket, then handed the rest to Pascoe. 'This is all the francs I have. Make it last, for if I have to make a withdrawal at a bank, I'm fairly certain the ruse will be up.'

Algernon took the purse and inspected its contents, then gave a low whistle before snapping it shut. 'Are you certain you want to go incognito? You could have a riot as yourself.'

Arley shook his head, part of him still marvelling at the focus of the crowd. 'Just keep attention diverted so I can have some peace.' He rummaged through his satchel, leafing through the papers from Elise. 'The first thing we should do is head to our accommodations. Then we can work on a plan for each day—'

'You there!' Algernon barked in his rough French as he pointed at a scrappy boy wearing rough hemmed trousers and a too big flat cap. He flipped a coin through the air and the boy snatched it so fast, Arley barely saw his hand move. 'Keep an eye on our luggage, and there's two more of those when we get back.'

The boy bit the coin and then, with all the menace of a blood hound, clambered onto their trunks and perched himself atop them, slightly snarling at everyone nearby.

'Now...' Algernon clapped his gloved hands together. 'After all that excitement, I need a drink.'

Arley hated parties. Hated gatherings, crowds, ballrooms, fundraisers, and his least favourite activity, the theatre. Every conversation always wound back to some discussion about an upcoming debate in the house, and could he be relied on for his support, or to an introduction to some insipid debutante, or for a request for patronage to a new cause.

And being patron to the Society for the Promotion of Civic Morality and the Adherence to Proper Values already taxed his energy, thank you very much.

Arley scanned the shimmering surfaces of brass, glass and mirrors in the brasserie. So many reflections. Himself hunched over the bar shimmered back as a curved distortion. Another visage of himself wrapped around a post. A flipped image in the glass. He hunkered down a little more.

'Your grace,' someone called. 'What would you like to drink?'

'The house specialty, of course.' Algernon clapped Arley's shoulder. 'And the same for my friend, Monsieur West.'

Duke Osborne hated parties. But how did Monsieur West feel about them?

The barkeep sat two glasses of lurid green liquid before them. Algernon picked his up, clinked it against the remaining glass, then tipped it back. Arley held his glass before him, entranced by the vividness under the gas lights.

'What on earth is this?' he asked.

Algernon gave one of his all-knowing smiles, the sort Arley was learning was a sign he was about to impart some lesson. 'Absinthe. Also known as the green fairy.' He splayed his hands before his face, like a magician in a market, his face animated, his fingers a performance. 'The elixir of the bohemians. A gateway to creative transcendence, and an unraveller of the sorrowful.' He lowered his tone and leaned close. 'Possibly, a bringer of visions.'

'It's a hallucinogenic?' Arley half lowered his glass.

'Not really,' Algernon said, with a theatrical, confidential hand raised against his cheek. 'But after five or six, the writers claim what they want.'

Arley raised the glass and narrowed his eyes as he inspected its contents.

'It's an experience. Embrace it. Embrace this new Paris, Monsieur West.'

Monsieur. Mister. A man. The incredible novelty of it sent a jolt of elation through Arley, and he couldn't help but mirror Algernon's grin. Ejecting reason, he threw back the liquor. It burned, then ran sweet. He slammed his glass on the counter. 'Another!' he called.

The barkeep looked to Algernon, who hesitated. Arley frowned. 'Don't push your luck,' Arley snarled.

Algernon's lips twitched, before he threw back his head and laughed the freest, most rambunctious laugh Arley had heard in his life, and then he was there too, laughing with his new friend. 'Another!' he called, and when the barkeep deposited their drinks on the counter, they raised them in unison, and clinked them together.

'Welcome to Paris, Monsieur West. Let's create that diversion.'

From brasserie to cabaret to café to dance halls, they all passed in a flurry of luminescent brass, green fire, laughter, and excitement. They crossed to the left bank, and in some room with low ceilings, lit by candles in jars, Arley found himself at the piano and set the entire room ablaze with his playing, and three doors down, during a cabaret, Algernon climbed onto the stage to join the show, every hand clapping in time to his heels.

He hadn't had fun like this since he was...

Since when?

Exhausted, but not in the usual *people are fucking awful* way, Arley leaned into his palm, his elbows propped on the bar in some tavern, somewhere. He didn't even know what side of the river they were on. Left bank? Right bank? He didn't care. An ache pulled at his thigh and his back throbbed from sitting in robustly made chairs. He felt used and energised and properly wrung out.

Marvellous. Beyond marvellous. Euphoric.

Using his thumb and his forefinger, Arley raised his glass from the bar and let it swing, as if hinged. 'Your grace,' he said, the false title rolling off his lips with ready ease and a snicker. 'I thought you said it was a myth that the green fairy brought forth apparitions.'

Algernon leaned his back against the bar and rested his elbows on the wooden counter. 'It is.'

'Then why do I feel as if I am seeing an angel?'

Like a portrait, his vision had a slightly green vignette to its edges, honing his focus on a woman on the opposite side of the room. A wisp of a beauty—delicate, thin, with barely any breast to alter the line of her body, she was dressed in bottle green, with ribbons the same shade as the winter mist on the river wound through her golden hair. The candles and gas lamps sent a slightly luminescent glow over her, and Arley had a sudden flash of her looking over her shoulder as she ran from him, laughing, with the long rays of afternoon sunset caressing her skin. The lights loved her. She could have been a thread of spun sugar, the last petal of a rose, a fragile plate of crackled glass that could shatter with barely a breath, but for the defined lines of her exposed arms. Strong, lean muscle showed beneath her tight dress sleeves, and when she half turned, her posture was steady and poised. A contradiction of delicateness and strength. He couldn't tell if his heart had stopped beating or if it moved so fast, he could no longer feel its reverberations against his chest. Everything in the room softened, but she remained as crisp as an autumn leaf.

Algernon leaned in close. 'A lady like that does not come cheap.'

'Cheap?' The splendid vision greyed. Arley looked to his companion in confusion.

'Look at her frame, her stance, her beauty. She is a woman of the stage. An actress, or maybe, a ballerina. And everyone knows how the ballerinas make their way in the world.'

'She's a prostitute?' Arley asked. A kind of possessive anger growled in him.

'Don't be so uptight, or so quick to slander. Labels are different here. Paris is more pragmatic than London when it comes to these arrangements, and there is a hierarchy to everything, even in this newest of people's parliaments. Yes, there are the prostitutes of the streets. But above them are the *grisettes,* or the dress makers. They work for the tailors and couturiers, sewing the best of Parisian fashion. They spend all their coin on frippery and lace, hoping to attract a man who would like to see them regularly and will pay for the privilege, maybe give them a life away from their sewing. Above them, are the *lorettes*. These women have found a man who will provide her with an apartment, and a small allowance, on the understanding that she keeps his company exclusively. Then, there are the *courtesans*.'

'A courtesan?' Arley knew what the word meant, but Algernon had spoken it with a curl of pleasure to his tone, suggesting more than the base translation to the English *mistress*.

'A courtesan is the epitome of her trade. She does not seek companions; they beg of her. She does not select the highest price; she sets her worth and then lets the men scramble to try to find the funds. Princes have gone bankrupt trying to win the affections of a Parisian courtesan.' Algernon tapped at the counter. The barman placed down two more glasses of green. Arley squinted, then winced. 'So, what say you?' Algernon's voice dropped low, his tone confiding. Arley had to close his eyes to make out his words. 'Because Monsieur West is unlikely to have the funds required to entertain such a lady and her companion, but a duke has coffers far more accommodating and may be willing to help a friend.'

Arley once again found the slender beauty across from him. Buying a woman's *time* wasn't unknown to him. Love affairs were messy, pointless things, and he preferred to keep his mistresses on short contracts, when he bothered with them at all. And was there much difference between the men who paraded their daughters before him, hopeful for a match, only seeking their own gain, and a woman who charged a price? At least his paid company had some kind of say.

Every previous arrangement fell away, dissolving into his past like smoke. He wanted to possess her, wholly. He wanted no other man to touch her, ever. And his coffers were deep, far deeper than even Algernon could imagine. Could he have her, for a night? For always? A ringlet rested on her bare shoulder, and the most violent flush of envy tore through him, because he wanted that patch of skin for himself, wanted to stroke it and kiss it.

'Do it.' He pushed the glass away, no longer wanting to be addled. 'Call her over. I will pay any price.'

Chapter Four

Vivianne didn't need to scan a crowd to know that she was being watched. It was part of her profession to know when she still held an audience's attention, whether on stage or in a brasserie or dance hall. She held her pose. Rolled her shoulders back a little and raised her chin, all to accentuate her best features. She went through the motions almost without thinking, for even though she had said she did not want to solicit company this evening, the more pragmatic, hungrier part of her knew she could not be so recalcitrant. She tilted her head a little and discretely scanned the room to locate whoever was watching.

Nicole tugged on Vivianne's arm. 'It's that duke! And he's looking at you!'

While Nicole had taught her so much about the stage, Vivianne feared she would never teach Nicole about discretion. She followed her friends poor attempt at a subtle gesture and found the man that had sent Paris chattering.

Like a carbon copy of an illustration from a book, like every noble she had entertained in the foyer de la danse of the Palais Garnier, the duke was... a duke. He had a thin twisted moustache and wore an immaculate black suit with a beautiful but understated waistcoat. He watched with the arrogant smugness of a man who took what he wanted from the world, but something in his gaze differed from the usual observations. Probing, but with no desire. He leaned over and spoke in another man's ear. Vivianne followed the action.

They often had sycophants following them, the dukes and wealthy men, but usually they were not so young. Not so well made. And not so raw in their stare. He wore the ugliest waistcoat she had ever seen. The salmon pink and navy collided to make his skin a little sallow. Half lidded eyes spoke of fatigue, and a slight intoxication, but still they flamed with desire. More than desire. Rampaging, unashamed lust.

It was the honesty of it that caught her. No games, no pretence of power. He wanted her, and in the grim set of his jaw, she could tell he meant to have her. She'd seen it over and again when a man took a liking to a dancer. His face spoke a language she understood to fluency. A prickle ran through her that started in her stomach and radiated through her chest. He was so different from the subscribers who filled the foyer, without hairs in his ears or a beard to scrape her chin.

'Come, Vivianne. You may be done with dukes, but I am not.' Nicole grabbed Vivianne's arm and hefted her to her side. The two of them bumped through the crowd until they pulled up just close to the duke, where Nicole released Vivianne, then stumbled forward and crushed against him. He caught Nicole in his arms, and with a sly smile, helped steady her.

'Pardon, monsieur.' Nicole's eyes fluttered as she traced a finger down his sleeve. 'I tripped on my skirts. I did not mean to bother you.'

He swooped, draped an arm over her shoulder and drew her against him. 'Not monsieur. Your grace.'

Nicole should have joined the melodrama and not the ballet, because her eyes widened, and her mouth formed a perfect circle of surprise. 'You are a duke?'

'A burden, carrying so much expectation, but yes. I am.'

As predictable as a farce, Nicole flattered as the duke prompted, his self-aggrandisement as grand as his title. Vivianne slid onto a seat at the bar. The man who had been watching her slid a glass of Absinthe before her.

Vivianne hadn't drunk all night, as she hadn't the coin to spend on liquor. And despite every effort from Nicole, she had been a reluctant companion, unwilling to flirt and have her drinks for free. She picked up the glass. 'You were watching me.'

'You are beautiful. Even more so up close.' Apart from a slight stiffness, he spoke flawless French, much better than his friend. Perhaps that was his place in the entourage. Translator.

She spun the glass between her fingers, watching the light change its hue from illuminated to dull, then back to brilliance. 'They call Absinthe the scourge of Paris. Did you know? Some doctors say it is poisonous.'

'Poison? Algernon said nothing about poison, you should not drink that. I'll get you something else. *Garçon!*'

He leaned across the counter. Vivianne threw back the glass and embraced the bitter burn. He paused, frowning.

'This is Paris, monsieur. We play with death every day.' She dropped the glass to the counter and spun in her chair to face him. 'What do you want, and how much will you pay?' She should not have been so crass. But her toes ached for a place on the stage, thumping hard against the boards, not suspended in the air so she could eat.

But she needed to eat.

He tugged at his cravat. 'I expected a courtesan to be a little less direct.'

Vivianne kept her expression neutral, even as inside, she wanted to explode with laughter. He thought her a courtesan?

'I, ummm... I would like a little of your company,' he stammered. 'If you would consider it. If you would accept my gift of...' He looked over her shoulder, before his awkwardness dissolved into confusion and panic. 'Algernon? Your grace? Where did he go?' He looked from her to the barkeep, then half stood to scan the room.

Even Vivianne was impressed at her friend's speed in separating the duke from competition. She put her hand on his arm. 'Nicole will look after him. Your friend is safe.'

'Safe? I don't bloody care if he's safe, he's got my...' Still frowning, he gave her a sheepish smile, and fidgeted with the cuffs of his sleeves. 'It's hot in here.' He tugged at his collar. 'Would you care to join me for a walk?'

When she first came to Paris, Vivianne had the luxury of choice. Of flitting from opportunity to offer, of laughing and flirting and indulging herself. But then the war had come, and the siege, and the revolution, and her choices had evaporated like a summer puddle. He was handsome, yes, and had the potential to be charming. And she could not lie to herself—his slight worship flattered the memory of the woman she had been. But flattery would not fill her belly, and nor would it give her a roof, or a bed.

'Monsieur, I gather you are new to the brasseries. Perhaps to Paris. The women here are only interested in your company if you attach a coin to it. And as your friend has been buying your drinks, I have my doubts that you have sufficient to hold my attention.' She pushed herself from the chair and braced herself for the chill walk back to her small apartment.

'Wait!' There was something sweet in his tone that made her pause. Something fresh, and genuine. He clapped at his trousers, his coat, until finally landing on his cravat. His fingers tickled the folds of silk until he found his pin. He struggled with the fastening, before freeing it and holding it out to her, like he was presenting a blossom he'd plucked from a bush. 'I have this. Perhaps it is worth a little of your time?'

She took the pin from his hand. The stone was substantial enough. Likely imitation topaz in a brass setting. Possibly worth a few francs. Enough to feed her for a day or two, maybe give her time to gather the stamina she would need to face the uncertainty before her. 'This will grant you...' She twisted it playfully, like the courtesan he thought she was. 'A walk to the river. Nothing more.'

'Just a... just a walk?'

'*Oui*. A walk.' She took hold of his arm and pulled his ear close to her mouth. He smelt of dust and travel and faded cologne, and his casualness cast an intoxicating contrast to the regular suffocation of rosewater and snuff. But a friendly smile and a pleasant scent could hide devious plans. It never hurt to be certain. 'And only a walk. If you attempt more, I will slit your throat.'

He gave a slow nod, then with an exaggerated gallantry like she was a lady, and not a woman who had just threatened his life, he patted her hand until she relaxed her grip. 'A walk in the moonlight with the most beautiful woman in Paris sounds like the perfect way to begin my stay. Shall we?'

It was only the city of light on the north bank, where the lamps glowed steady and the candles lit the windows of the wealthier homes as they embraced the night-time passions of the rich. On the south bank, and especially in the Quartier Latin where they walked, shadows chased after one another and layers and layers of darkness dappled the haphazard stone streets.

Away from the heady, pulsing noise of the wine sellers, Vivianne's companion seemed to fold into himself. He flicked a nail against his thumb.

'Monsieur, so anxious. Why?'

'Well, I… I normally meet women in different social circumstances. I'm not quite sure what to say.'

'You could start with your name.'

He laughed, low and self-deprecating. 'I suppose I could. Arley. Arley West.'

'Vivianne Chevalier.'

'Does anyone call you Vi?'

'*Non.*' He tightened at her abruptness. She leaned into him. 'I have always been Vivianne, even as a child.' She'd given this city enough. The thought of sacrificing half her name for its convenience was too much.

'No one ever calls me Arley,' he said, his words running into one another in a rush. 'I sometimes wonder if my parents agonised over my name, only to have everyone call me West, or...' Their heels clicked the stones as his words trailed. 'Algernon thought you might be an actress. Or a dancer.'

'A ballerina,' she said. Although who knew for how much longer.

'I've never understood the theatre. To get all dressed up to sit in the dark, watching people talk or listen to music. It always seemed pointless to me.'

'That *is* its purpose. Men of means, they can flaunt their wealth. For those who cannot afford an actress's favours, it allows them to dream. The theatre is built on lies, but at least it is honest about it.'

'Honest lies?' He chuckled. 'I can see the appeal. A man may be fooled, but—'

'At least he knows he is being fooled.'

Their next few steps settled into a comfortable silence. Normally, men talked. Normally, women like her listened. It was what they wanted—flattering conversation that convinced them of their uniqueness before the inevitable power play and manipulations began. She settled into his slightly slower rhythm and eased into his ambling step.

'You picked a poor night to walk with a pretty face. The moon is so hidden, you cannot see it.'

'Most women are more coquettish about their appearance.'

'I know it is pretty. There is no reason to pretend otherwise.'

'It is very pretty... but that's not why I wanted to walk with you. You looked so fragile, but also, so strong. You are a dichotomy. It intrigues me.'

Vivianne had always weighed men by their worth, their title and value. Their influence within the Palais Garnier. She assessed her future with them in terms of stability, promotion and if they would put food in her belly. Monsieur West had nothing that would help her. Awkward, so much so that he almost didn't know his own name. Shy. No, not shy... reluctant.

'If you prefer, you can speak English, Arley. I will understand.'

He huffed a surprised laugh. 'Another fascinating aspect to Miss Chevalier. How so?'

'I spend a lot of time with English men. I found it convenient to understand what was being said of me when they thought I was not listening.' They were closer to the river now, and the slosh of the water against the stones carried louder on the night air. Although he kept hold of her arm, a tension rippled through him, and he bowed his head. 'You are judging me,' she said. 'But you shouldn't.

We are not so different. Both of us are reliant on the whims of dukes. We each pander in our own ways.'

'I was not judging you. I am confounded by your honesty. It's not something I've come across. I spend my life amongst manipulations and deceit.'

'*Vraiment*? Because I was judging you. What kind of man comes to Paris on his friends' purse?'

He could have taken offence. He should have because she meant it as a barb. His words had appealed too much to her understanding of the world, were too much in symmetry with her own jaded views. This type of intimacy was unfamiliar to her. It both pleased her and sent a ripple of fear along her spine.

Instead, he laughed and bumped against her. 'Brutal honesty. Why?'

She shrugged. 'You cannot pay. Pretence tires me. Why waste my energy on pleasing you?'

'You are failing because I am enjoying your attempts *not* to please me. You are not as clever as you think.'

The ludicrousness caught her off guard, and a laugh, not staged, but from beneath her ribs, burst out of her. What to make of this man? The sweetness of his chivalry, and his light playfulness awoke a nostalgia for her girlish dreams of love, and when those had faded, of companionship.

'Already we have reached the river, and the Pont Neuf.' She stroked the wear of his elbow. 'I think it has been so long since I walked these streets, I have forgotten how short a distance it is. I fear I have overcharged you. But I am without coin, and I am too tired to walk anymore. Perhaps to keep our deal even, I could allow you a kiss?'

'A kiss?' He spoke like he was weighing the value of it. 'You French kiss on each cheek all the time. Why should I pay for something you give away for free?'

'Not *la bise*,' she said, with a laugh. 'A proper kiss.'

'On the lips?' He took a step closer and bowed his head. 'And you will keep my pin, and the debt between us will be settled?' he asked. The clouds shifted. Moonlight caught the ripples of the Seine, and their light danced in his eyes.

'*Naturellement*,' she said.

'And you will not owe me anything?'

'You will be free to indulge in Paris as you like,' she replied.

'And I would not see you again?'

'There would be no need.'

He took her chin between his thumb and forefinger and tilted her face up. 'I do enjoy kissing beautiful women. Especially those with clever mouths.'

He drew close. Mere millimetres away, his breath rushed over her cheek. He stroked her bottom lip with his thumb. Vivianne couldn't remember ever being treated so gently. Her heart pattered. She closed her eyes.

'I don't want it.' The warmth of his closeness was replaced with a rush of night air as Vivianne stumbled forward into the almost kiss. He turned with a flourish and crossed his arms over his chest.

Anger and embarrassment fizzed in her belly. 'You are turning me down?'

'Your kisses are expensive. I would like to renegotiate our deal. I think, for my pin, I would like something else from you.'

'You will not get more than a kiss,' she said, ire flaming as she pulled his pin from her pocket, ready to throw back at him. 'And you do not get to say where it goes.'

'Is that all you think about?' His lips twitched, as if suppressing a laugh. 'I have a confession. I am not here just as a friend of the dukes. I am here for my employer. I work for a travel company. I need a guide. Someone to show me Paris. A Parisian to show me Paris.'

'There are books at every *magasin*. Surely there is a guide book in your hotel.'

He waved his hand in dismissal. 'I only have a few days. Certainly not time to visit every location listed in a book.'

'I do not have time to be your tour-guide,' she snapped, his rejection still smarting.

'Then you do not want this.' He plucked the pin from her hand and spun it between his fingers. It caught a slip of moonlight, and instead of absorbing the glow, it glimmered. Real? A stone that size would be worth more than just a few francs. It would be enough to keep her in bread and wine for months. 'I want you to show me ten must see sites in Paris.'

'Five,' she shot back. Her pride refused to let him dictate terms, no matter how good they were.

'Seven.' He held out his palm.

She matched his posture, and he gave her hand a firm shake. 'I have rehearsals in the morning,' she said as she released his hand. 'Meet me at the Palais Garnier tomorrow afternoon.'

He removed his hat and spun it through the air, then bowed low. 'A pleasure doing business with you, Vivianne. I look forward to more of your company.'

As he walked away, a moonbeam chased his heels as they rippled a puddle, like he drew the light of the universe into himself. And even though her hunger ached, a small part of her thrilled at the thought of seeing him again.

Vivianne shook her head, chiding herself for becoming caught up in his charm. He would have some intention, would make some demand of her body. Men were like that. It was just how they treated women like her.

Seven places. Vivianne made a mental map of her city and picked the fastest route that she could draw. He was far too dangerous. Lingering in the company of Monsieur West would not do her any favours.

Chapter Five

Arley leaned back as the man pressed the razor against his throat. He tried to relax against an unfamiliar hand. The man scraped the blade against his neck, not as delicate as his valet, but twice as steady. When he paused to wipe whiskers and soap on his cloth, Arley swallowed, trying to moisten his parched throat. Tonight, no Absinthe. No anything.

He could dress himself—he had travelled, before, after all—it was the shaving that worried him. And after the journey across the Channel, his stubble was coarse, and after all night visiting brasseries, taverns and wine bars, he did not trust his hand.

At least the apartment at the Hotel du Louvre had been comfortable, with thick drapes that kept daylight at bay, allowing him to sleep through the morning. Only a dull ache at the base of his skull remained, and the fresh coffee that had been sent up was already banishing the dredges of the night before from his body.

How deeply he'd slept. Enveloped in the soft bedding, and with no thoughts riffling through his mind, stirring up unease, squeezing his chest, he had slumbered through the night. Was that how most men slept? Without worrying about conduct, or proper behaviour? Without replaying conversations in their mind, wondering if they had made some encouragement they shouldn't have and if they were going to be bound to some promise they didn't intend to make?

Or was it that the only thought his incessant mind wanted to play on loop was the memory of the captivating Vivianne Chevalier? She had drenched his thoughts, and there was no room for anything else.

A woman he couldn't have, even though he wanted her desperately. Had such a thing occurred before?

The genuine transparency of the entire situation was beyond refreshing. An honest lie. He liked how she turned down Monsieur West. How she laughed with him when he was amusing and didn't when he missed the mark. How she treated him as an equal. No, as less than an equal. As beneath her.

She had a price, which he could not pay, and there was no debating on the issue. No manipulations. And for the first time, he felt like he might pass time in the company of someone who saw him as he was.

His name was Arley West, instead of *your grace*.

A thump sounded at the door, followed by some muffled complaints, before it swung open. A bleary-eyed Algernon stumbled through. He steadied his hand on a settee.

'Where's my coat?' Arley snapped.

Algernon raised his hand, frowned, and half closed his eyes, his finger moving as if sliding through memories in his mind. 'Absolutely no idea,' he said, then flopped onto the settee. 'What are you doing here? Aren't these the duke's rooms?'

'Don't push it, Pascoe.'

Algernon smirked, mumbled something that could have been *touché*, then half rolled to rest his elbows on the side of the lounge. 'How was your courtesan?'

'A fabulous conversationalist,' Arley replied, still curt. Algernon closed one eyelid, as if processing. 'You took my purse. And my means to pay.' He tried to draw anger, but the emotion was unwilling. 'How was yours?' he asked, not really interested.

Algernon's mouth broke into a wicked grin, and he leaned back on the settee and swung his feet over its cushions, before tipping back his head. 'Magnificent,' he said, then closed his eyes and began to snore.

Arley shrugged on his coat, then gave Algernon a firm shake. 'Money,' he demanded.

Eyes still closed, Algernon fumbled with his pocket and passed him a considerably lighter purse. 'Don't spend it all at once,' he murmured, then snored again.

Arley clipped it open, fuming. A little less than half of the francs he had brought remained, but still enough. Enough for... anything. Anything he wanted. For an afternoon with Miss Chevalier to extend into an evening...

Arley fished out half a dozen coins. He flung them onto Algernon's chest, tucked the remaining funds into his pocket, and headed out into the city.

When he had come a decade before, Paris had been a city in flux. Demolitions and constructions were moulding the city into a new vision, that of Haussman and Napoleon III. Scaffolds had lined the streets, bricks had both been stacked and tumbled as the narrow medieval alleys were wiped away. Whereas London always seemed determined to progress only if it was dragged kicking and screaming, Paris rushed headlong into any idea it had, good or bad, but with such wholehearted, obsessive passion that when everything was done, no one seemed to remember that there had been other choices.

And now the construction continued, a combination of completing the vision from a deposed emperor and rebuilding the shattered wreck left by the war and its own citizens. Dust showered from shells of buildings, as workers struck at walls and threw down old doors and shutters. A twinge in his chest brought forth the memory of when, only seven or maybe eight years before, the old houses on the opposite side of the street had been torn down. Then it had only been two houses, both sprawling, ancient things, even older than Number 10, with a paddock linking them. One place had been owned by the immovable Mrs Crofts, the other leased by Lawrence and his wife.

At the time, the change had jolted Arley every day he stepped out of his own, unchanging home. Now, he'd become accustomed to the towering wall of replicated white townhouses and their occupants, that he barely remembered how it had been before.

Would Paris, one day, forget all the places that had been demolished? Would she, too, move on?

The opera house had been little more than a lattice of frames and scaffolds, and while some official who had shown him the city all those years before had tried to describe the vision, he'd been too disinterested to allow imagination to fill in the gaps. Now, knowing it held Vivianne, and that it mattered to her, he paused between the construction, activity and dust of the Avenue de l'Opéra to take it in. Opulent to the extreme, he couldn't decide if it was garish overstatement or architectural brilliance. The entire building glistened bright against the vivid hue of a Parisian sky. Apollo, the sun god, sat perched atop a central dome, and gold sculptures glinted. Tall columns flanked the front, and below them was a long row of decorative arches. Poetry, music, drama and dance—he recognised each carved relief, and the busts of the master composers—Beethoven, Mozart, Auber, Bach, and others. The entire façade was a homage to music and performance, layered in myth, symbolism and achievement. Would he impress Vivianne if he showed her how he understood her building? That he could read it as easily as a child at their letters? He had studied classics at Oxford, after all. All that effort would finally be of some relevance to his life.

He tapped the coins in his pocket. Maybe there were easier ways to impress her. He'd made his deal the night before only thinking of how to keep her in his reach. He could suggest they skip her tour completely, and he could take her back to his rooms, turf Algernon out, before satiating the hungry fantasies that had plagued him all night.

Tourists and gawkers milled outside the opera house, but there was no sign of Vivianne. Impatient, he stalked the laneway, searching each feminine face for her. At the back of the building, a plaque set in a sandstone archway read *Théâtre de l'Opéra—Administration*. The stage door. Maybe she meant for him to wait for her here.

Arley leaned against the block stone column. Its ridges rubbed at his shoulder blades, and here in the buildings shadow, the cool March air pinched his skin. A man wearing a black coat and swinging a solid cane entered the building. A few light-footed girls followed. Another man. Arley scratched his temple, then coughed against the city dust. He went to the door and tapped. It opened a crack. A grubby ear emerged, and against the dark it appeared disjointed, like it was hovering in the shadows.

'I, errr... I have a meeting with Miss Chevalier,' he said.

The ear disappeared. In its place, a hand, palm up, fingers rubbing together, emerged.

'She's expecting me,' Arley growled. He only had 5-franc coins, and he wasn't handing one of them over to a doorman.

Thick lips with a hint of stubble moved into the gap. 'Subscriber number?'

'Subscriber? I'm just visiting.'

A tongue flicked out, and the mouth chuckled. Arley straightened and prepared himself to be given admittance, when all body parts disappeared, and the door slammed closed.

He knocked. No reply.

He thumped. Silence.

'I will have you know,' he began, inhaling his self-aggrandisement, 'I could have you—'

He caught himself in time. Duke Osborne could make such complaints and be heard. Arley West could not.

He shoved his hands in his pockets, kicked a stone, then leaned back against the pillar. He scrunched into his coat, searching for some protection against the cold.

A few more men passed. Women. Girls.

Arley had never had to wait on anyone before.

Waiting was tiresome.

'Monsieur?' A bright, peaked face angled itself into his line of vision. The woman from the brasserie, who had been there with Vivianne and left with Algernon, smiled at him. 'You are the duke's friend, yes? Are you cold?'

'A little,' he grumbled. 'I have a meeting with Miss Chevalier.'

'Lucky her,' she said, tilting her head. 'Follow me, I'll take you to the foyer de la danse. You can wait for her there.'

Vivianne's friend introduced herself as Nicole, and with a light tap and a word, secured his entrance into the opera house. He trotted behind her as she wove through the slightly darkened staircases and hallways as they moved both deeper and higher into the building. He'd never been backstage at the theatre before, and as he warmed, his annoyance melted, and he could not turn his head fast enough to follow the maze of movement and noise. Lights fluttered, doors opened, giggles erupted, and deep voices bounded. Sweat and heat mingled with urgency. Every breath smelt like lust.

'There are more men here than I expected,' Arley said as they moved to one side of the hallway to allow a line of dancers to pass, their muslin skirts brushing against his knees. 'Are they teachers? Do they work here?'

'Subscribers,' Nicole called over one shoulder. 'Patrons of the theatre. Their membership gives them special access to watch rehearsals and meet with the dancers after a performance.'

'What stops them from going into the dressing rooms?' he asked.

Nicole laughed. 'Nothing.' She led him around another corner. 'Here is the foyer. This is where the dancers stretch before and after they go on stage.'

He hadn't expected so much opulence for a backstage space, but the gleaming gold, brass and marble room was like the building's façade had been inverted and pressed against the walls. An enormous, multi-layered crystal chandelier caught the light and dispersed dazzling fragments of light over the ceiling. Marble columns framed tall mirrors, and brass bars had been fixed at set intervals around the edge of the room. Before one mirror, with her hand on the bar, stood Vivianne.

She hadn't seen him, or if she had, she made no acknowledgement. Wearing the same light, diaphanous muslin skirt, fitted bodice and white stockings as the dancers in the hallway, with a bright blue ribbon tied at her waist, Vivianne stretched and placed her ankle against the bar. Arm extended, she curved over, until her fingers first brushed, then reached past the tip of her ballet slipper. Arley followed the delicate sweep of her muscles as they tensed. She twisted her body and moved deeper into the stretch.

Shrouded in white innocence, she looked all at once feminine, graceful, and terribly exposed. A flick of her skirt, and he caught a flash of the back of her thigh. Arms raised above her head, she moved like a lily caught in a breeze, petals flinching, her stalk wavering, yet fixed firm. Every gentle movement, every delicate gesture seemed a lie, as clearly every inch of her body was composed of sinew and strength.

She held her ankle in one hand and stretched it over her head. *Heavens*. He could suffocate right there and not care.

To compose himself, Arley dragged his gaze from Vivianne, searching, clutching for any small thing to hold his attention. On the far side of the room, a man dressed in black filled a corner like a shadow. Straddling a simple wooden chair, he rested his elbows along its back and leaned forward. Arley didn't recognise him, although he knew the cut of his clothes, and the arrogance of his pose. Another noble, or if not titled, someone of wealth, who was used to getting what they wanted.

He made no charade at other business. Just sat. Ogling.

The crystal extravagance of glass and brass moved from lyrical to disjointed. An uncomfortable burst of shame shot through him. While the room was designated for the dancers and set aside as a place for them as they moved between the stage and the dressing rooms, in reality, it was not their space at all. It was an extension of the performance, and today the sole audience was the man in black. And Arley.

The long black ribbon tied at Vivianne's neck flittered as she bounced onto her heels, its tips kissing the air as she spun. When she spotted him, her lightness fled. A protective scowl turned her lips as she rolled her shoulders back. Arley shot a look at the man seated in the chair, who now turned to watch a group of dancers who skipped in, chattering as they took up their places along the bar. He wanted to despise the man for his lasciviousness, but how could he? Hadn't he rushed to become flush with coin? Hadn't he thought to pay his way to her bed, and as she strolled across the room toward him, he still wanted her so badly. Her expression had softened, but it was now a mask. Something deeper in him, more aching, wanted her to look at him like she had the night before when she had offered him a kiss. He wanted her to like *him*.

'You are ready for your tour?' she asked as she pulled a blue, fitted jacket over her arms and tied it at the waist. 'Five places—'

'Seven!' he cut her off, then shoved his hands into his pockets. 'The deal was for seven. Seven places to broaden a young person's mind. To introduce them to artistic culture. But not impoverish their family. And not create any scandal.'

'And here is your first stop. They must come to the ballet. *Voilà!*' She spun and followed a line of dancers who had disappeared down a flight of stairs. 'I will meet you outside once I am dressed. Six to go!'

CHAPTER SIX

Garnier, Colonne Vendôme, Tuileries, Louvre, Pont Neuf, Notre Dame, and then she'd bid him *au revoir* at the grand department store Le Bon Marchè. The night before, Vivianne had mapped the route in her mind. She'd seen this city torn apart and rebuilt more than once and knew every path and alley. The perfect list, it covered everything any English person visiting Paris wanted to see, or some version of it. She could have taken him to the Arc de Triomphe—the English always liked to see it, because then they could talk about their victory over Bonaparte like it mattered to her—but it was too far out of the way. And that would be eight places, and Monsieur West had only negotiated seven. By nightfall, she'd have that pin, then she'd sell it and keep her cupboards full as she figured out what she would do once she no longer danced at Garnier.

She had changed into a burgundy walking dress of a shade that hid the muck and dust from the street, and it swished against her walking boots. The uneven stone pushed hard against the thinning soles, the discomfort serving as a reminder that she could not afford to be distracted by handsome men with shallow pockets. She needed to rid Monsieur West from her life, and with the itinerary she had chosen, she could do that in one afternoon.

'Steady on,' he puffed as she headed toward the rue de la Paix. 'It's a tour, not a race.'

Vivianne strode on. It wasn't her fault he wasn't used to traversing the streets. He probably went everywhere with his duke in a carriage.

'Colonne Vendôme.' She gestured at the large bronze column as they passed. 'Now you have two.'

A bell rang, and the door to a bakery opened. Vivianne's stomach protested at her pace, and her mouth watered at the crisp smell of fresh bread. Maybe after she sold that pin, she'd go to a tavern, and buy bouillon, bread, and ale. She could fill her stomach properly and not just tease its edges.

At rue de Rivoli, she made a sharp turn. 'The Tuileries Gardens makes three. Up ahead, is the Louvre, and then you will have four.'

'Now just wait.' He grabbed her arm and spun her to face him. The combination of cold air and warm exertion made his skin flush. His cheeks were full with health, and his blue eyes ignorant of hunger. 'You can't just point at places. I have a guide book that does as much. There has to be a reason somewhere is included, remember?'

'These are all beautiful sites in Paris. Is that not reason enough?'

'Better than that. More specific. I need a story, not just a dot on a map. You can't just point at the Louvre and say "There's some art." It has to mean something. There must be a painting or sculpture in there that you love. If you could show a visitor just one artwork in all of Paris, which one would it be?'

Vivianne tapped her foot. 'One artwork?'

'One. The sort to inflame a ready mind. To capture the heart of the city.'

Inflame a ready mind? Nothing inside the Louvre would do that. The directors who controlled access to the salons ensured that nothing in there ever changed, even as the city bucked against stagnation. They had developed their taste decades ago, and sought to inflict it on everyone, driving artists with any shred of vision to hunger and compliance.

She should drag him into the museum, point at any oil in the Grand Gallery, and then be back on their way. But the sincerity of his request unsettled something in her chest. He did not want to see Paris. He wanted to see *her* Paris.

'If you don't like the painting, it still counts,' she said.

His mouth twitched. '*Naturellement.*'

'Follow me. I will show you my favourite picture in all of Paris.'

As they strolled along the promenade above the river, unease and hesitation pushed out Vivianne's self-righteousness. She should have just taken him to the Louvre and told him what he wanted to hear. Even for a

Frenchwoman, her passion pulsed too strong. Yesterday, it had seen her lose her position. Today, she might lose the small salvation fate had offered her.

Watching from her periphery, Vivianne tried to take the measure of the man who trailed beside her. She knew men: her life, her career, her existence depended on reading them faster than their eyes could wander her body and assess her face. While they undressed her in their mind, she stripped them bare in other ways. Would they be cruel? Have proclivities she was not willing to indulge? Did they have funds? Would they be generous?

But this man was a jumble. His clothes screamed poor taste, but his stance was confident, almost arrogant. He wore only one piece of jewellery of any value yet gave it up like it were a button. He wanted to kiss her, and more—all men did—but had instead sought her company, and her knowledge. A concierge could have given him a list of places to visit and left him free to enjoy his time abroad, but he was determined to undertake his mission himself, and to do it well.

'You take your work seriously,' she said as they settled in beside one another.

'I take everything seriously,' he replied. 'Last night was the first time in a very long time where I haven't been serious.'

'I think you were not very serious when you bought that waistcoat.'

He laughed. 'No, I suppose I was not.' He plucked at a button. 'It was Algernon's idea.'

'The duke?'

'Yes.'

'You are an odd friendship.'

'We are.'

The river carried the cries of the traders and merchants, and applause from the floating theatres rolled across the water. A tourist boat chugged past. Vivianne walked into a pocket of sun and paused. The wind could grow cold here, and without a coat, she shivered. Not wanting to leave the sunshine, she gestured at a man standing before them. Arley leaned against a post and followed her gaze.

Almost always there was someone painting on this stretch of the Seine. Today, it was a man in navy pants and a green coat and wearing a flat cap to contain his black curls. He had worn cuffs, dirty shoes and a sublime, lost expression. He sucked the nub of his brush, then dabbed at the palette held aloft in one hand, his focus on the canvas as intense as any master.

'This painting?' Arley pointed at the man and his easel.

She nodded. 'It is my favourite.'

'But it's not finished.'

'You didn't say it had to be finished. You said a painting to inflame a ready mind. *Voilà*.'

He crossed his arms. 'I don't think I've ever seen someone paint outdoors before.' A slight frown furrowed his brow as his lips thinned in concentration. 'What's so special about it?'

Vivianne searched his expectant face. She had dragged him down here at his prompting, and now he wanted an explanation. Would he understand? Or would he, and his pin, storm off? She had no stories of symbolism or teachings from art schools to offer. She could only try to explain how the painters made her feel.

'It's not that he paints outdoors that makes him special, although that is something, yes? Look closer. He does not paint kings, or myths or gods or grand stories. He paints the people. This one, the customers at the café. Others sketch in the brasseries, or in the gardens, and watch the city as it goes about its day. Some go into the fields outside the gates and paint the peasants as they work. There is no lesson on religion, or history, or nationalism. It is just... life. Life after sadness. Life after the war. You wanted me to show you my Paris. This is it.'

Vivianne waited for him to argue. And maybe he should, because it wasn't as if he could go back and report to his company that this painting, this corner, should go on the itinerary. But he was trying to turn the city into a checklist, and that was not how Paris worked. One immersed themselves, inhaled it, let it seep into their veins. It was an experience, not a list of things to do.

At the café, a man with a monkey perched on his shoulder played an accordion. The strained melody held the familiar mix of sadness and hope that every song seemed to have in it these days. The monkey's tail curled around the musician's nose. He sneezed, and a discordant, compressed jumble of notes filled the air. The café patrons laughed, and the musician chuckled, then scratched his pet's head. Arley laughed, and when he turned to her to share the joke, his eyes sparkled.

'I'm not one for people. Mostly I find them... problematic.' He shuffled and thrust his hands into his pockets. 'However, you have me. I don't know how, but I will put your outdoor painter on my list. We have three places left. What is next in your Paris?'

She had been going to take him across the new bridge, and from there, onto Notre Dame. Ever since Hugo published his book, everyone was obsessed with the place.

'My Paris?'

He nodded. Vivianne scanned the city skyline of the south bank, with its old, haphazard lines and the flat black tiles of the new buildings. And while she could not see them from here, in her mind she ran the alleys and haunts, saw the people, their joy and their misery. There was no way to just *show* him that.

'My Paris takes time.' She threaded her hand around his arm. He crooked his elbow in response and tucked her against his side. 'And after all morning at rehearsals, I am as hungry as a wolf. We will have our next stop tomorrow. Right now, you can buy me a drink at the café. Let us sit, and talk, while we watch the man paint.'

CHAPTER SEVEN

Arley flexed his hand against the stone wall. Taking a slow breath, he descended a few feet more, before recalibrating in the darkness. A soft glow extended up the narrow, spiral stairs, but the candle, and Vivianne who had hold of it, were already on the lower level and out of his sight.

'*Plus vite*, Arley. Faster.'

'How on earth,' he said as he inched his way down the last few stairs, 'Can you manage that descent in all those skirts?'

'I am a ballerina. I have excellent balance.' She pushed herself to her toes in demonstration and swept an elegant hand before her. 'Take a moment and let your eyesight fully accept the darkness. You will need your senses for this.'

How far underground had she taken him? The air, tight and stagnant, lacked the freshness of the city above.

'This isn't a ruse to rob me, is it?'

Her laughter lit the blackness, while her smile, the first clear thing he could focus on in the flickering candlelight, loomed macabre. 'You only have one thing I want, and you have left it at your hotel. Don't think I hadn't noticed.

And if I was going to rob you, I could lead you into any number of alleys across the city that are easier to make an escape from. Maybe, when we are done, I might lure you into one of them with the promise of my kiss.' She pouted and tipped her head to one side. 'Except you don't want it. You want my Paris instead.'

He very much did want her kiss. The day before at the café, as they watched the man paint, and drank wine and ate bread dipped in oil, she had relaxed a little. She spoke of the changes she had seen in the skyline, hinted at the war, gushed about the stage. Bright, animated, every word from her full, rose-pink lips was a revelation. That night, alone in his four poster, with no thought or care of what had become of Algernon, he had obsessed over her lips. Their taste. Their eloquence. If he grasped her chin and pressed his mouth to them, would she respond? Or would she push him away, demand her payment, and never speak with him again? Tantalisingly out of reach, the only way he could have a kiss or anything from Vivianne was if she gave it. Because if he had to place a price on her now, he would be unable too. She was irrevocably, completely priceless.

'How is your vision? Can you see anything beyond me?' Vivianne asked.

Arley blinked away the last of the shadows. The surrounding walls glowed, but they weren't flat and even, like the stone in the stairwell. White, uneven curves, bumps and lines reflected the light, while gaping sockets and cavities drew in the darkness. Bones. The walls were made of bones.

'What the hell?' Arley took a step back. They'd passed beneath a marble sign suspended above the entry, proclaiming *Arrête! C'est ici l'empire de la Mort.* (Stop! This is the empire of Death). He'd thought it the prelude to something poetic. His heels bumped the arched entry and he half slumped awkwardly into the recess. Vivianne laughed. She grasped his hand and tugged him to his feet.

'My Paris is not always light and pretty pictures. Fear not, the dead cannot hurt you. Welcome to *les Catacombes.*'

The ceiling just above his head, so close that if he reached he'd be able to press his palm against it, was stone scraped and gouged by tools, as was the floor. The two earthly extremes were linked by the most macabre walls imaginable. Bones: femurs, fibula, humerus and tibias, but mostly skulls, dozens and dozens of them, were stacked in a tight, interlocking pattern. The walls seemed to stretch on forever.

Vivianne interleaved her fingers with his. She wore kid gloves, soft with age, and the leather felt warm against his skin. She kept a tight hold and led him forward through a winding alley as her candle cast a haphazard circle around them.

'Before the first revolution,' she said, her voice taking on the tone of a confiding storyteller, 'the cemeteries around the churches became too full. The people were always sick. The king, Louis XVI, who later lost his head, ordered that the cemeteries be emptied, and the remains brought here, to the old quarries. At first, the bones were just tipped in, but later, the workers stacked them, to make some order.

And they made them beautiful. Millions of Parisians.' She trailed a gloved finger along the wall. 'The poor of Saints-Innocents. The aristocrats that fell to the guillotine. The tyrants of the Terror. All of them are here, all together. Invisible, yet exposed.' She tapped at a femur. 'This could have been le Duc d'Orléans. Or a humble peasant. We will never know.'

From the day he had become duke, Arley had felt the pressure of self-preservation. Like himself, his father had been the only legitimate son, and while there were enough branches extending backwards throughout the family tree to ensure there would be a presumptive heir out there somewhere, the weight of the line had always been on his shoulders. Like his death would create some catastrophe.

'Doesn't it scare you?'

'The bones? *Non*. There are no ghosts in *les Catacombes*.'

'Not that.' He stared hard into the vacant cavities of nose and sockets that once would have been a face. A man or a woman? If they were alive, what colour eyes would look back at him? 'Dying. Before your time.'

Vivianne huffed. 'There are worse things than death. Hold this.' She held out the candle, and he grasped the brass holder. She hesitated, took a half breath and, bending back her wrist, unfastened her buttons. 'I was sixteen when I arrived in Paris, determined to find a place on the stage. I had danced my way from my home to here, but when I got an audition, I was not good enough. The petits rats, the young girls of the ballet, they train from when they are five or six. I had no form, or technique. But I had passion. But I cannot eat passion. I had to work.'

She loosened each glove finger, before tugging it free, then rested her naked hand against his cheek. She trailed her fingertips across his skin. He inhaled soft roses and powder, but her skin rubbed as hard as stone.

'They call them the *grisettes*. The grey. That is the uniform they wear. Grey skirt, grey shirt, grey skin… They work long hours beneath the floors of the fashion houses, only seeing the sun through dirty windows, yet all the beauty of Paris rests on them. So many young girls, like me, come to the city with dreams, but they cannot grasp them fast enough to fill their stomachs. So many are lost. Disease. Absinthe. Despair. Their families cannot take them back, and even if they could, they are too ashamed to go home. And the city of light, she is a loving mother and a cruel madame all at once. The lucky ones find comfort and warmth in the rich silks of her skirts, but for most, after Paris has amused herself, she discards them like ash from a cigarette. Burnt. Useless.'

He went to place his hand over hers, but she snatched it away.

'My skin is so coarse, I do not need a thimble when I sew. But I am lucky. I met Nicole, and with her help, I learnt the technique I needed. I practiced every day during the siege, and when Garnier opened, I got my audition, and now, I have my stage.' Her voice cracked a little, and he waited as she waded through her sadness. 'But the girls who are still there, hoping for a man to free them, for an opportunity that never comes… That is a fate worse than death.'

'They dream of marriage?' he asked.

Vivianne laughed. 'You speak like a man holds his greatest affections for his wife.' She slipped her hand back into her glove and fastened the button. 'They dream of setting their own price. Of having a choice in who they take to their bed. Of security.'

All her elegance and strength, her delightful wit and her pragmatism seemed to leech from her as she spoke. The candle flame cast dark pockets under her eyes, and just out of the reach of its glow, her skin paled. A tight fear gripped him that she might melt and disappear against the backdrop of bones and skulls, like they might claim her for their own. What would become of her after he left? What man would take his place in providing for her?

Shame, rich and gluttonous, coursed in him. He had carried the burden of the dukedom from a time before his memories were solid things but had also been sheltered from so much. When death sent jolts of fear through him, he really meant his own. His self-indulgence at his own fate suddenly made him ill. Why would he be worried about the loss of another? He'd long ago accepted that one day his mother would go, but that was borne of the reality of having already experienced his father's loss. But who else in his life did he hold so close that the idea of their erasure send as profound a fear through him as his own? No one. He held no one close.

His knees buckled, and he went to steady himself against the wall, then pulled back when he found a skull from a long-ago lost person. People had likely wept for them. Who would weep for him? His chest tightened, his gut clenched, sweat heated and cooled his skin, and he turned hot as he shivered.

'Arley?' Vivianne took a step toward him.

He dropped the candle and the light guttered. 'Take me to the surface,' he said.

How they clambered up along the narrow winding stairwell, he could not say. They burst into the open. Gasping, like he'd been drowning, Arley gripped an iron bollard and half bent as he coughed through the easing suffocation. He crumpled to the ground, rested his head between his knees, and breathed. Vivianne crouched beside him. She placed her hand on his back.

Embarrassment swirled through him, making his head spin even more. 'I can't believe that happened. I can't—'

'*Chut!*' she said, and in time with her word, she made a little snapping motion with her fingers to silence him. 'It happens. Maybe we don't put *les Catacombes* on your list?'

'Perhaps a bit much reality for a poor Brit.'

A light smile twisted her lips as concern sunk her eyes. He saw it so rarely that he recognised it instantly. Right now, he was nothing, no one, a man with a pin. Monsieur West had so little to offer. Yet, she cared.

Strong, compassionate and as beautiful as an uninterrupted sunrise—Vivianne Chevalier was the most magnificent woman he had ever met.

Her grin turned indulgent, and she weaved her arm through his and leaned into him. 'Can you stand? Because you are in luck. Not far from here is something much better than *les Catacombes*.'

Still woozy, Arley let her tug him to his feet. She pulled him close against her. She was far stronger than she looked, and he relied on her steadiness to help him keep his balance. His feeble footsteps fell into hers as she led him along the paved footpath. After a few minutes of silent walking, they arrived at the entrance to a garden. Luxembourg Gardens, full of green life and tall trees, children rolling hoops and people stretching on benches in the sun. A tableau of life, so stark a contrast against the streets of death that he now knew wove beneath their feet.

'So that I know for next time... What upset you? Was it the dark? Or the bones? Or something else?'

He forced a breath of Paris spring, and while his chest at first resisted the cold, slowly, it melded, and relaxed into the freshness. How to explain the jumble? How to explain the emptiness he had felt, and also the twinge of fear that something might happen to her? How death had never been about him, and yet it had shaped his life, not with grief but with expectation?

'When I was ten, I almost died. I was skating on a pond. It wasn't fully solid in some patches, although it looked it. I fell through.' The icy grip, the compression, the piercing needle like shards of ice that had sunk into his body resurfaced in his memory. 'It's not often I remember. But when I do, it can be a little... intense.'

It wasn't that moment that compressed him and made him tremble. After he had been wrenched from the ice, he had been wrapped in blankets and bathed back to warmth and then shuddered in his mother's arms before the fire. Admittedly, he hadn't skated since. Hadn't done so many things since. Not from fear, but because he had fully come to understand that he existed as something beyond himself. As he'd been pulled from the water, the first words he had heard were, 'Not the duke.' His governess had been in tears, not for him, but fretting that she'd be dismissed and never find another position. The doctor had been called and entered the house with the grand announcement that he was there 'to see his grace.'

Only his mother had said his name, Arley.

He was simultaneously so important, and also, irrelevant.

He was still mouthing his words when Vivianne interrupted his thoughts.

'You felt vulnerable.'

'Incredibly,' he replied.

'And scared, but worse... judged for being scared.' Her eyes, blue flecked with grey, the same shade as the clouded sky, shone with understanding. 'I know what it is like to be on display. Not just on the stage, but all the time. The secret is not to hide from it, but push through, until you find the moment where it doesn't matter anymore. When you remember what made you want to be there to begin with.' She released her hold and took a few steps forward on the path, before spinning to face him. 'Take dance. In the foyer, with the patrons and the other dancers and the prima ballerinas, all I can think about is how if I don't dance well, I may not impress that subscriber who was watching, or I may not be considered next auditions. Like the world hangs on the performance.'

She paused, closed her eyes, and inhaled. The slight tension around her eyes softened, and the tightness around her jaw slackened. 'Then, they go, and for a small pocket of time, it is just us. All the dancers. All together. And all at once, we remember what we love and why we are there. The air hums with the remembrance.' She extended her arms into two graceful half circles, in front of her chest, then raised one arm above her head, then the next. 'On the stage, the lights are so bright we cannot see the audience, only hear them, and then the orchestra starts to play, and they are gone. And the only thing left is the dance.' She held out her hand, palm up. 'Dance with me, Arley. Forget the world.'

The sky cracked with a jagged fork of lightning, and thunder rumbled. 'I think it's going to rain.'

'And?'

'We might get wet. We could catch a cold.'

'A cold. Is that so terrible? Don't tell me. You might sneeze yourself to death. Do not worry, I will hide your body and scrub your bones clean and secret you into *les Catacombes* so that you can be hidden and on display all at once. And then, in death, you will have peace with the world.'

'It seems pointless to have peace if I'm dead,' he said.

'It does.' She stretched her hand a little higher. 'So dance with me, you stupid man. No one will care.'

Rain pattered, his chest rebelled, chill water snaked its way beneath his collar and traced an icy line down his back. Never much used to discomfort, his body railed against the cold and urged him to shelter. He took her hand, and she squeezed him, hard. Umbrellas popped into life around them, a few people gave a light scream then scattered, but Vivianne did not ease her firm hold on his hand.

'Would you like to waltz?' She adjusted her stance in his arms, and with a light pull, beckoned him to take the lead into the first few steps. 'Or maybe a cotillion.' She released one hand and spun away. 'Or the polka.' She twisted back into him. He caught her and moved with her momentum, swaying slightly as he let laughter link them. The light mist over her hair clumped and dampened, a curl clung to her cheek and between them, their damp clothes cloyed and suctioned. Her bodily warmth leached into him. He spun her in a circle beneath his arm, and she pirouetted like she was on stage, her laughter dancing like the drops on the air. He tipped her back, and she raised a playful foot, before he pulled her against him and then her lips were on his.

Like an eternity concentrated into a flash, Arley lost all sense of everything. There was no dampness, or cold, no fear, no life or death or even himself. Just her. Her sweetness. Her grip on his coat. The small of her back beneath his splayed hand. Her lightness.

They broke apart. 'You thief,' he said, feigning effrontery. 'You stole a kiss.'

'I did not. I gave you one.' She frowned. 'My kisses are very expensive. You should be grateful I am so gracious.'

'You think my kisses are free? Because they are not. They are so expensive that I don't think you can afford one. You would need ten pins to afford one of my kisses.' He gripped her chin. A daring amusement sparkled in her eyes. 'I have no choice but to steal it back.'

Arley caught Vivianne in his arms, and as he dipped her, like some dashing knight on the stage, she squealed playfully until he brought his mouth to hers. At first, he kissed gently, mirroring her, but when she linked her arms behind his neck and pulled him closer, he tightened his hold. Her lips parted, and he accepted the invitation to kiss deeper, slower, with a languor like they were caught timeless and hidden, not bent into a sublime embrace in the middle of a gravel path beneath the dripping trees in the Luxembourg Gardens. A brazenness roared in him. How fantastic to catch a beautiful woman in his arms and kiss her, grasp her hips, tangle his fingers in the damp ribbons in her hair and not give a damn.

Vivianne pulled him closer. Arley raised them both to standing. With a delicate nip of her lip, he set her free.

She took a step back, blinking fast, and reached her hand through the air as if searching for a pillar to steady herself on, but finding none, instead swayed. She shook her head until she focused on him, and her slightly dazed expression darkened to annoyance. 'That was too much,' she snapped. 'You get six places now. No more.' She pushed back her soggy hair, spun on her foot, and marched away.

'It was worth it,' he called to her retreating back. She waved her hand in the air in dismissal. Arley touched his lips. They still burned. He inhaled, trying to imprint the smell, the taste, the sensation of Vivianne into his memory. 'Completely, frustratingly worth it,' he mumbled to himself, then began the long walk back to his hotel.

Chapter Eight

'You are doing it again.' Nicole said. She stood beside Vivianne at the bar, the pair of them watching each other in the mirror. Nicole bent, then extended onto her toes.

'I am not.' Vivianne could have played coy, but she knew what Nicole was alluding to and she wasn't in the mood. 'I am only showing him the city.'

'Every time you pin your hopes on a man, they disappoint you. This one will be gone soon. You should be looking for your next meal. Another duke, or a merchant from the patrons. Not playing guide to some worker *Anglais*.'

The shape of Nicole softened and blurred. Vivianne steadied herself on the bar. Her *petit déjeuner* of bread and coffee had been hours ago, and now, her belly protested at being ignored for so long. But her diminishing funds did not stretch to lunch, so she had arrived at Garnier with a grumpy stomach.

Today would be her last day with Arley, and by days end, she would have coins in her pocket. And she would see the back of the Englishman with no prospects, soft lips, and hands that set her skin aflame...

Vivianne blinked hard and brought her vision back to Nicole. The kiss had been nothing but a moment's lapsed judgement. *Never* again.

He had smelt as she imagined an English garden to be like. Fresh, light, and sweet. Arms that held her like she was delicate, lips as firm as a demand. He teased at her thoughts, as did the soft rasp of his chin, and the sweet prod of his tongue.

Vivianne wiped away the succulent memory. Never, *ever* again.

In the short time since Garnier had opened, dancers, singers and musicians had been catapulted to notoriety. Paris threw off the years of war, revolution and deprivation, so that she could embrace frivolity and joy. Men sought to catch the ascendent star and make them theirs, and many a naïve ballerina had confused the attention with love, only to find themselves abandoned and heartbroken when a new star caught everyone's attention. The men who came to the theatre were a currency. Dancers who forgot were likely to find themselves without support and without a stage.

It would not be her. She knew the price. She paid it too often.

'*Excusez-moi, mesdemoiselles*. Flowers.' Guillemot, one of the men who manned the stage door and was known to take coin from infatuated men to deliver flowers and gifts to the dancers, stood in the archway into the practice room. In his arms he held a bunch of red roses, dark as blood and crisp as paper. Against the pragmatic wash of the walls, and his tattered black suit, the blossoms exploded with colour.

Vivianne's heart held her chest captive, its slow beat dictating her breath. She'd never been sent flowers before. Had Arley thought of her lips, as she had thought of his?

'For you, Mademoiselle Nicole.' Guillemot held them out. Nicole gave a high cry, then skipped across the room and gathered the blooms into her arms.

Vivianne's stomach rumbled and with it, her indignation. What horror to feel such envy, such bitter green jealousy for her friend who had plucked her from obscurity and provided her with the opportunity to bring her toes to the stage. But as much as she detested it, she could not control the swell of exasperated frustration and contempt that moved through her as she traced the beauty of each delicate rose. The duke had sent her flowers. Nicole brought the bunch to her perfect nose, and as a petal kissed her lips, she closed her eyes to inhale not just the majestic fragrance but the promise of something more. Of a future.

'Love is not for us,' Nicole said as she laid the roses on a chair and returned to the bar. 'I know he is charming, but he will not send you a bouquet like that. He cannot afford them. And if he cannot afford roses, he cannot afford the rest of you.'

Nicole stayed in the practice room, while Vivianne went to change. She'd already spent too long with the Englishman, enjoying too much of his company as they walked the streets and talked. The firm line of their negotiation had created a barrier around what men normally wanted from her—her body—but with the change, other parts of her had become exposed, and he grabbed them before she could protect them with a price. He brought out her humour, cared about her opinions, followed her advice on which restaurant should go onto his list because it had the best soup, or the freshest bread. And yesterday, to see a man crumble before her, sharing his vulnerability, then watching the rain wash away his stiffness… had she ever been treated that way? Kissed that way? Not since the days of the siege, when her hands had been needed for helping and her feet had walked endless stretches of despair had she been wanted for something *more*.

But this was a new Paris, with new rules, and this play between them had to stop. Or he'd need to start sending her flowers, even if it was with the duke's coin.

Today, she'd show him one last place. Then, she'd say *au revoir*. Today, she'd keep her distance. Her body *and* her mind.

Changed, wearing her sturdy boots, Vivianne descended through the layers of Garnier until she arrived at the stage door, then stepped outside. Although the sun blazed, the wind bit, and she pulled her shawl around her as she stepped out into the chill. The breeze blew much colder than the day before, and a few flecks of sleet swirled on the wind.

Arley stood waiting, leaning against the stone arch. Even hunched into his collar and with his cap pulled down over his curls, he was beautiful. With the door's creak, he looked up. His face fine cut, like crystal, brightened, his smile alone enough to shatter light.

Non, Vivianne. One last place. You need to move on.

'Don't you own another suit? Can't your duke buy you a nicer waistcoat?' she huffed as she trudged over the stones. As she approached, he straightened, pulled off his cap and held out a handful of flowers. Daffodils, tulips and ranunculus, their stems not cut, but torn, and held together only by his palm, instead of with paper and ribbon. 'Did you steal those?' she snapped.

'Define steal,' he said. He pulled them back a little, toward his chest, like a shield. 'They made me think of you. They're so bright, and pretty. I wanted you to have them.'

The petals shifted and their hues merged into each other. Like the windows of Sainte Chapelle, where she had planned to take him that afternoon, where all the colour and light of the world would bathe them. Her stomach roared. Her head thumped.

'Vivianne?' Arley took a step closer. His brows furrowed, and fear shaped his features, like in *les Catacombes*. Her knees buckled beneath her. He took another step as he held out his arms. The flowers scattered. Pink, peach, purple, blue sky, green leaves, yellow stone, Arley's ugly waistcoat, his black coat, all of them swam and blended, before they smothered her in darkness.

Snippets of movement, of Arley, a carriage, and being hoisted upstairs and through doors flitted in her memory. The mattress beneath her was too soft to be her own, the fabric against her cheek too smooth. And she rarely had enough money to afford fuel for a fire, yet one cracked, and the room smelt of its warmth. And the sheets—fresh, like a garden. She knew the feel of a stranger's bed. Arley had brought her to his hotel.

Two voices filled the room. One thumped her heart. The other gripped her chest. She kept her eyes closed as the fuzz of their words found form and clarity.

'She is not infected.' The cruel officiousness... it could only be a doctor. Vivianne sent up a silent prayer to return to the blackness.

'What do you mean, infected? Is she sick?' Arley asked, his voice leaden with worry.

Vivianne gritted her teeth as the doctor laughed. 'I do not think she has a street disease. That's what you want to know, isn't it?'

Eyes scrunched, Vivianne willed herself not to move, not to even alter her breath. She felt raw, as all of her heartache and her transgressions were spread as wide as a three sous whore's thighs as the doctor so nonchalantly spoke of her, her body and her place in the world.

'Why did she faint?' Arley asked. His tone was level but edged with disdain. For her or the doctor? She could not tell.

A button clipped, clothes rustled. A door opened. 'The ballerina's do not always eat,' the doctor said, his voice a dismissal. Feet scuffed carpet, voices mumbled, a door closed. Vivianne dared to half open her eyes.

More luxurious than she expected, she lay on a wide, four-poster bed. Heavy drapes were fastened at each corner. The suite extended to beyond the point where her vision found form. Arley turned back from the door as he raked his fingers through his hair. He'd removed his coat and waistcoat and now rolled his shirtsleeves to just below his elbows. He moved slowly across the room, then eased onto the bed beside her.

'I didn't want to take you into the theatre,' he said as he rested a hand on the covers, over the little mound made by her feet. The intimate weight was a comfort and reassurance against her fears of his judgement. 'In case they wouldn't let me stay with you. Sorry if you were scared. I didn't know what else to do.' He tapped at her with a slight agitation. 'You don't eat?'

'Not by choice,' she rasped out.

He lurched from the bed and went to a small table stacked with glasses, bottles and carafes. He filled a tumbler with something amber, then returned and passed it to her. She took a sniff, then a sip. Armagnac. It burnt her nose and throat, but settled in her stomach, and sent her veins racing.

'You have no money because I held back the pin? Demanded more of your time?' His words were only half questions, as he seemed to speak more to himself, his voice heavy with self-recrimination. 'Why didn't you tell me?'

'Tell you I am half starved? Give you more power than you already have? There is never enough of it for men like you, is there?' Vivianne braced herself against the bed to better face him. How dare he judge her when she had given him far more than she had any man. 'You want my truth? I have only been playing the part of a courtesan. But I have not had the attentions of a patron for some time.' She pressed the uneven cut of the crystal against her palm, before taking another gulp and pushing herself up. 'I will leave.'

'You will not.' He lay alongside her on the bed, kicked off his shoes, raised her head as he slid his arm beneath her and pulled her against his chest. 'I have ordered soup, and bread. Some cheese. I can have them send up some wine if you like. Or coffee.'

'The duke will pay?'

He laughed. 'Yes, the duke will pay. He may be an inconsiderate arse, but he would not want you to go hungry.'

She should have resisted, but why? His shirt cotton rubbed soft against her cheek in a feather light caress against her skin. She let her eyes grow heavy and curved into him. Stroked at his chest. Not rough like his coat, his shirt fabric had a tight weave, with perfect shell buttons, and was softer than any fabric she'd ever worn. Luxurious and of a quality that she only knew as clothing the bodies of men.

Not just any men.

Men of means.

Chapter Nine

Arley woke to a slab of sunlight across his face, a stiff cock and the most beautiful woman he'd known toying with the button at his throat. Vivienne trailed her fingers over his chest and drew lazy ribbons on his skin. She grazed the tent of his erection, before walking her fingers over his body again. When she unfastened his top button, he gave a small groan.

The night before, after eating, and barely talking, Vivienne had fallen asleep in his arms, and he'd breathed her until sleep claimed him. During the night, she must have removed her skirts, as she sat beside him in only a light, threadbare chemise, the fabric so thin that her pink areola cast a slight shadow against the muslin, and the small points of her nipples made bumps against the fabric. Midway through the night, uncomfortable and overheated, he'd tossed off some articles of clothing. With a sheepish realisation, he looked down to see he was clad only in his underwear—tight fitting white underpants that reached past his knees, and a fitted white undershirt. He made a half grab at the sheet, but Vivienne tugged it away.

'Vivianne, I cannot pay,' he said, holding fast to the lie.

She smiled, her eyes sparkling. 'Then you will be in my debt, instead of me in yours.'

'You don't owe me for helping you—'

'*Chut*,' she cooed and pressed a finger to his lips. 'I want to.'

She unclipped another button, and kissed the small exposure, then another button, and kissed lower still. She sat up, stifling a giggle. 'Please take this ridiculous underwear off. I cannot while you are dressed so.'

Arley didn't think he'd ever undressed so fast in all his life.

Vivianne's golden hair, all tousled and loose ringlets, like it had been brushed by the wind, trailed over one shoulder. Little wisps tickled his skin as she kissed him, kissed his neck, licked the depression below his Adam's apple, then circled his nipple with her tongue.

'Were you dreaming of me, Arley?'

Her tongue traced a slick line through his centre. She nipped at a slight softness around his stomach, then grazed her teeth across the indentation between there and his hips. He pushed back against the pillows and let a hum buzz his lips, the tingle a mirror to the purr she sent through him.

'Every night since I first saw you. And each day feels like a dream too.' He could barely give the words voice, but she had spoken her truth to him. He was not ready to tell her everything, but he could tell her that. To let himself be vulnerable. It seemed only fair he give her back a little of that power.

Her light pink tongue flicked, and she shuffled herself to the side and scooped her hair over her shoulder so that it cascaded behind her like a tumble of spun sunlight. On all fours at an angle to himself, her toes peeked over the edge of the mattress. The expanding morning light showed the silhouette of her body beneath her chemise.

'Are you always so quiet?' She trailed her tongue along his shaft. His cock jerked in reflex to the sensation.

'Measured,' he scratched out, even as her tongue circled his knob. 'Controlled. All the time.'

'You will not be measured this morning,' she said.

Her hand wrapped around his cock, and he arched into her palm, and when she took him into her mouth, his whole body groaned. He propped himself up a little to watch. Her tongue flicked at the crest of his knob, before she took him deeper into her mouth, and a stroking hand met her lips.

Arley sat up a little more. The sight of her teasing mouth wrapped around him sent another jolt of wicked pleasure. Like the kiss in the park, she was giving herself, freely, and he wanted to be with her and to give her pleasure in return. And perhaps he was not ready to have the balance between them settled. He stroked her back, brushed his palm over the delicate curve of her spine, and over her taut arse. Bunching the chemise to one side, he slipped his hand between her thighs.

'Dear heavens. You shave?'

She released his cock from her mouth. 'All the dancers do.' And she took him into her mouth again.

No stiffness about fucking, no faux formality, just lust and sweat and desire. She rolled her hips as he stroked her wetness, her moan rippling through him as her head gently bobbed with the movement. He slid a finger inside of her, pulsed into her body, found the rhythm of her body and settled into the synchrony. He stroked the slight roughness of her intimate stubble, then teased at her, before plunging his fingers into her body again. But it was not enough. He wanted more.

He rolled her slightly, so that they lay side to side, and Vivianne did not release him from her mouth, only gave a muffled squawk against the motion. His stomach pressed into her chest, and the lovely small mounds of her breasts and hard nipples indented his skin. Grasping her thighs, wrestling her damned chemise aside, wishing he'd demanded she shred it as she'd stripped him, he pulled her close and pressed his mouth to her sex.

Bodies entwined, her thighs pressed against his cheek, she rolled against him. Salt, tang, sweat, sweetness, lust, woman and heaven, he licked, and supped as famished as she had been the night before. He teased her delicate nub, tasted it, drew it into his mouth and suckled, as if drinking her down, like she could quench the uncertainty and unease he always carried in him. Her moans rippled tremors of energy. He felt like every part of him was caught in the storm of her passion, and it battered every bit of him, even as she sent the most unparalleled bliss through him. Her body writhed against his, her thighs clasped his ears so tight that he could barely hear her moans, only feel them vibrate through his chest. All he could see was her skin, the cleft of her arse, and the rumpled edge of the sheets. He inhaled a breath of her, then fucked her with his tongue. She smelt of want, and desperate need, and abandon. From his cock to her mouth, from her chest to his stomach, from her thighs to his mouth, and the sweet heaven of her cunt, they formed a chain of lust and longing made of the most wicked abandon. Arley teased his tongue until he found her nub again. No, not nub, nothing so short and crude, her clitoris, a beautiful word shared between their languages, like it had been made for this moment. Her gentle firmness pitted his tongue, her flavour an elixir.

He could stay locked in this moment forever. Arley dipped into her again, her sweet heaven coating his tongue. She thrust a little, her mouth riding his cock, sucking tighter, taking him a little deeper.

He craved her, even as he pleasured her, he wanted to impress her and wipe away the memory of any other man. He wanted to make her feel good. He'd spent his life immersed in morals and rules, a sentinel of proper behaviour, as a damn patron to a society that turned gossip into a virtue. Now consumed and saturated by her, the freedom of the past few days surged and melted into the moment. Encased with practical, base desires, he flicked his tongue against her clitoris, suckled it, nipped her, just a little, eager to learn, to feel what she liked and to do it again and again. He wanted to feel her scream against his cock, and he wanted to shout his muffled ecstasy into her body.

Her body pinched a little as a tremor shuddered through her, but just as he went to plunge his tongue into her again, she disentangled herself from him, dragged her chemise over her head and flung it to the floor. She turned to grip the bedpost, her back to him, her knees apart.

'*Baise-moi*,' she ordered over her shoulder. Fuck me.

'I cannot pay...' he stammered, even as his cock twitched in rebellion against him.

She fixed him with a look that was half lust, half fury. '*Baise-moi*,' she repeated. 'Now.'

Arley crawled the length of the bed, drinking in her nakedness, before tasting the back of her thigh, licking the top of her cleft and kissing the line of her spine, mouthing each vertebra, he imprinted the texture of her skin on his tongue, melding her scent, taste and sensation into a fluid memory. Moans, like little mews of delight, tumbled from her lips. He breathed her scent of jasmine and sweat, licked the salt from her nape, and kissed her till he was drunk, catching snippets of her mouth as she curved to his body. He took her hips, aligned himself to her wetness then plunged into her as deep as he dared. A stream of garbled French spliced with groans and gasps filled the air. He tried to catch her words with his kisses, a mix of street slang alien to him and words he knew, most of all, *Je veux plus*, she groaned, over and again, and *Je te veux*.

I want more.

I want you.

Oui, oui, oui.

Somewhere between losing himself in her groans as much as his own, he heard her demand, 'Louder, Arley. Shake down the walls.'

She tensed and her thighs clenching against him as she cried out, as if she had only aching moans left in her vocabulary. Arley fell into the essence of her, his climax rebounding through him, and as her trembling met his, he groaned, at first biting his lips as he always did, forcing restraint into every moment of his life, before he released it, and let himself be loud, like she wanted. He threw back his head and half howled her name, and in reply, she amplified, her shouts of harder, faster, louder melding with his own. Who cared if he was heard? Who would gossip about a liaison between a no name clerk and a ballerina? He was just a man, lost in the body of a beautiful woman.

She bent slightly, eased back against him, and he pushed deeper and spent as she trembled. She jerked with energy, her release the twin to his. He'd never felt so in sync with another. Never felt so connected, so raw. Fucking had always been primal, a physical necessity, the quenching of a base desire. As Vivianne arched, her body relaxing, he clasped her hips and pushed just a little deeper to hold the ecstasy a little longer. Everything about her felt different to anything he'd known before.

But beneath the pulsation of release, the ebb of desire, the satisfaction of seeing her posed before him in total surrender, the gift of her body stirred something else. A feeling that had been there from the first time he'd made her laugh, had grown as she'd shown him her city, and with it, herself.

There were a hundred ways to admit that he was lost, and maybe with his cock still buried in her was the crassest form of realisation, but surely...

Surely, there was no better way to...

Dare he say it...?

To fall in love?

CHAPTER TEN

When Vivianne opened her eyes as the last blissful shudder ebbed from her body, the first thing to come into focus was her white knuckles still wrapped around the bed post. She'd lost control. Been so flooded with desire she'd demanded he fuck her.

And how he had. Every stroke of his cock had been heaven, every kiss, every lick, every touch focused on her, and her body, and she'd forgotten that just like a dance, fucking was a performance.

No one had ever kissed her between her thighs before, caressed her skin, savoured her lips, cared what she felt, and with the newness of the feeling, she'd lost herself. And *mon Dieu*, he'd finished inside her.

She'd given him control.

Vivianne never lost control. Never allowed her own pleasure to dictate her actions with a man. It was too dangerous. They already had all the power, and to give them her desire was a pathway into jealousy, pathetic obsession, and eventually being discarded. No man kept a woman once she adored him. She clutched for her familiar anger or exasperation to level at him, or at herself, but with the lusciousness of her orgasm still trailing over her skin, like a hush of velvet, she could not rouse the emotion. She grasped for something else, to find a feeling to use as a shield, but all she found was the weakness of happiness. An empty ache blanketed as she spiralled into his spell, and a cold rush of fear chilled her.

Arley, still inside her, gave a satisfied sigh. He ran his palm down her back, and his light, feathering stroke sent a quiver along her spine. He brushed the hair from her neck and curved to kiss her nape. Thin tickles erupted, and she had to stifle a giggle. Chiding herself, she pushed it down.

'I don't think I've ever felt like that,' he said. 'Never enjoyed it so much. I—'

'Don't spoil it with words,' Vivianne snapped as she twisted away. He fell back against the mattress and opened his arms in invitation, a stupid, satisfied smile on his beautiful face. She should slide off the bed and dress, race home to wash, but instead, she crawled along his length and collapsed against his side. He gathered her in his arms and she settled against his chest. The rhythm of his breathlessness matched hers with gasping synchroneity.

Arley stroked her hip, then pressed a kiss to her temple. Her racing heart stumbled.

Non, non, non. She would not. She could not let herself feel anything for this man. She had to choke down the feeling in her chest. Had to snuff it out before it starved her.

She'd woken with the thought to seduce him. He may not be as rich as a patron, or have influence, but he wore nice shirts, had steady employment and with the duke, probably had good connections. And he liked her, that was abundantly obvious. And when she watched him as he slept, she had confessed to herself that she was not ready to let him go. So she'd thought to show him the pleasure she could give. Make a new arrangement. Renegotiate their deal.

Perhaps she could salvage her plan.

Vivianne twisted in his arms and rested her chin on his chest. Everything about him felt so uncomplicated and easy. So gloriously simple.

'Monsieur—'

'Arley.' He nudged her, a slight grin giving light to his sleepy, half-closed eyes. 'Why so formal? Especially after *that*.'

She would not be drawn into that look. She drew little circles on his chest. 'You are leaving soon, yes?'

'Now that I have my list, maybe tomorrow.'

'Do you think your business will bring you back to Paris? Perhaps often enough that you might need to keep a small apartment? Something simple for your convenience?'

'Vivianne...' His tone had that preparation for dismissal, and it hurt more than any other rejection she had received, even more than failing her auditions. But unlike those times when she bowed her head and walked off stage, this time, she would not allow herself to be set aside so easily.

'At least think on it. Just a little? Because I am tired. Tired of Paris and the games she plays. I am almost too old for the ballet, and I will die before I go back to the *grisettes*.

I know the promise of a courtesan means little, but I give you my word that I will keep your bed warm only for you.'

'This journey was an exception. My work is in London. I will not need to come back here often at all.'

Vivianne squirmed, desperate to put some distance between herself and his body.

Arley gripped her and held her in place. 'You did not let me finish.' He took hold of her hand and brought it to his lips and pressed a kiss into her palm. 'All my life I've been what I was told to be. With you, for the first time, I feel free. Like a person I do not know. I don't want you in Paris, I want you to come home with me. But not as my mistress. I want you to be my wife.'

'Marriage?' The word made her dizzy. Not since she'd been a naive girl leaving her village had she felt like that was a path for her.

'Would you like me on one knee?' he asked, and before she could reply, he pushed himself up, slid over the side of the bed and crouched on the floor, both ridiculous and stunning in his nakedness. 'Or on two knees, begging like the fool I am. Or perhaps I should lie prostrate, like the courtiers of old before their queen.'

'Get off the floor.' She couldn't help but laugh as she pulled him back into the bed. He claimed her mouth, and she welcomed his stealing of her kisses. She splayed her hands over his back and felt him growing hard again against her thigh. 'It's been days. You cannot marry someone you've known so short a time.'

'People marry after knowing each other less. My mother had one conversation with my father before they were promised.'

'And were they happy?'

'Completely miserable. But we will be different. We have some energy between us, a connection. Surely that is something worth building on.'

In less than a week, he had taken everything. He had her power. Her heart. And yet as he watched her, waiting for her answer, he looked as fragile as a taut length of thread against a blade.

'You will tire of me. Men always do,' she said.

'And you may tire of me. And maybe we will be old and tired and cranky together. But at least we will have tried.' His joviality faded. She ran a shaking finger over his lips, still disbelieving the words spilling from them. 'I feel it,' he whispered. 'In your touch. In your kiss. In your body,' he growled in her ear, and a warm shiver skated from where he kissed her to her toes. 'This is right. Let me give you more than rent on an apartment. Take my name. Marry me.'

He asked her like she had a choice. Like her response mattered.

'*Oui*,' she said, at first uncertain, then as the awareness blossomed in her, she had to snuffle her surprise, her delight, until it burst out as laughter and joy. 'I will. I will marry you, Arley West. I will be your wife.'

CHAPTER ELEVEN

Arley pushed the slip of paper across the counter, along with a 5-franc coin.

'For Mr Phineas Babbage, Number 1 Honeysuckle Street, London.' He tapped the note. '*Urgent*.'

The man rolled his eyes, and muttered what might have been *Anglais* under his breath.

Likely everything sent by telegram was urgent.

Despite the man's condescension, Arley grinned like a lovesick schoolboy. The most miraculous thing to happen in his life had been condensed to dots and dashes. He'd thought about messaging Cecil and asking him to arrange the first reading of the banns, but if a message was delivered to Number 10, who knew who else would see it. He didn't want to be greeted at the train station by a hoard of reporters.

Arley stepped out of the telegraph office and into the place du Théâtre Français. It writhed with early morning energy and anticipation. Carriages, omnibuses, people on horseback and those travelling on foot filled the wide boulevard of the Avenue de l'Opéra. In the distance, spring sunshine reflected off the roof of Palais Garnier.

He'd wanted to tell Vivianne who he was as soon as she'd agreed to marry him, but something had held him back. He'd spent his whole life as Arley the duke, and a morning as just Arley, stretched out in bed with the first blossom of love still unfurling in his chest, had been too rare and too beautiful to taint. And her slight hesitation as she asked for small luxuries, negotiating their future as she negotiated everything, had been so endearing, he couldn't bring himself to break the intimacy.

All he had promised her was himself, his heart, and a future without hunger. She shone so vivacious and brilliant, he felt a grey shadow beside her. She'd been lied to so much, broken and manipulated. And he'd lied to her, too. He hadn't meant it. Somehow, it had all snowballed.

But his truth would change her. It would give her the world. The moment he disclosed himself should be special, more than a casual conversation where he slipped in, *oh, and I forgot to mention, I'm a duke.*

His revelation should be magical. Memorable.

On the train, maybe? Too boring. On the steamer? At short notice, as Monsieur West and lacking connections and influence, he'd only been able to secure a second-class ticket. She'd think him insane if he took her to their berth and then announced himself.

When they arrived at Number 10. That would be the perfect moment. When she could see the street, the villa and their future for herself.

Why just tell her who he was when he could show her?

Chapter Twelve

'Paris never forgets, Vivianne.'

Nicole spoke her warning into the mirror, meeting Vivianne's eyes in her duplication.

'I don't care what Paris does,' Vivianne snapped back. 'I am leaving.'

'You think you will be happy in his little English world? You will not fit. He will grow bored. He will keep a mistress.'

Over the morning, between rolling, laughing, and kissing, Arley had described his home and his life, and to every request she made, he agreed. A new dress every birthday. A garden where she supposed she would learn how to grow vegetables for their kitchen, as her mother had done. Someone to help with the laundry. But over and over, his love.

In the light of the rehearsal room, Nicole spoke the deepest fears that Vivianne had buried. But her friend was young and had opportunity before her. Dukes sent her roses. She had the luxury of hesitation. Of waiting for a better offer. His promise carried more than a glint of happiness. It contained days of food, and comfort, and warmth.

'What do you want of me? I will never be the prima ballerina. I will have successful auditions less and less. I am tired of being hungry, of groping dukes, of princes without courts and the shredded nobility who come here to pretend the old days remain. I am going to be a wife. Why can't you be happy for me?'

'Because this is not an opera, where a boy falls in love with a girl he just met. This is life. He will have some secret.'

'I cannot go back to the *grisettes*. And if I am wrong, he will not be the first man to have lied. To have filled me with false promises then ran as they shattered. And if that happens, I will find a way. But maybe, I might be happy.' Vivianne choked back tears, imploring her friend to understand. 'Perhaps your duke will bring you to London one day, and I will see you again?'

They stood, eyes on one another in the mirror, as they had stood for so many years. With a turn, and a swish of muslin, Nicole spun and launched herself at Vivianne and wrapped her arms around her neck in a tight embrace.

'Remember me? In your boring little cottage?'

'I will never forget you,' Vivianne said as she pulled her friend tighter. 'Never.'

As Vivianne walked from the opera house, her heart thrummed as fast as an allegro. She carried a small bag of her few possessions. A spare dress. Her ballet slippers. Any jewellery she'd been given was long sold. Maybe Arley would buy her something special for their engagement.

Maybe he would be all the terrible things Nicole had said he might be.

She caught sight of him first, standing, awkward and alone outside Gare du Nord. He stared at his pocket watch while tugging at his coat sleeves, then scanned the crowd with a slight agitation.

What of her dreams?

What of dance?

What of *Maman*?

All of her life would rest with him.

Arley spotted her through the crowds, his expression shifting from concern to relief.

He had a garden. He hated parties. He liked simplicity.

She skipped across the street and took his arm, and he tucked her hand into the crook made by his elbow.

'Miss Chevalier, may I escort you to England?'

She gave one last look at the Paris sky and the roofline she had seen pulled apart and rebuilt so much she barely recognised it from how it had been when she'd arrived.

'Monsieur West, I would be so delighted if you would.'

Like the last note from a soprano, the train whistle rent the air. The rhythmic chug of the pistons formed a humming beat beneath Vivianne's feet, and her toes tapped the carpeted floor of the train carriage. Across from her, leaning back against the plush red seat, Arley sat with a copy of *Le Figaro* half concealing his face. His glasses—just for reading, he had assured her—perched on his nose, and the paper rustled as he turned the page.

Vivianne touched her fingers to the window. Paddocks, stone walls, stone cottages and people hewn just as rough stared up at them. The occasional dirt lane, a church on a hill, a graveyard, they all flashed in and out of view as the train sped through the countryside, hurtling them west, away from Paris and toward her future across the Channel. In all the years since she'd been gone, so little had changed. A cloud of black smoke from the train engine obscured the view, before clearing again.

Arley stretched his back then turned another page. She hadn't thought he'd wear glasses. Nicole's words teased at her again. Was this his only secret?

'When were you born?' she demanded.

He peered over the top of his paper. 'Pardon?'

'How old are you? How many years?'

He half smiled. 'I am thirty-three.'

That made sense. Young enough to be agile, old enough to be bored with novelty. 'And you work at a company for travel?'

'Something like that.'

He watched her over the top of his paper, then slightly raised his brows in expectation. Vivianne swayed as the train slowed a little at a crossing.

'Where is your duke?' she asked.

'You know, I'm not sure. I had completely forgotten him. You drove any other thought from my mind.' He shook his paper out. 'I'm sure he'll find his way home.

I haven't known him long, but I fear he'll be like a bad penny. Always turning up.'

Vivianne hunched back against the chair. She could read, but not well, so had little to distract herself from the gnawing doubt at her impetuousness. For not the first time in her life, she had placed her future in the hands of a handsome man.

The countryside of her childhood ripped by, and even though she knew the railway line was kilometres from the little stone cottage and barn she had grown up in, she couldn't stop herself from looking for it on the horizon.

'Tell me again about our house.' She didn't want to sound scared, but the unsettled fear that bubbled wouldn't calm.

Arley lowered his paper, then laid it aside. He placed his glasses beside it on the seat, then swung himself across the little cabin to sit beside her. He pulled her against his side and interleaved her fingers with his. 'In our garden, there is a tree in the yard that is so old, my grandfather used to climb it. I used to sit in it some days and watch the happenings of the street. And maybe our children will climb it too.'

Vivianne stiffened, her chest tightening. 'Children?'

Arley squeezed her hand. 'I had always hoped. I barely knew my father. But my mother remarried when I was older, and even though we did not always get along, we were something of a family... their happiness made me crave it for myself. I never truly thought it possible until I met you.' A little of the colour left his face, and his smile wavered. 'Is that something you want for yourself? To be a mother?'

'I have spent so much of my life trying not to be one.' The warmth in his eyes didn't fade, but it turned sad, and disappointed. 'You want to make a family? With me?'

While she had heard his words *marry me* clear enough, the exact window they would open for her hadn't fully bloomed in her mind. But now, chugging through the countryside, Paris behind her back, the vision of a new life cleared in her mind. A little house, with a garden, and now, the picture he painted included small pieces of her heart, playing, calling her by a new name. *Mother*. No. They would not call her Mother. They would call her *Maman*, and she would teach them her tongue. Nerves, hope, fear, excitement, all of it rose and while she could have screamed, she instead let out a nervous giggle. '*Oui*,' she whispered. 'Yes, I do.'

Arley raised her hand to his lips and kissed her palm. 'I knew. As soon as I saw you, I knew.' He twisted his hold, then kissed her wrist. A flutter ran through her. 'We could start trying now?'

He folded her collar back, revealing a little more skin, and teased his tongue over the exposure.

'You want a bride with a swollen belly?' Even as she spoke of reservation, her body keened.

'I have already sent word ahead by telegram. The first reading of the banns will be this Sunday. We'll be married in less than a month. No one would know.' He scraped his teeth, then nipped her skin. 'Do you know how hard it has been to sit here and read the paper and not throw your skirts over your head?'

He planted kisses behind her ear and nipped at her earlobe. It all felt too good, too perfect, and the pleasure he ignited clanged like warning bells.

'This is rash. You are infatuated. It happens to the dancers all the time.'

Arley sat back and studied her face. 'I am not infatuated. When we reach London, you will understand my haste, but trust me, I've never been more certain of anything. I know love from having lived so long with its absence. From watching, but never feeling. And I know it hasn't been long, but there is a pull between us. A thread.' He tucked a finger under her chin and drew her closer. 'And if I marry you, I can kiss you all I want and not have to pay.'

She tried to resist, but it was incomprehensibly true. She did feel alive in his arms, she did feel a magic in his touch. He spoke of love so casually, and why not? Why not rush into its arms? Why not surrender?

Why not, indeed, fall?

Arley tugged down the blind and checked the brass bolt. He leaned back against the door and pressed his hands flat against the wood. 'It scares me too. I came to Paris to write a list, and now I am bringing home a bride.' He swallowed hard, and his bravado flickered, then faded. 'The more I have you, the more I want you. You are a shining light. An extravagance. But will I be enough for you? Just as I am?'

Confidence and hesitation, bravado and uncertainty, his fingers trembled as he raised them to his throat and tugged at his collar. He fumbled with the first button and exposed a small triangle of chest.

In a mirror to his movement, Vivianne unfastened her own top button. Then the next. Eyes locked on hers, he continued to work at his shirt, tugged off his waistcoat, then stripped off his top layers in one movement. But with the sweep of his arm, he banged his knuckles against the roof of the carriage, and with a twist, and a squawk, he stood, half bent, with his undershirt tight caught at his chin.

'Dash and sod it,' he mumbled into the layers of clothing bunched around his ears, then twisted and knocked into the door. The blind rattled against the glass, and he gave a pitiful yelp.

Vivianne stifled her giggles as she jumped from the seat. When she found the tangle of caught clothing, she slipped it free. Still laughing, she kissed his neck, and cheek, and when she found it, his mouth, nose and eyelids.

Arley shook his clothes from his wrist. 'I was trying to seduce you. I just look like a fool.'

'I am not difficult to seduce,' she said, still laughing, then caught herself. And she saw, reflected in his eyes that would not meet hers, his vulnerability.

She traced a line from the dip at the base of his neck, between the firmness of his chest, and over the tautness of his torso. 'For a man who spends his days at a desk, you are very impressive.'

'I row. On the Thames.' He found the buttons of her bodice and slipped them free. The slow seduction altered its pace and shifted to fast and haphazard. Together they grappled, wrenched, fumbled and freed, kissed and gasped and drank each other. Bumped teeth and noses and laughed like youths fumbling behind a hay shed. There was nothing delicate about it, no seduction, no performance or pretence. Just raw and needy, and as Arley sank back against the seat and unbuttoned his trousers, and she dropped her skirts to straddle his thighs, her body thumped with that same yearning that had made her bend before him and demand he conquer her. He pushed the last layer of cotton from her body.

His expression took on that sweet awe, like in the wine bar when he had made his plea for a walk with his pin. 'You are so delicate. I am worried I might break you.' He ran his palms along the length of her torso, over her ribs, brushed her nipples and took one in his mouth. Vivianne arched into the attention, moaning with bliss. 'And then you spin on your heel, or laugh, and catch me unawares, and all I see is strength. And I just hope you don't break me.'

Suspended over his body, her sex pressed against the tip of his cock, Vivianne paused. A soft curl fell over his face, and she pushed it back, searched his eyes and kissed him, slow and deep. Her tongue searched his, teased at his tip, tasted his earnestness and breathed his love. She drew it into her body and let it wash through her, affection and desire meeting as strangers before melding into a shuddering embrace. When they separated, she had to blink fast to hide her tumult, but a tear spilled free and ran cool down her cheek.

'Is something wrong?' he asked as he wiped it away with his thumb. 'Do you want to stop?'

How to explain? Sex, fucking, bodies rutting, desire, none of it held any mystery for her. She was no maid. It was far from her first time. It wasn't even her first time with Arley. But never had she felt so stretched and exposed, so completely vulnerable, her heart ripping itself from her body as if magnetised to him. She'd never loved, truly loved, in a way that might destroy her.

'*Je t'aime.*' It came out hoarse, her voice as rough as the meaning soft. '*Je t'aime.*'

Arley took a slow breath, then stole her promise with his lips. '*Je t'aime,*' he whispered. 'From the moment I saw you.'

As she lowered herself onto his shaft and welcomed him into her body, Arley gritted out a clenched groan. He held her tight against him, his heavy sigh coursing and melding them. Thighs tightening, she rose along his length, then lowered herself, enjoying his deepness, the sensation of his hardness in her, but most of all, the flutter of his eyelids as he tipped his head back and grunted to the ceiling.

'Do you ever fake your pleasure?' he asked, then nipped her lips.

Vivianne rolled her hips, then settled lower. Her bottom rested against his thighs. 'Fake?'

'Pretend. Make the right noises.' As if embarrassed, he hid his mouth close to her ear. 'Do you pretend to orgasm?'

'You are as fragile as a petal.' Vivianne rose again, and this time, thumped down hard against him. He shuddered as he dug his fingers into her hips. 'Not with you. Not yet.'

She had meant it as a deflection, a jest, but Arley tensed. He grasped her chin and drew her face close. 'Never with me. *Compris*?'

For a moment, she wanted to shrink. To roll her body from him, to bend from his intensity and hide. But he held her chin tight, his blue eyes searching, pleading.

She nodded. 'Never, my love. Never.'

No caring, no performance, only jolts and thrusts, they bucked and swayed with the train's momentum. Arley braced her as they slowed to cross a bridge, and he guided her to closeness as they arced into a sweeping bend. Vivianne rested her arms on his shoulders and teased her fingers through his hair, drank his lips, all while riding him hard as she chased her own pleasure and release. Even his grunts fell away, and when he pinched her nipple, and bit her ear, she thrummed against him, faster, until she tipped her head back and howled at the ceiling.

'Shhh,' he half laughed as he smothered her cry with a kiss. 'People will hear.'

'I don't care.' The last of her own perfect storm eased, and spent of her own energy, she sought him, kissed him and held her thighs taunt as he thrust into her. 'Again. Make me come again. Finish with me.'

Arley pushed his hand between them, stroked her clitoris, moving his hand deftly in time with her body's movements. As they knocked against each other, he groaned her name and gripped her body to hold it in one place before pummelling into her with unrestrained abandon. She cried out as another wave rose and washed over her, and releasing her hold on him, she surrendered into his hold as he gripped her. Vivianne arched back, presented her body for his feasting, and let her arms hang limp by her side as he sunk into her with a few heavy, concentrated thrusts.

How could such pleasure come from one man? *Mon Dieu*, he was exquisite.

The air in the carriage cloyed, and as she blinked herself into awareness, all she could smell was humid muskiness. The windows perspired as thin snaking beads trailed lines down the glass. She kissed a matching droplet from his forehead.

A faint tap came at the door. 'Is something wrong in there?'

Vivianne snuffled a cry of surprise, and hunched against Arley, who wrapped his arms around her.

'Nothing is amiss. On your way,' he said.

He sounded so bold, so authoritative, that she had to lean back and take him in again.

'What is that voice?' she asked with half a grin. 'One minute you are a mouse, and now, a lion.'

'Just my voice.' He tugged her close against him and stroked her hair. 'Oh, Vivianne. I can't wait to bring you home.'

Chapter Thirteen

Not yet. Just not quite yet.

Vivianne sat perched on the edge of the seat as she peered out the window. She rocked easily with the hackney's roll, even though Arley felt every bump.

The last two days had been exquisite torture. They'd travelled by train to the coast, then caught the steamer from Calais to Dover, before catching another train to St Pancras. Amid the bustle, he'd found a cab, and hauled Vivianne and her small bag inside. The entire time, he expected someone to recognise him and spoil his surprise, but somehow, they'd managed the entire trip.

It had likely helped that they barely left the cabin on the steamer. The more he had her, the more times he lost himself in her body or held her against him as she slept, the more of her he wanted. A lifetime would not be enough. Her light, her laughter, her playfulness. Her everything.

Should he tell her now, by the park? No, not just yet. When Number 10 came into view. Then, he'd tell her.

Vivianne sat composed, her head occasionally turning as they passed a tall building, or a gathering on the street. Her fingers tangled into each other, and occasionally bunched her burgundy skirt. It was the nicer of the two dresses she'd brought with her. Soon, he'd give her an entire wardrobe. Jewellery, gloves, hats. Anything she wanted.

With a light shiver, she pulled her shawl closer around her shoulders. They'd left a Paris with blue spring skies, but arrived in a darkly clouded London, heavy with rain and gloom.

'It's not always like this,' he said. Vivianne looked across at him with a frown. 'The weather. Some days are sunny. And then it's just as pretty as Paris.'

'Oh dear,' she said.

'Oh dear?'

'Already you are speaking to me of the weather. I really am to marry an Englishman, aren't I?' A playful glint lit her eye, and she turned back to the window. The cab took a sharp turn, and Vivianne twisted as she turned to follow the sign that read *Honeysuckle Street*. Miss Delaney's villa passed by his window, while opposite, they passed the townhouses. Babbage, Hempels, Mrs Crofts.

'These houses are so beautiful. Much grander than I expected. This is your street?' she asked.

'It is.' He tried to conceal his excitement, but a smile tugged at his cheeks.

She slid across the squabs and leaned over him to peer out the window. Under her breath, she counted. '*Numero quatre. Numero huit... dix*?'

The cab slowed as it approached the gates. Arley leaned out and gave a wave. The gates opened, and the hack continued up the short drive. Slips of sandstone and slate roof flashed between the trees.

'I don't understand.' Vivianne moved back across the seat and pressed herself into the corner on the far side of the cab. 'You said you had a cottage, with a garden. Do you live in an apartment?'

'I have not been entirely truthful with you. About my house. And my occupation.' He shuffled in his seat to face her. He reached out for her hand, but she did not take hold. Instead, her gaze flicked between him, to the window, then back to him. 'I haven't lied about Spencer and Co, and why I was in Paris. That is true. But I'm not a clerk for the company. I'm an investor. I have a seat on the board.'

Vivianne's mouth opened. Closed.

'My name *is* Arley West, but not mister, or monsieur. And no one ever calls me Arley. Most of the time, people call me "Your Grace."'

Her eyes widened. Why was she not speaking? Surely, she had deduced what he was trying to tell her.

'Vivianne, I'm a duke.'

Slap.

Her hand cut across his cheek just as the carriage came to a halt before the door.

'Steady on!' He touched the spot where her palm had connected, stinging from indignation more than pain. 'I didn't plan on meeting you, and I had to be sure I could trust you. I thought you'd be excited.'

'You're a duke?' She started at a timbre he knew, but at *duke*, her voice went up an octave.

'Yes,' he squeaked. Where was his duke tone? He dug, scrambled, searched for it.

'A royal one?' she asked.

'No. Thank heavens no. Just a regular duke.'

'A regular duke.' She raised an eyebrow. 'Riddled with debts? You had no money. I am no heiress. I have no inheritance.'

'I have no debts and I don't need to marry an heiress. I have investments beside the company, and the estate. I pay my accounts.'

The driver gave a low, meandering whistle. Vivianne stayed bunched on the far side of the cab. She crossed her arms across her chest, and her lovely little breasts rose and fell fast as she took small gasps of air. 'Will you keep a mistress?' she asked, her voice cracking.

'No, heavens no. I love you.' He slid across the seat and pulled her tight body against him. He rubbed at her back and tried to coax some relaxation into her muscles. 'Vivianne...' He tipped her chin up and looked into her clear eyes, the same colour as a stormy Parisian day. 'Are you scared that because you are not noble born, you will find it hard to be a duchess?'

Vivianne pushed herself from him and straightened in her seat. Forget about the anger of before, this was pure, blind fury. Dear lord. *French* fury.

'How dare you?' A squall edged each word, slowly building to a tempest. 'I am a dancer of the Palais Garnier. I have been tiptoeing around nobility for years. I will not just be a duchess, I will be the best duchess London has ever seen.'

She was fire, passion and abandon, the most beautiful composite of everything lacking in his life. 'You'll be my

ALIVIA FLEUR

duchess?' He tried to match her fire with seriousness but failed, and instead of stifling his smile, it spread. 'Instead of Monsieur West, you'll settle for Arley the Duke?'

She huffed. 'Of course, I will, you stupid man.' And before he could offer her his hand, she wrapped her arms around his neck and kissed his lips, his nose, his chin. She gripped his cheeks in her hands, then pulled back. 'You lied to me?'

He nodded. 'I didn't set out to. I needed to know you loved me for me.'

She prodded him in the chest. 'Don't do it again.'

They tumbled out of the carriage, and finally on solid stone at the entrance of his home, he pulled her tight. He lifted her toes from the ground before spinning them both in a half circle. She gave a short squeal, then kissed him again. She was the air in his lungs, the bright sun he had craved and already he knew she would make his dreary days light. She would be the companion to his loneliness. She had seen him with nothing and loved him. With everything, they would be so happy.

A sharp cough came from the doorway.

Arley placed Vivianne on her feet. 'Cecil. This is Miss Chevalier. We're engaged.'

Cecil visibly drew on all his years of experience to not let the surprise in his eyes reach his voice. 'Very good, your grace.'

Arley grasped Vivianne's hands in his own. 'This is Cecil. He runs Number 10. Anything you need, anything, ask him, and he'll help you.' He held out his elbow. 'Care to see your new home?'

Cecil coughed again. 'Given that a hackney has just driven through the gates after witnessing your jubilant homecoming, and is now circling London, do you think it might be prudent to pen a message to your mother, your grace?'

Cecil's words sent a jolt of reality through him. He wasn't an invisible clerk visiting Paris anymore. He was a duke. And telling his mother about his engagement by telegram, followed by a letter, was better than her hearing from a speculative report in *The Tattler*.

'You're right.' He pressed Vivianne's hands to his lips, kissed them briefly, then released her. 'Cecil, take Miss Chevalier to the front room. Tea, coffee, food—are you hungry?'

She shook her head.

'I won't be long, then I'll give you a tour.' And with a final kiss, he parted from her, and made his way to his study.

In his brief absence, the mass of letters had multiplied. They may as well have been rabbits for their prolificacy.

Diligent, dutiful Cecil had separated his correspondence into two piles. One, the towering mountain of inane invitations, the other, just two letters—one from Winton, the other from Tillman, likely a quarterly report.

Arley sat at his desk and pulled a sheet of paper before him. As he reached for his pen, a thin manilla folder slapped onto the desk before him. He startled, then looked up. 'Do you have to be so dramatic?'

Phineas shrugged. 'If one can be, then why not?'

As far as everyone knew, Phineas worked as a bank clerk. An occupation so pedestrian that no one even bothered to ask which bank he was employed at. And everything about the man screamed mediocrity—his dress, his hair, his looks, his conversation.

Phineas did not work at a bank.

Phineas was a spy.

Arley had never asked what branch or department he answered to. He doubted Phineas would have told him. The man was inscrutable. His defences tumbled only once a year, around Christmas, when he would become thoroughly soused, make nonsensical statements about life and love, and then collapse into his chair and sleep through until Boxing Day. Then, he would emerge from his townhouse, pick a fight with Lawrence Hempel, and the rhythm of life would return.

Phineas fell into the chair on the other side of the desk and stretched a foot over his knee. 'I put this together after I got your telegram about the banns. Did you know she's a—'

'Ballet dancer. Yes, I'm aware.'

A half smile tugged at Phineas's mouth. 'Likely nothing more problematic in there than what you already know, then.'

Arley flipped the folder open and scanned the page. A line of dates ran down one side, and beside them was a list of disjointed names, places and events, but with the web of Vivianne's conversations, he strung them together. Her arrival in the capital from the countryside. The outbreak of the war. The siege. The Commune. *After*. Arley flipped the cover over and pushed it across the table in disgust. 'I know what she was, and I don't care. When did you become a moral crusader? Been attending meetings at Number 5 in my absence, have you?'

'I didn't do it for you,' Phineas sniped. 'And not from some misguided sense of morality. You might not give a damn, but investors and potential clients won't have the same outlook as you. And your contribution to this business might be pocket change and a trip abroad, but it means more to others. What do you think would happen to Iris if this company failed because of your bad press? Hasn't Elise lost enough?'

Arley sunk into his chair with a huff. 'Are you getting soft?'

'There's a difference between being soft and being an inconsiderate arsehole.'

An uncomfortable pang of guilt stuck in Arley's chest. Phineas was one of the few, possibly the only man in London, who didn't care for his friendship or seek his favour. That's what he liked about the man. Mostly.

Arley crossed his arms. 'I'm not the first peer to marry below his station. What about Hamish?'

'Iris exceeds him in wealth and wits. And this has nothing to do with station. She's a *ballerina*. There's not a nobleman or wealthy merchant in England who doesn't appreciate the implications of the word.'

Arley took up his pen and scratched out the first line of his note to his mother.

'I'm happy for you,' Phineas continued, although his tone held no hint of joy, and his mouth didn't turn up a smidge. 'But you know how this city works. And how it works for you. You've been the most sought after bachelor for more than a decade, you turned your nose up at every debutante, and now you're getting married, to a French commoner no less. The society mothers and fathers will have opinions. If they can't get to you, they'll get the company, and then the press will maul what's left. You can't just ignore public opinion. You'll have to give them what they want.'

'And what will they want?' He slammed his pen onto the desk, then huffed as a spurt of ink splattered across his note. 'Why must they want, what do they possibly need from me?'

'To be entranced, of course. To fall in love. To have hope that even though it wasn't them this time, maybe the next time, it will be. But also, you need to make them accept why you chose her. Show them she is from them, but above them. Special. A woman born into ordinariness, but somehow, still destined to be a duchess.'

'A common duchess? This is worse than the mini grand tour. The world is untethered.' Arley ran his hand down his face. Annoyingly, Phineas was right. 'What do I need to do?'

'She can't stay here. Not until you're married. And she can't live with just anyone. She needs to stay somewhere appropriate, with someone who has an unblemished reputation. And she'll need to be presented, at court. And taken out. Show her off a little. Let everyone see what you see.'

'I'm not showing them that.'

Phineas rolled his eyes. 'No need to brag.'

Arley chuckled, then choked off his mirth. He'd been so caught up in his own escape from society, from London, enjoying his happiness, that he hadn't considered how things might play out when they got home. So fixated on their future, he'd neglected to consider the path to it. London had gossiped like a hencoop after his mother remarried and he knew the criticism she'd worn, but her and Tillman had been independent, happy to leave the city and able to weather the loss of society's approval. The clients Iris was hoping to win over to the business, with the promise of education, and sophistication… he was part of that promise. And no self-respecting, aspirational merchant with dreams of marrying their child up the social ladder was going to send their offspring off to the continent with a company whose board member had come home engaged to a French courtesan. Rather than reassure them, he would represent every terrible fear they held.

'She'll need a back story. A cover. Want me to put something believable together?'

'Nothing too elaborate. Just simple.' Hands clasped behind his back, Arley wandered to the window, only half registering Phineas as he spoke of possible histories for Vivianne.

Outside, the weather had cleared a little. The trees filtered the sun as it shone onto the road and sidewalk. Who might be appropriate for Vivianne to stay with? Benton, directly opposite, was still abroad, and *no*. Far from appropriate. Odette? While she managed her own reputation with care, it was too big a risk. Iris had enough to deal with, and while she had steadfastly navigated her own scandal, she'd really only been accepted back into society because Hamish had drawn on his limited senses and married her. The Hartright kerfuffle was a memory, but still one muttered about in drawing rooms when the conversation lulled. Vivianne needed more than just acceptable, and a nice place to stay. She needed to be linked to the *right* type of someone.

Across the road, Spencer ascended a staircase. Scratched at the black door. Waited. After a long minute, he slipped through the wrought-iron fence and scampered away. The door opened, and a stiff butler huffed, then closed the door again.

Someone respectable.

Someone believable.

And completely beyond reproach.

Chapter Fourteen

A duchess.

She was going to be a duchess.

Not a duke's short-term lover while he was visiting Paris. Not a duke's mistress. But a proper,

titled,

married to a duke,

duchess.

Vivianne shook off the idealistic complaint of her younger self. Of the woman who had run the barricades and had tended the wounded during the siege. That woman had known hunger, but also did not know how much worse was to come. And just imagine the good she could do. She could sponsor artists. She could commission plays. She could invest in the theatre. She could do so much.

And not be hungry.

'Do you have a preference, my lady?'

Vivianne looked at Cecil. He'd been speaking for so long, she couldn't even remember at what point her thoughts had trailed off. 'I do not,' she said, drawing on her memories of all the pomp she had seen at Garnier.

'No thought at all?' he asked.

Vivianne shook her head. 'I trust your opinion. Like Arley does.'

'Very good. I shall fill the ballroom with octopi and order you a bed made of cheese.'

Vivianne startled. 'Pardon!'

Cecil gave a low chuckle. 'Just testing, my lady. I could tell you were distracted and could not resist a little joke. I was asking if you would redecorate your rooms before you are married, or would you like to address that after?'

Vivianne eyed the man. Dressed in a butler's livery, he presented himself with exactitude. His greying hair had been combed to obedience, and not even a button on his waistcoat dared to sit askew. Despite his officiousness, a hint of warmth underlay each word, and there was a kindness to his smile. She decided she liked him.

'You know, I am not a lady,' she said, her voice low even though it was only the two of them in the parlour. 'All of this is very unexpected.'

'I gathered,' he said drily.

'Monsieur West did not—'

'His Grace is not one for theatrics. Or flamboyance.' He took a step closer, his voice also lowering. 'Forgive my lack of propriety, but it is refreshing to see him so taken with another. I have known him all his life. You must be something.' Cecil stepped away and stiffened back into formality. 'Now. Should I arrange a decorator for your rooms?'

'Rooms? There's more than one?' Her entire apartment in Paris was only one room. Her house growing up had only been one room. What might a person do with more than *one* room? 'Can I see them?'

Cecil bowed. 'Follow me.'

The sitting room where Cecil had led her for tea had not been far from the villa's entrance. He led her back through the foyer, along a wide hallway with vaulted ceilings and portraits hung frame to frame. Stern men, slightly less stern ladies, men in military uniform. Vivianne scanned their faces for a hint of Arley. Maybe, his eyes in this one. Maybe, a hint of his chin. She hadn't ever seen pictures of her own family. She had only known her forebears through stories told by the hearth. His ancestry looked down on her as they passed. What would they think of her? That one, with an extra pronounced frown, probably not much. Another looked as if he'd thoroughly approve—but in a way that made her skin crawl.

She raised her chin against their stares. She did not care for their opinion. All that mattered was what Arley thought. And he loved her.

They ascended a staircase, its walnut brown steps covered in carpet that sunk beneath her street boots. The smooth balustrade ran sleek under her hands. She'd taken off her gloves in the sitting room, but now tapped her pockets to find them and slipped them back on. Her hands were too rough, too unrefined to touch wood so luxurious. Her hems were thick with dust and grime, and as they hushed over the carpet, she could almost hear every loop scream in offence. She patted down a ruffle on her blouse. She should have asked to change.

At the end of a long hallway, Cecil paused before two tall white doors. Vivianne craned her neck. They must have been twice her size. Each panel had been carved and decorated with delicate mouldings and edged in gilt trim. He took each long gold plate handle in hand and pulled the doors wide.

Slips of light sliced between the curtains. Vivianne waited for her vision to adjust to the murky grey. A dresser. A mirror. Doors. Curtains. Immaculately clean to the point of sterility, the air in the room swirled not with dust, but with inactivity.

'Can I have some time alone to look? To think?' she asked Cecil.

Cecil gave his already familiar bow. 'Of course, my lady.'

Vivianne held her breath until the door snipped closed, and then she had to stuff a knuckle into her mouth to stop herself from screaming. Hers. A room as big as her apartment in the Quartier Latin, just for sleeping. She dashed across and flung the curtains open. The window behind was twice her height, made of small squares of glass and a wooden frame coated thick with cream paint held each one in place. Outside, a small courtyard garden with a large oak tree and winding paths shivered with early spring. Sunlight cascaded in, and the wallpaper, dressed in gold leaf, winked with life. A dresser, a mirror, some chairs... where would she sleep?

Two sets of doors—not as tall as the main one that led into the hallway, but of the same white and gold style—filled the wall. Vivianne opened one. Shelves, rails, hangers, drawers, all empty. A wardrobe. She smothered a giggle. Her one spare dress would look utterly bereft in here.

Heart thumping, Vivianne opened the other door and stepped inside.

Her little bed in Paris had one purpose—sleeping. Almost as narrow as her body, made from curved steel, its mattress stuffed with horse hair, it, like sleep, had been purely functional. Other beds—in hotels or rented apartments—had other purposes. Like the bed in Arley's hotel, this one had four tall posts, and the drapes were all tied back at the corners. As wide as three of her beds placed side by side, piled with pillows, covered with a rich red brocade coverlet with gold trim that skimmed the floor, it sat squat in the room, placed central against a wall. The same wallpaper as the other room gleamed. There were no paintings in this room, no photographs on the walls. Like it had been wiped clean, and the previous occupant erased.

What colour curtains? What paintings might she hang? Who, in this room, would she be?

A squeal snuck out, then morphed into a scream, and her feet tapped out a frantic release against the floor, and she grasped her skirts and ran across the room, *one, two, three, four, five* entire strides needed to cover its length, then she launched, spun and landed on her back into the mattresses gentle embrace. A room of her own. A soft bed of her own. A man who loved her, who she loved in return.

She propped herself onto her elbow to survey it all. Directly opposite her bed was another door, although she did not need to open it to know where it led. That would be the door to Arley's rooms. Before, she had imagined the two of them sharing, as they had on the journey, not living separate sleeping lives. But what did that door mean?

Would he come in each night to claim her?

Or would she be expected to broach the barrier herself?

Would she use the lock when she wanted to be alone?

Would she ever want to be alone?

Vivianne hugged her arms across her chest and fell back, giggling like a maid and giddy with excitement.

'I gather I am forgiven?'

Vivianne rolled onto her side. Arley pushed himself off the door frame and, hands in his pockets, swaggered across the room.

'You must beg my forgiveness,' she said.

'And what is the price of your forgiveness?' He stood before her, all tall confidence and ruffled edges, caressed by the golden light.

'I want my kiss. The one that you stole at les Jardins du Luxembourg.'

'You stole from me first,' he countered, mocking, then launched himself onto the bed beside her with a low growl. With a bubble of explicit joy, Vivianne shrieked with laughter as he clambered over her, kissing, nipping and caressing. 'Where can I return this most expensive kiss? Here?' He nuzzled into her neck. 'Or here?' Moving lower, he trailed his lips across her chest. 'Or perhaps, much lower?'

Anticipation spread as Arley shuffled himself down the bed as he pushed her skirts up. With a slightly rough desperation, he brushed a crooked finger between her legs.

'Will you still shave for me even though you no longer dance?'

'Pardon?' Her sharp tone cut the air. She pushed her skirts down. 'I cannot dance?'

'You can dance. Just not ballet. Not forever. Just until things settle.' Arley rolled onto his back. 'It's not my choice. But reputation means so much in this city. It's for the company. If our competitors learned you were a dancer, they might leverage it against us. They could suggest we would not provide the *right* type of enlightenment. And that would hurt us.'

'But you don't need the company or the money. You said as much.'

'I don't. But Iris, my neighbour... It was her idea. The last year has been a trial for her. This business was her dream. If she lost this, she'd be heart broken.'

Arley spoke with such care and quiet admiration. How could she refuse his request to help a friend, when she herself had had so few of them, but relied on them so completely?

'I cannot stay here, can I?' she said.

Arley took up her hand and pressed it to his lips. 'I've asked a neighbour if you can stay with her. She's a little moralistic, but that will help. She's only across the road, so you'll still be close. It's not forever. It's just for a few weeks. Then, we'll be married, and things will go back to how they were before.'

The cold flush of reality filled her stomach. She'd known her life here would be different. They'd talked marriage, family, a little cottage, but somewhere inside she had never quite pulled together the thread that she would no longer dance. She knew the English were uptight—it was why so many of them came to Paris, to indulge in the freedom.

Vivianne pushed a curl from his forehead. 'I will do this for you, and your friend, *mon amour*. Soon, things will go back to how they were, yes?'

Vivianne slid to the edge of the bed. Arley caught her by the waist. 'You don't have to go immediately,' he cooed in her ear. He dropped to the floor, knelt at her feet, folded back her skirts and eased her knees apart. 'I cannot let you leave until I return your kiss.'

'Disgraceful.' Vivianne forced the word out between pursed lips, drawing on all her experience of the stage to keep from smiling. 'And then what happened?'

'It's really not polite to discuss in front of a future duchess,' Lady Tatton said. 'But rumour has it, she dropped her handkerchief on purpose. Thoroughly scandalous.'

The Society for the Promotion of Civic Morality and the Adherence to Proper Values met in the front sitting rooms of Mrs Crofts home every Friday, and as fiancé to the society's patron, Vivianne was a particularly honoured guest this morning.

I didn't mean to agree. And it was so long ago, I don't know how to back out. But it's finally useful. It will help with your reputation.

She wouldn't mind if they actually discussed scandalous gossip. But they seemed obsessed with minor trivialities and lapses of protocol. They would likely dissolve into vapours if they came to Paris.

Arley would hear how tedious this was. He would pay for making her suffer so.

'Item number 17: larrikins in the park.' Mrs Crofts wore black. Black beads on her day dress, black combs in her hair, black net gloves and a black jet buckle at her waist, as if she were a fresh widow unexpectedly plunged into mourning. But at Number 5, there was no hint of a Mr Crofts, living or deceased, anywhere. No picture on the mantle, no remembrance locket around Mrs Crofts neck, no painting of a man that looked like he may have been a match to the matron. The only hint that someone had actually made her a *Mrs* at one time in her past was a thin gold band on her left hand that showed between the triangles of her gloves.

Mrs Crofts spoke with a forced formality. She stood central to the room, before the empty hearth, and tapped her glasses to the meeting agenda. 'It has come to my attention...'

Vivianne leaned closer to her new acquaintance. She seemed too young to be captured in such a place. She should be out, dancing, walking in the sunshine, or laughing with her friends. 'Do you enjoy these meetings?'

The woman looked to her hands clasped in her lap. 'Not particularly. I only joined because His Grace was patron. My mother thought I might get the chance to meet him. Impress him. But he never comes. And now, I suppose it wouldn't matter if he started attending. First Lord Dalton, and now Duke Osborne. I don't suppose there will be any young men mother will approve of left soon.'

'Is that why you come? To find a husband?'

The young lady frowned. 'What else would I do during the season?'

Lady Tatton was maybe a few years younger than Vivianne, but the gap between them could have been decades. She had always wondered about the women that the men left behind when they came to the city of light. Hated them for their security, and their gullibility. She hadn't expected to find them so bereft, and just as powerless as a *grisette*.

A knock at the door interrupted Mrs Crofts' monologue. The butler addressed Vivianne from the door.

Dieu merci. Arley had come to save her. She made her apologies as she left, trying to ignore the wistful looks of the women who's slightly envious gaze followed her.

Arley would hear what a bore he had placed her with. He would regret it. After she kissed him. Then she would tell him her mind. She stepped outside onto the landing but instead of her fiancé, she found Cecil.

'His Grace is detained,' he explained. 'But I have orders to escort you to Number 10.'

'Why?' she asked.

'He made me promise I would not tell until we arrived.'

Vivianne raised her eyebrows. 'Surely you have learnt that I am not fond of surprises.'

Cecil rolled his lips to suppress a smile. 'Very well. You have an appointment with the tailor. The couturier if you prefer.'

Arley had promised her a new dress, and something for their wedding. 'A good tailor?' she asked.

'The very best.'

Vivianne clasped her hands together. Her calluses rubbed through the worn leather. 'I do not mean skill. I mean character.'

'His Grace thought you might enquire as such. Yes, my lady. Good on *both* counts.'

Vivianne scrunched at her dress, the fancier of the two she had brought, and one she had made herself. Simple, and modified to Parisian fashion, but compared to the lushness of fabrics and embroidery in Mrs Crofts's sitting room, incredibly austere.

'What am I to order?'

Now Cecil did smile. 'Anything you desire.'

They walked the short distance to Number 10, and once inside, Cecil led her to the front room by the entrance, the same room she had sat in the day before. But now, it looked like a couturier's showrooms, the sort where she had once toiled beneath the floorboards.

A young woman bobbed a curtsy and gestured to a low wooden box in the centre of the room. Vivianne stepped up and spun in a small circle. Ginghams, satin, flannel and cottons draped the furniture, while open tool boxes filled with glass beads and buttons covered the floor and tables. Feathers, beetle shells, silk thread and leather swatches, she recognised all the fabrics and ornamentation from her time with the *grisettes*. Three attendants stood waiting, all with a pencil and notebook in hand. A man with a mass of measuring tapes draped around his neck circled her. He pressed one finger to his cheek.

'Nipped waist. Not much chest. Short stature.' He took one of her gloved hands and extended her arm before her. 'Lovely long limbs. And a very pretty face. I can work with this.' He clapped his hands twice. 'Mary-Anne! Measurements.'

A woman stepped forward and slid a tape around Vivianne's waist, then her chest, around her bottom, then her hips. Each time, she called a number over her shoulder.

'They are not my numbers,' Vivianne said. 'They are too low.'

'Inches,' the tailor called across the room as he flipped through swatches of fabric. 'I would love the precision of your French millimetres. Perhaps one day?' He picked up a length of silk and raised it to the light. 'Colours?'

'What of them?' she asked.

He gave an exasperated huff. 'Which ones do you like?'

When not on stage, she mostly wore navy, burgundy, and bottle green, the colours that hid the dust and dirt of the city. Practical shades for a woman who tended her own linen.

She was not that woman anymore.

'Could I see something in pink?' she asked. The tailor snapped a finger and pointed. A woman gathered a length of fabric, the same shade as a summer peach, and presented it. Hesitantly, Vivianne stripped off her glove and stroked. Muslin, with a soft, fine weave. She'd barely feel it against her body. 'And blue? Not dark, but like the sky. And violet. Yellow. And all the colours, I want to see them all! How many can I have?' she asked, her words now tumbling with excitement.

'I have instructions to measure you for as many as you think you need,' the tailor replied.

'How many... I do not know how many. Cecil, how many do I need?'

Cecil tipped a little to the side to address the tailor. 'The future duchess needs a *full* wardrobe.'

What full wardrobe meant, Vivianne did not know, but it sent all the staff into a flurry. Papers shuffled and fell, fabrics unfurled, boxes opened, and the tailor scribbled frantically in his notebook.

'My lady, what do you think of these beads?'

'My lady, see this charmeuse.'

'My lady, would you like tea?'

'I am not, my lady, *exactament*,' Vivianne said. 'Do you have that flannel in mauve?'

How glorious, how completely indulgent to stand in one place while the most languorous silk tumbled over her chest, as a bolt of velvet rolled across the floor, as a feather was tucked behind her ear and a string of beads slithered over her shoulder.

But what to choose? Which lace? Which silk?

'I cannot decide,' she said. 'They are all so beautiful.'

'Do not think too much of the colours, or combinations. That is my job. Think of place, and presence. When you step out, how do you want to *feel*?' the tailor asked.

Vivianne flung her arms wide and turned in a half circle. 'Like the prima ballerina!' All the ladies gave a cheer as the words exploded from her. She hugged herself with joy. It was all so *perfect*.

'I did not approve Venetian lace.'

Vivianne's breath caught in her throat. 'Arley!' she exclaimed, then flung herself across the room and into his arms. 'It's all so beautiful!'

'Propriety, Vivianne,' he said in a hush as he gently pushed her to arm's length. 'I thought you might like a walk. With a chaperone, of course.' He shot a look across at the tailor. 'Do you have everything you need?'

The tailor nodded. 'Everything and more.'

Hand tucked into his familiar elbow, and followed by a watchful Mrs Crofts, Vivianne let Arley lead her down the drive and out into his street. He pointed at the long row of townhouses as he described each occupant in turn. 'The green door is Benton Hunter. Still abroad, thank heavens. He has a tendency for disruption.'

'I like disruption,' she said.

'Not his type. For a man trained in diplomacy, he is awfully lacking in it when at home. Between him and your host are the Miss Hartrights, Petunia and her niece, Elise. Spinsters, both of them.'

'Spinsters? But I have seen Elise. She is so young.'

'Scandal hurts more than the person who courts it, I'm afraid. Her sister didn't mean it, I'm sure. And the fellow at the heart of it... I met him once. He seemed like a good man. Certainly better than the one she was engaged to. But in this city, gossip weighs more than reason. And poor Elise bears the brunt of it.'

As they walked, he told her about the house being renovated to take lodgers for the company, and the story of the old woman who had lived in Number 6, which was now a vacant block only inhabited by a grey cat with a white tipped tail who scampered between the rubble, to the brown brick where the woman who was the brains behind their business lived. With a shout, the door of Number 3 opened, and a bundle of children tumbled out into the street and raced toward the park. And trailing her and Arley the entire way was an attentive Mrs Crofts.

'Your Mrs Crofts is a proud defender of my virtue. Perhaps someone should tell her she will need to sail across the Channel to find it. I have not seen it for many years.'

Arley smothered a laugh. 'I suggested one of her staff, but she insisted on seeing the duty through herself.'

'Why do we have to be chaperoned at all? It's not as if we haven't—'

'Shhh!' He glanced over his shoulder, before giving her a conspiratorial smile. 'Heavens, don't remind me. I think about it constantly. It's insufferable, how much I miss you. But appearances matter. People gossip at the slightest thing.'

'So if people knew I had your cock—'

'Vivianne!'

'In my mouth.'

He wiped his hand down the length of his face and gave her a mock look of frustration.

'They would be offended?'

'Yes, they would be.' He bumped his elbow against hers. 'I will not sleep tonight.'

'Good. You deserve to suffer for sending me away.' Vivianne toyed with her glove button. 'You could have had your pick of those innocent misses. And lovely ladies, too. I thought I would despise them, but I do not.'

Arley stilled her fidgeting fingers with his broad hands and turned her to face him. 'I did not want some innocent miss. I chose you, and when I was just a humble monsieur, you chose me. Nothing else matters.'

Vivianne pushed herself onto her toes, craving his lips. With a glance over her shoulder, Arley turned his head. She lowered herself again.

'I have something for you.' He pulled a small, folded booklet from his coat pocket. 'It's an etiquette guide, to help you with your presentation at court next week. It lists everything you need to do, and what to expect.'

'You are lucky the queen's throne is empty. I would not bow if she sat in it. Why must I do this again? Can't I just marry you?'

'Being a duchess has certain expectations, and one is that you have been presented at court. And the people want to see you. Be impressed by you. They want to make you their star.' He waved the booklet. 'Do you need to rehearse?'

Vivianne pushed his hand away, then gave his cheek a playful tap. 'I can hold an audience. I can curtsy. Do not worry. Everything will be perfect.'

CHAPTER FIFTEEN

Sweaty, thick and stagnant—Arley could not recall the air in the corridor of St James's Palace being so stiff when he had attended his levee and been presented at court. But then, that had been over ten years ago, and only men attended the presentations of their male peers. The presentation of the debutantes and newly noble wives took place at Buckingham Palace, and not only did the families attend, but also every austere nobleman seeking a rich wife from the merchant class, and the more comfortable titles looking for an equal, in status and wealth.

'Pardon me,' he grunted as a woman wearing a skirt as wide as the hallway pushed past, and her mountain of ribbons and ruffles sent him clinging to the wall. He'd never get to the drawing room in time if he had to battle through all of this.

'Your Grace! This way.'

Hamish Dalton, dressed in perfect court dress except for a hideous waistcoat, stood at the end of a corridor, munching on a biscuit. A few crumbs landed on his coat, and he flicked them away with a frown. Arley pushed through the press to join his neighbour.

'Do you use the same tailor as your friend? That Algernon chap?' Arley asked.

'Not usually. This is old. I wanted to look all perfect for Iris, and then this morning, she dared me to wear it. I think she was battling nerves when she said it, but I couldn't back down from a challenge.' Hamish snickered. 'Met Algernon, did you? I haven't seen him in weeks.' His hand disappeared into his coat pocket, then reemerged holding another biscuit.

'Given he's travelling on my purse, I imagine you might not see him for a few weeks more.' Arley nodded at Hamish's hand. 'I didn't realise they'd started serving refreshments at these things.'

'Bertie, pay for food? Unlikely. Gena was worried I'd get hungry. She made me take provisions.' He tipped his head. 'I think it's this way. Iris and your fiancé are in the same group. We should be able to sneak in a side door and find somewhere to watch.'

For all the world looking in, the presentation at court was a grand spectacle, a moment of triumph, an arrival. Its reality was crowded corridors, sniping parents and bored princesses who pretended to care. Arley had attended some out of a sense of duty his first few years in London but had quickly shrunk from the spectacle when he found himself as much on display as the women in white.

And that hadn't changed. As he and Dalton moved down the hall, heads turned, while hands and fans raised to conceal gossip.

'Have you been to one of these before?' Arley asked.

'Never. Iris is one part incensed, three parts terrified that, as a newly noble wife, she has to be presented. If she'd known what she'd have to take on, I'm not sure she'd have married me.' He chuckled. 'And everyone seems to have forgotten that my father never bothered to have me presented. Poor Iris. It's like she's carrying the burden for both of us.'

The three of them were practically of an age, Arley perhaps a year older, but how different their childhoods had been. Hamish had been the forgotten spare heir. Iris, as the adopted daughter of the unconventional Albert Abberton, had been both doted upon and given an extraordinary amount of freedom. Iris and Hamish had spent their childhood sneaking about the street, seeking mischief and making it when it could not be found. Arley, already a duke at six years of age, had spent his brief visits to the street inside Number 10, toiling at lessons, learning politics, and becoming equipped to manage all the structures of his future. By the time he had come to London at twenty-one, ready to step out in his own right and fulfil his father's legacy, Hamish was sequestered in the country and Iris was abroad with her father more often than she was at home.

They reached the drawing room and jostled their way into the crowd. Across from them, on a dais, Prince Albert sat beside his mother's vacant throne, while on the opposite side of the empty chair, sat his wife, the Princess Alexandra. A scarlet carpet runner stretched the length of the room, disappearing through an archway at either end, like a train track, shuttling debutantes from innocent obscurity through to station marital availability.

Hamish tapped Arley's arm. 'Here they come.'

They started as a blur of white. Fluff, feathers, lace and flounces, they formed a long glowing line that disappeared into the darkened distance. Iris led the group and took a visibly nervous inhalation as she stepped beneath the archway. A few visible curls of auburn hair burnished against the white of the three feathers that sat atop her head, the simple crown of a woman married and being presented as such. As an unmarried woman, Vivianne would have two.

Iris paused, looked up and perhaps caught sight of Hamish, as a grin tugged one corner of her lips. Beside him, Hamish took half a step forward, craning his neck to better see his wife.

Once, he would have felt a bitter jealousy at such subtle affection, but now, he almost glowed at seeing it. Like he was part of some club.

As Iris reached the space before the royal couple, a page dressed in red with a singular tall ostrich feather atop a tall black fur bonnet, moved to stand beside her. He extended his arm. Another page lifted the edge of her long, white train. Together, the trio walked to stand before the throne. Iris dropped into a curtsy and lowered herself until her feathers brushed the floor. She held the pose until the page draped her train over her arm, and then she rose to standing. With a confident half turn and a wink at her husband, she continued along the red-carpet runner and out into the adjacent reception room.

Hamish retrieved another biscuit from his pocket. 'I'm going to find Iris,' he said, then took a hearty bite. 'She did well, didn't she?' and before Arley could reply, his neighbour wove between the other onlookers and was gone.

Arley tapped at his side with his fist. This was how he always wound up. Surrounded by people, yet alone.

He scanned the line of debutantes and wives waiting to be presented until he caught sight of a familiar stance, and the slight fidget of a poised, gloved hand. As the group moved a little further along, the delicate, perfect profile that squeezed his chest and turned his ankles to jam flashed into view, then disappeared behind a much taller debutante's puffed sleeve. He shifted his position to try to spot her again. Her gaze found his for just a moment. Sunshine and storm in a look, the brief connection sparked a fire inside and he let the realisation settle that now, he wouldn't be alone. He would have someone who loved him, just as he was.

How he missed the closeness of those days in Paris. Missed her lips, the yield of her body when he pressed against her, missed how she arched as she climaxed, and how she dug her nails into his back. He missed her giggle when she made some joke and he finally caught on. He missed her hand around his elbow.

Duty, propriety, all the structures of his life had filled the week since they'd returned, and that combined with the watchful eye of Mrs Crofts meant that moments together were brief and observed. But boxes for her new wardrobe had been delivered, some to her rooms, others, to her temporary lodging across the street. Soon she would be just a panel of wood away from him. His wife. His duchess. His forever.

The line of debutantes moved forward. Now he could make out the sleek cut of her bodice, and the fullness of her skirts. More ostentatious than what he thought she'd pick, her skirts half swallowed her, and she resembled a doll, set atop a puff of cream. She stroked the embroidery and smiled to herself. He'd made her happy. And that made him happy, too.

'I heard you had gotten engaged. She's quite pretty.'

Arley scrunched his fingers into a frustrated fist. 'Winton. What brings you here?'

Arley cast about the room, but all eyes remained fixed on the line. How had he even been allowed in? But of course, this was Winton. He always found a way. Roguish to the point of charming and bearing such an uncanny resemblance to their father that the older nobles visibly turned in confusion when he came into a room, Winton would have greased, eased or begged his admittance. It was what he did. He found the simplest path through life. He had all the freedom of being a duke's son with none of the responsibility.

'You, of course. I wanted to say congratulations, and all that. I was going to send you a gift, but I'm a little light at the moment. And you likely have everything you need.'

Arley had learned of Winton's existence the same way that his mother had learnt that her husband had kept a mistress—when his will had been read. He'd settled a house, some investments, a small allowance and a plea for compassion on the pair. And with the obedience of a duchess, his mother had continued the payments to them, and once he came of age, Arley had taken on his father's wishes and done the same.

His bastard half-brother walked through life with the ease of a man with wealth and no burden. Six years his senior and taller than Arley, Winton's dark hair stuck out at all angles. His uneven grin coupled with broad shoulders and his well-meaning, if slightly gullible nature, made him a favourite, despite his birth and the rumours that he was tupping every second nobleman's wife. Everyone loved Winton, and they could. They didn't have to pay his bills.

'You have an allowance.' Arley shuffled sideways to better follow Vivianne. 'You should have received it just weeks ago.'

Winton rubbed the back of his head. 'Funny story. I wound up in this card game at the Hog and Thistle. I swear I had a solid hand. Solid! But then, bloody Kenneth, Earl Bamford's fourth son, do you know him? I don't suppose you do. He had three aces, and I only had two! I lost it all.'

Arley's teeth ground so tight together, it was a wonder he didn't bust a molar. 'No more, Winton. You need steady employment. You need to make some kind of contribution to society.'

'And what do you do to contribute?' Winton's tone turned defensive, and a little dark. Arley knew him as an occasional angry drunk, where his affability turned to anger with jeyklesque speed, but had never known him to bite whilst sober.

'I sit in the house. I make laws. I'm a duke, for heaven's sake,' he said.

Winton grunted but said nothing more.

'Miss Vivianne Eloise Katherine Marie Chevalier,' announced a page.

The few extra names had been Phineas's idea. A way to add some mystery, and hopefully, muddy the trail.

Vivianne stepped forward. She swayed slightly with each step, until she took hold of the page's arm, then steadied. She stepped forward before the vacant chair. The room quietened. Necks craned. She adjusted her posture, then dipped into a curtsy, and bent forward.

Not deep enough.

Not low enough.

Her feathers did not brush the floor.

Such a small thing, yet it set the room to hum with the observation. *The French woman will not bow.* She tried again, this time dropping lower, but her skirts puffed with air, and still she did not reach. Her arms flailed. Arley wanted to cry out, and he tried to push through the crowd, but the audience was too fixed in their stance, salivating and hungry, their bodies a wall, and before he could get to the edge of the group, Vivianne toppled forward. Her skirts gave a tiny *floof* as the air left them, and she lay sprawled as her delicate toes kicked at the air, like two tiny pink fish in a white, rippled sea.

Winton laughed, his great donkey like guffaw setting off a chain of cackles, which rose into a crescendo. Even the royal couple had to work hard to smother their amusement. Arley forced his way through the crowd and tugged Vivianne to her feet, then he whisked her along the carpet to the fading symphony of criticism and spite.

'He pushed me,' she hissed as he hurried her into the foyer.

'You just lost your balance,' he said, hoping to calm her.

'I am a ballerina of the Palais Garnier.' Vivianne twisted from his grasp and prodded a finger into his chest in emphasis of each word. '*I do not fall.*'

'A ballerina?' They had almost knocked into Iris and Hamish, and as Iris looked between the two of them, her cheeks paled. She was too well travelled, too worldly to miss the implication of the word. 'You are a dancer? From the opera?' She scrunched her skirts. 'And after last year—' She looked to her husband, then to the floor at Arley's feet. 'Your grace, I would never judge, but the press does not care for our happiness. Elise walks a tightrope and may never be free from her sister's scandal. My name is completely hidden from any advertising we do. Our reputation rests on your connection to the company. No one has morals as stringent as the masses. I am sorry to be so blunt, but if this were to become public, it would ruin Spencer and Co.'

Vivianne huffed something like *Anglaise* under her breath, but all her rage left her. She was too good, and Iris too vulnerable, for her to hold her ire.

'I had thought of this,' Arley muttered. 'Which is why...'

The mood of the room shifted. Not so much a chill, as a shift of focus, as if everyone's attention had gone from the trivial and mundane to the magnificent. A few groups in the far edges turned from their conversation. Palace staff slowed their step. Hamish stopped chewing. A voice, rounded, cutting and firm, low enough to be indiscernible to others in the room but crisp enough to penetrate his ears perfectly, came from behind.

'A telegram. You actually thought it appropriate to deliver your news via dots and dashes?'

Arley shut his eyes against the roll of guilt and annoyance in his stomach. 'Now is not a good time for this conversation.'

'Arley William Victor Charles Ferdinand Francois West, you will not educate your mother on the appropriateness of time.'

Barely scraping five foot in height, with a rounded figure, bright blue eyes, dark curls and an indomitable stare, Arley's mother had a way of looking up at the world while simultaneously making it cower. The youngest of three duke's daughters, she had been raised to be a princess, but her father had settled for making her a duchess when the royal family found brides amongst the European courts. Widowed at twenty-four, she'd been a crumpled, paranoid mess for most of his early life, and had handed off his education to headmasters and advisers who liked the idea of moulding a duke to have in their pocket. When he was fourteen, she'd found love, along with her voice, and had plucked him from the influence of others. But the lost years were lost, and while they'd found common ground, they'd never quite gotten along.

His estate manager and stepfather Tillman hovered behind, his slow country smile dawning. 'Hallo Arley,' he called, with a bright wave. 'The new tractor arrived.'

His mother pulled him to her chest, held him for half a breath, then released him just as quickly. 'That was appalling.'

'Vivianne just needs to—'

'I'm not blaming *her*,' his mother quipped. 'I read enough on the train and filled in the gaps with my experience. You sent a kitten to face wolves. Heavens Arley, it's been a quiet news week. They're hungry for anything.' Arley's mother strode forward, grasped Vivianne's biceps and twisted her into the light. Vivianne squirmed as his mother clasped her chin and angled her a little. Arley half expected her to push up Vivianne's gums to check her teeth, like she might one of her prized thoroughbreds. Vivianne squawked, and his mother released her. 'You can't just put a woman in a fancy dress and throw her into society.'

'I don't care about society,' he grumped back.

'That is irrelevant, as society cares about you.' In the rush to remove Vivianne from the presentation room, his coat collar must have folded over, because now she straightened it, and tugged at his hems. He brushed her away. She crossed her arms, and gave him her signature, penetrating look. 'You've always liked to nudge. Antagonise the *ton* just a little, then retreat to your villa. But it's only ever been just you. Now it is not.'

This is what came from stepping out of his small circle. From listening to his mother's suggestion that he meet people outside of parliament. From responding to Hamish's request for help and for getting caught up in the *bonhomie* of it all.

But if he hadn't, he wouldn't have met Vivianne.

'We'll be married soon, and it won't matter. They'll find someone new to gossip about,' he said.

'They will most certainly not. You think you know everything, but you only know this town as a duke. They will want to know everything about her. They will follow her fashion. Ask what she is reading. Report on who she bets on at the races. Where she buys her ribbons.' His mother threaded her arm through Vivianne's, before she patted her hand. 'Don't listen to him on these matters anymore. And call me Lorelei. Come my dear. Let's make you a duchess.'

When reflected in the water, the spires of the Houses of Parliament seemed to stab their little spikes into the grey pall of cloud, all rippled and distorted in their mirror. Arley leaned into the motion, sunk his oar below the water, then heaved again, enjoying the short propulsion from the movement. The river was busy with other sportsmen rowing, sailboats, cargo and traders, and even though it smelt of oil, dead fish and stagnation, in his little skiff, tugging on the oars and sluicing over the water was one of the few places outside of his home where Arley found a slight peace with the world.

In just a few weeks, he'd spend more time inside the house than he did anywhere, even home at Number 10. And that included sleeping. Between the debates, committees, reviewing reports, the sitting house filled his life with direction and purpose that was somewhat lacking in the winter months. Even before proxy voting was abolished eight years before, he had attended every day and taken his work seriously. He owed it to his family's legacy.

Had his father paddled across the Thames, contemplating life inside the house? Arley knew the man had rowed—he'd been a founding member of the Ilex Rowing Club, which, as a graduate of Oxford, Arley could also join. It was one of the few scraps of certain information he had. A mere sliver of knowledge to supplement the shadows of memory of a tall man full of gruff words and long, appraising silences. Arley pulled back on the oars. His biceps flexed against his shirt sleeves.

He'd spent his life gathering snippets about his father as he sought to construct some kind of visage of who he had been, and from that, try to create some kind of definition of how to be a duke. He'd had so little to base his life on.

Big Ben pounded the air with its rhythmic tolling of the hour, as a horn from a passing ferry echoed over the water. Arley sunk one oar, and the surrounding ripples swirled and glugged as he leant into the motion as the skiff turned. His father hadn't even bothered demanding a spare heir from his wife before he'd relocated to town to live a secret life of domesticity with his mistress and their child.

Had Arley—quiet, preferring solitude to groups, always forcing himself into his inheritance—been a disappointment from such a young age? Or had his father only been waiting for Arley to grow older to teach him what he needed to learn, for a day that would never come as he'd died too soon?

Or was Winton—charming, and so striking in resemblance to the man that he could have been his twin—simply who he preferred?

The skiff bumped against the deck. Arley wobbled a little as he disembarked. He dragged his boat onto the bank, then squatted to tether it to the rope. Since Ilex had moved from Chelsea to Putney, he'd rented a small storage shed and a change room close to the Lambeth launch from a local publican. It allowed him to spend snatched moments on the river, when he needed some peace to recalibrate, and remain close to the house. And the publican kept it quiet that Arley used his rooms. He was a good man. Or at least, a good man for a fee.

'Morning, your grace. Have you seen the evening edition?' The publican pushed the paper across the bar. 'Seems Goodman took a turn during the night. His doctor has advised he retire.'

Arley's father had been good with numbers. That fact was the first to have come into Arley's life. Arley was better with languages, so he'd forced himself to learn the machinations of budgets and spend. Because his father had also wanted to be Chancellor of the Exchequer, even though it had been decades since someone from the upper house had been appointed to the post. A position one couldn't demand, regardless of title or connections, it took work, preparation, and a hefty slice of luck when the opportunity came along.

Winton may have gotten their father's attention, but Arley had his legacy.

This was his chance to fulfill it.

CHAPTER SIXTEEN

Future Duchess Takes a Tumble.

Those looking West for inspiration on what to wear might want to consider a more pared down approach, as conversation coming from the presentation at court yesterday reveals that big skirts are big trouble...

'There are no menus in *The Tattler*.' Lorelei plucked the newspaper from Vivianne's hand, folded it into a tight rectangle and placed it on one of the low tables that dotted the sitting room of Number 10. 'None you should serve, anyway.'

'You said I had to know what is happening in the city, for connections and arrangements. How will I know otherwise?' Indignation bubbled beneath her words. 'And I did not fall. I was pushed.'

Lorelei held up a silencing hand. 'The truth does not matter. Don't read the articles. They will not help you.'

Vivianne could charm a diplomat with a half-smile. She could hold a line in perfect unison with the *corps de ballet* and move as one with the other dancers. And she could balance on one toe and raise her other foot above her head. But she feared she would never learn the intricate dance of relationships, etiquette and behaviour that Arley's mother detailed to her as they worked together in the sitting room at Number 10.

'It would be quicker if you would just tell me what to serve,' Vivianne grumbled.

'If I tell you, you will never learn, and I will never leave, which would be a tragedy.' Lorelei delivered the dire prediction with the same abrupt monotone that she used for almost all conversation. 'Arley and I like each other better when we are at a distance. And I have no interest in occupying a house with a newly married couple.'

'Your grace—'

'Lorelei.'

'Being a duchess is not what I imagined. The attention. The restrictions. Arley says I cannot dance.'

'You can dance. Just not the ballet.' Lorelei circled Vivianne, slapping her fan into her palm. 'Again.'

Vivianne lowered herself into a curtsy.

'Too low. I said a royal duke, not a foreign prince. Do not adjust your chin. *Never* smile.'

Vivianne flexed her fingers into her new gloves. After hours of bobbing and reciting names, lines of sweat raced down her back. Unlike at Garnier, where she wore light muslin, in here she wore a heavy day dress with layers of petticoats, a bustle, and adorned with ruffles and bows. Her gloves hadn't moulded to her hands yet, and even the gaps between her fingers felt clammy. Vivianne plucked her buttons and stripped one off. Lorelei took her hand and twisted it into the light, frowning as her eyes traced her calluses and toughened skin.

'Never be without your gloves in public. That includes in spaces with staff. You can never remind them of themselves.'

Vivianne huffed as she shoved her hand back into the stiff leather.

'The Earl of Foxingford...' Lorelei paused.

Vivianne trawled her memory. 'Unsuccessfully tried to woo the wife of Baron Ludgate. He still thinks of her, and in a way he should not.'

'And therefore...'

Must she take on the burdens of earls and ladies, along with her own life? 'Therefore...'

'You can never invite Lady Foxingford and Lady Ludgate to the same event,' Lorelei said, her tone prodding. 'Unless you want fireworks. Which you do not.'

Vivianne tapped the names off on her fingers. 'Foxingford. Ludgate. Never together.'

'And while Ludgate is a supporter of McGlinty, he will never vote with him unless given the opportunity for...'

Vivianne's head throbbed. Lorelei continued to circle her as she spoke. A tap at her wrist to adjust her posture was followed by a tug on her skirt to neaten her hem. Since the disaster of her presentation the week before, this had been her days: receiving lessons on deportment, learning the intricacies of relationships and practising her curtsy *again*.

No wonder the people of France had beheaded so many of the aristocracy. Not because of the oppression. But because they were all so tedious.

'People, presence, persuasion, Vivianne, in everything you do. Understand the people you are interacting with. Always be mindful of your presence. You are a duchess—you curtsy to no one unless they are wearing a crown. And always understand what you want from a situation, or you will find yourself twisted into some commitment that does not suit.'

'This is ridiculous!' Vivianne shook her skirts and stormed to the window. The sun had broken through the clouds, and she longed to sit in the garden, or walk through the park. To find a café and sit and watch the promenade. But like yesterday, and the day before, and every day since her failure, she was contained. 'Do people not attend parties just for fun?' she asked.

Lorelei sighed with her now familiar exasperation. 'People, yes. Duchesses, no.'

The faint crunch of wheels on gravel sent a jolt through Vivianne. Each day, she hoped to catch a moment with Arley, but maybe one in three she saw him. His days took him from home to parliament early, and while she often lingered as late as she could, she was often back in her room at Number 7 and looking over the street from the opposite side of the road when his carriage turned into the drive. His voice echoed in the entryway as his shadow moved past the arched entrance before he followed. Frustrated and agitated, he issued orders to a short man beside him as he handed over his hat and gloves to Cecil.

'I did not say I would vote with McGlinty. I said the opposite.' The man, holding a pencil and notebook, bobbed beside him as he scribbled. 'And I need to meet with Viscount Pemberton to discuss his current support.'

The man she'd met in Paris had moved with a slight uncertainty. But this Arley spoke with determination as he rattled off names and orders, before the group moved out of sight, his voice fading with their footfalls.

'He is making a bid, then,' Lorelei said.

Vivianne looked to the duchess. 'A bid?'

'Launching a political campaign. He wants to be Chancellor of the Exchequer. Fulfill his father's unattained dream,' she explained. 'The memory of that man hangs over him still.'

'Is being a duke not enough for him? He wants more?' Vivianne asked.

'It's not about *more*. It's about legacy. His father wanted the appointment, as his grandfather held it, but died before he could achieve it. At some point, Arley took it on as his mission. Legacy doesn't weigh men like Arley or his father, it sustains them.' Lorelei turned to Vivianne. 'And you will be his counter. The lightness that brings important connections to dinners. The modest beauty that is described in the press as his steady keel. The gentle elegance that softens his hard edges. You can help him in his ambitions. That is what a duchess does. We are far more important than men realise.'

'But he's a duke. They don't just give him what he wants?' Vivianne asked.

'He is not the only duke, and that is not how the house works. Certain privileges are available to him, but not everything. He's too reserved for the shoes he's intent on filling. His father was more... sociable.' The air turned stiff, and Vivianne wasn't sure what emotion edged Lorelei's words—pride or resentment. 'People expect a performance from a duchess.' She gestured at the archway that her son had just vacated. 'This world will be your stage. And when the audience is gone, you will be his retreat.'

This Exchequer was for Arley what the prima ballerina was for herself. It needed more than hard work, or commitment. It needed influence. Ambition. Opportunity. The pang of the lost dream still bit, but now, she could help Arley achieve his dream. He could have his heart's desire, which she had not been able to grasp for herself.

'I think you are ready.' Lorelei's brisk tone broke Vivianne's thoughts.

'To be a duchess?' Vivianne asked.

'Gracious, no. For an outing. Gather your things. We are going to the stationer. You need invitations.'

'For what?'

Lorelei smiled. 'For the most talked about wedding of the season, of course.'

They should be elegant. No, ostentatious. No, demure. White, and innocent? Pastel and bright? Or dark and serious, edged in black, to show the importance of Arley's title.

'My lady, those are for funerals,' the assistant said as he turned the page in the sample book. 'May I suggest ivory and gold? It's a classic combination.'

The assortment of papers spread before Vivianne shimmered like stained glass in afternoon light. Lorelei, seated beside Vivianne on the chaise in the private room that the staff had ushered them into, gave no hint of preference or direction. Only watched, her sharp eyes following Vivianne's gloved fingers as she touched each little sample.

Parchment, vellum, heavy, light, embossed, hand painted, machine pressed. And then, what typeface? She had to focus hard to read, especially English, which she had learnt by ear, and so preferred the simpler letters. But should she request the more ornate style because it was more... well, more?

She recited Lorelei's mantra in her mind—*people, presence, persuasion*. Which one of these would impress people she did not know and convince them she was worthy of being a duchess?

'I think I like...' She tapped her finger between two samples, before pausing on a heavy parchment, with slightly rough, rustic yet beautiful edges, and the lightest gold fleck through the texture. 'This one. It is beautiful, no? And I would like the letters with all the curls.'

When Vivianne looked to Lorelei, she was trying to hide the faintest of smiles. She'd done it. She'd made a good choice. Despite its simplicity, her heart beamed. Her first success. Today, invitations. Tomorrow, she'd be running the household.

Perhaps not *tomorrow*. But soon.

The stationer opened a large ledger and folded over the pages. He took up a pen and began scratching out the order.

'What is the charge?' Vivianne asked. Lorelei had told her she'd need to watch the economy of the household. She could begin now.

'The... charge?' asked the attendant.

'For the paper, and envelopes. The printing. How many pounds?'

Beside her on the chaise, Lorelei shifted, and gave a subtle cough.

The attendant pulled out a sheet of paper and made some notes.

'I reckon it at £37. M'lady.' A slight gruffness edged his tone.

'*Non, non, non*, that is too much!'

'You are asking us to rush the work. Other orders may need to be delayed,' he said, defensive.

'I know this work, and the people who do it. Even for premium paper it should not be more than £10. Maybe even less.'

Vivianne squared her shoulders like she was on stage, frowned, just a little, and stared him down. He blinked fast, his mouth opening and closing as he looked from her, to Lorelei, and then down at his sums. 'I suppose we could reckon it at...' He scratched out a few more numbers. 'How does £7/6 sound? Better?'

'*Bien*. Much better,' Vivianne said.

Lorelei furnished the stationer with the details of the church, the date, and the numbers to be printed. Vivianne moved to the door and peered into the shop. It was full of activity—a man inspected small bottles of ink, young ladies giggled over pink sheafs of paper, a matron discussed fountain pens with an assistant. Vivianne took half a step into the space and inhaled. Dry parchment, the heavy aniseed like scent of ink, and the hubbub of people, city dust, soot and energy filled the air. For the first time since she arrived, Vivianne felt close to the people, their daily lives and grievances, their sorrow and joy. Perhaps she could stroll through the shop and brush shoulders with them. Maybe start a conversation. She could buy Arley a new fountain pen. Surely, that was something he would need.

But before she could place her boot to the wooden floor, Lorelei tapped Vivianne's elbow. 'We are finished here.'

Inside the carriage, Vivianne flexed her fingers against her gloves. She loosened the buttons and tugged at the fingertips. As Lorelei stepped into the cabin, Vivianne leaned back and watched the golden light inside the shop and followed the silhouettes of shoppers going about their day. The door snipped shut. The carriage bobbed as the footman climbed onto the box and whistled before they set off again through the streets.

'What were you thinking?'

Vivianne pulled her attention from the streetscape to look at her future mother-in-law. 'I was thinking about how busy this city is, but I see no one stopping to draw or paint. Do the artists work outside in London? Or is that only in Paris?'

Lorelei's steel gaze pierced Vivianne. 'I was referring to the shop. With the attendant. You bargained with him.'

'The price was too much—'

'Duchesses do not bargain.'

'But I know the cost of these things, and what they pay the workers, and—'

'If you have to ask, you cannot afford. And if you cannot afford, you cannot be trusted to settle your accounts, and if you cannot settle your accounts your future husband is open to bribes and persuasion and will likely attract attention from undesirable associates and is in no position to run the financial affairs of this country.'

'But I saved—'

'You saved nothing. The gossip train will be humming. Every assistant will now speculate if the future duchess will throw lavish or frugal parties. Will it be worth hunting out the best piece of game or fruits for her table because she will only bargain and argue? Will she want talented musicians, or just players who can hold a tune? Will other dukes and duchesses bother to attend? Or will she only invite the ragtag neighbours of that street?'

Vivianne placed her gloves in her lap and rubbed her rough hands together. 'Arley is very fond of his neighbours.'

'He is fond of many things that aren't good for him.'

'Like me?'

Eyes locked, Vivianne held Lorelei's stare, daring her to say what she herself felt most keenly in her heart. That she didn't belong, that she would never learn, that she wasn't good enough and would only ever be a duchess in name.

'It's been weeks, Vivianne. Don't assume to tell me you know this world better than I do.'

Vivianne dropped her gaze to the carriage floor. She crossed her arms across her chest, and while she knew her stomach did not growl, and she wore beautiful clothes, new boots, and travelled through the city in a carriage that smelt like cloves and lemon, her body and breath yearned for the dirt of the streets, the painters, the sunshine, Nicole, and the feel of the uneven stone through her heels.

When Lorelei next spoke, her tone softened a little. 'The fire that used to light your way? It will now blister your hands if you take your eyes from it. This is not The Marriage of Figaro, where it is fun to criticise the nobles and laugh at their stupidity. This is our life. From them but not one of them. You must never forget.'

Chapter Seventeen

Arley couldn't recall a Spencer and Co meeting ever being so ordered.

Maybe not ordered. There was no officiousness. No strict following of the agenda.

Only quiet.

Even the blasted cat, perched on the sill, watched him through narrow eyes, making not even a tail flick toward the milk jug on the table.

Arley sat in his usual seat, to the left of Iris, opposite Hamish. He took a breath. Cleared his throat. Searched for his duke voice.

But when he opened his mouth, what came out was slightly strangled, and off-key, like the nervous squawk of his youth. 'And on the printed itinerary before you, you can find the sites that would provide the type of tour that a young person might find enlightening. Their mini-grand tour. They certainly enlightened me.'

Hamish snuffled into his tea. Iris shot her husband a disapproving look.

Lawrence shook the paper, as if the motion might change the words. 'Watch the painters outside the cafés?

No parent is going to agree to that.' He squinted at the page. 'Does that say a visit to a subterranean cemetery?'

'I thought that one sounded intriguing,' Phineas drawled.

'What about watching the rain fall in the gardens?' Lawrence asked.

'Oh no.' Phineas shook his head. 'That is a terrible suggestion.'

Arley squeezed the rough papers in his palm, then slapped them onto the table. 'You wanted a tour to inflame a ready mind, didn't you? Enlightenment? New beginnings? Explore Paris after the siege? This is it. It's different from before. The place feels like it's on the cusp of something amazing. There's a weight and a lightness to it all at once. And if a young person is going to go there, it feels remiss to not expose them to all that energy. Going from site to site and missing all the places in between won't do that for them. Odette, surely, as an artist, you appreciate this list?'

The soprano pursed her lips as she raised the paper. 'I would like to see all these places. And to watch the rain fall in les Jardins du Luxembourg again.'

Arley settled back into his chair and tented his fingers across his chest.

'Which is precisely why you should not include them,' she continued. 'I have always felt that England is ahead with one foot, and behind with the other. Our clients need to trust us. We are unknown. We need to walk slow. At least for the first year.'

'The parents will expect something a little more structured. More supervised learning,' Lawrence said.

'But what about the speech Lady Dalton gave when we all agreed to be part of this? How travel could change a person and open them up to the world? That's what this is.' Arley slapped the pages onto the table. 'How will they learn if they're always bloody watched, always under scrutiny and never given a chance to damn well fly!'

Arley gulped air through the last of his outburst. The table held a collective breath. Iris lifted the sheet before her, her eyes flicking hesitantly across the page.

'I like Garnier and Colonne Vendôme. The rest is too vague. Too much of a risk. It won't appeal to our clientele.'

'I will ask Vivianne—'

Iris spread her thumb and forefinger across her forehead, before pushing her fingers through her hair. 'I have a book, your grace. I will send you a list to confirm that the remaining sites I think will suit are still standing. That will be enough. The tour leaders need to be trained. We don't have time for more. We will launch with what we have.'

Early morning at the start of spring was Arley's favourite time on the water. Before the river became too busy with traffic and the wake from passing boats made it difficult to get up a good pace. He balanced his oar across the skiff's breadth, then knelt to untie its rope.

'Why don't you ever race?'

Arley grunted his frustration. Damn publican. He should have paid him a special 'lie to my mother if she makes an enquiry as to my whereabouts' premium. His mother had a way though. The wealth of Croesus would not be enough to keep the man silent. She'd extract the information she needed, regardless.

'The Ilex Rowing Club doesn't race. Not in open competition, anyway.'

'You're very good though. You could join another club.' His mother took a quick step back as the wake from a passing boat washed over the deck, but the water still reached the circle of ruffles and turned the light blue trim of her gown dark. He'd been waiting for this conversation since she'd arrived. Over stiff dinners, and breakfast, she had said nothing.

'I don't want to hear it,' he grumbled, not looking up from his boat.

'That McGlinty has sided with Clarke? I won't tell you then.'

Arley swore under his breath. He'd hoped that despite their run-in last year, he might still have gotten the man's backing.

'Why are you doing this?' she asked.

'If you came here to warn me away from Vivianne, you have wasted a skirt hem. I'm going to marry her. And you cannot judge. It seemed to suit you to marry down.'

'Is that why you don't come home? Because I married Tillman?'

She was normally so stiff and formal, and the vulnerable ache of her words caught him. He'd left the estate for many reasons, but none of them were because of Tillman. He liked the man, and he was a competent manager.

Arley shook his head, embarrassed by the unintentional barb, but still not ready to back down. 'I came to town to have some peace from being the damn duke in the big house. From all those picnics you kept hosting.' He stomped to the edge of the deck. 'Besides, you never visit.'

'I was trying to help you make friends. After all that happened at school, I was worried you were lonely.' Arley's mother never looked away once engaged in a verbal spar, but now, her gaze flicked to the ground. 'I help more by staying away. They only cut me, not you. If I came to town more, they may not be so generous.'

Arley slung his skiff into the water and steadied it as it bobbed. His mother followed him across the deck.

'I know we lost years. I shouldn't have sent you to school so young. I didn't know what else to do. There are no guides on how to raise a duke. You may not believe it, but I am trying to help. She's unconventional, but she loves you. Do you think me so rigid that I cannot be happy for my son? I came here to speak with you because I want to know why you are making a bid for the Exchequer.'

'You know why. I've always wanted to win an appointment on my merits. It's his legacy.'

'If you want a wife who will further your ambitions, you should have chosen one raised for the task.'

How to explain that in this one part of his life, when it came to who he made his wife, he didn't want to be like his father, and that was because of her? 'I've never forgotten that day when they read his will, and Winton and his mother were named. You didn't even flinch. Just sat up higher in your chair and nodded. I never wanted a wife to think so little of me as to be completely unperturbed at my demise.'

'It was not an easy moment for me. I cried myself to sleep for more than a week.' She stared into the water, as if she might find redemption in its depths. 'But one cannot show emotion in those moments. It's too dangerous. I am trying to help Vivianne understand, but she is all fire and energy. She wasn't raised for this.'

The skiff wobbled as he balanced one foot on the edge. 'Then help her,' he pleaded.

Arley settled into his little boat and clapped his oar on the deck to hold it steady.

'I'll try,' she said. 'But remember, your father led two lives for a reason. Love and legacy are rarely companions.'

'They will be for me,' he called as he pushed off. 'Persist. I know she can learn. I believe in her.'

CHAPTER EIGHTEEN

Cecil opened the tall white and gold doors of the ballroom with the same pomp and flourish that Vivianne would expect for a queen. He crossed to the closest set of curtains, and with a hefty tug, pulled the heavy navy fabric open to let in a small wash of afternoon light.

Lorelei had tasked Vivianne with deciding on table arrangements, seating and decorations. She was to present a sketch for discussion tomorrow.

'Would you like me to light the lamps, my lady?' Cecil asked.

'I am not a lady.' Vivianne linked her fingers and stretched her arms above her head. Against the new corset and tight bodice, her spine cracked relief into the movement. 'Will it be a bother to light just some?'

Cecil gave a slight bow. 'Not at all.' He returned to the doorway, then twisted a knob beside it. All the sconces lining the walls blazed to life. 'His Grace had the lights switched from candles to gas some years ago. The glow is not as nice, but I don't miss the wax, or the ladders. Do you need chandeliers?' His hand hovered. She didn't, but Vivianne gave a conspiratorial nod. Cecil beamed, and turned another knob, and the chandeliers blazed into being, casting shards of light onto the floor and setting the crystal sparkling. 'I do not get to do that often these days. Lovely, isn't it?'

While not as beautiful as the foyer de la danse, the ballroom had been created with a peculiar mix of refinement and extravagance, a melding of a lost age of excess and a quiet temperament. The frescoes that graced the ceiling looked down with quiet contemplation, while gilt trim on the wallpaper and mouldings sparkled and reached, seeking ascension. Heavy drapes shielded four sets of evenly spaced windows. But of all the beauty of the space, what Vivianne took in most was the floor. Aged, polished wood gleamed in the lamplight. A delicate parquetry border of roses and leaves circled the room, the variegations of tone created by the wood type as brilliant as a bunch of fresh flowers. It was a floor created for one purpose. Dancing.

Vivianne's waistband cinched, and when she inhaled, her corset seemed tighter than before.

'Could I perhaps have some time alone to...' She gave a noncommittal shrug.

Cecil nodded. 'Of course, my lady. I will be a bell ring away if you need anything.'

Vivianne bounced on her heels as Cecil left the room. Once the door clicked shut, she turned her slipper clad feet into a line, heels together, toes out. First position. She slid one foot wider. Her bodice stretched tight over her back as she extended her arms to match her feet. Second. She stretched one hand forward, her body itching to move into third, but her bodice resisted and the bustle shifted her centre of gravity. She wobbled.

Vivianne had trained herself to the regime of the ballet, and now, the new order of elegant yet heavy dresses buffed and rubbed. The layers of gingham and cotton petticoats weighed heavier than they had all day and sent an ache through her shoulders and neck. When she couldn't move into fourth, she unbuttoned her jacket, and for good measure, removed her blouse. She tugged loose the pointless corset, as she had almost no breasts to support or restrain, leaving only her chemise, then unfastened her skirt and loosened her bustle. As each layer fell, lightness eased into her limbs. With a final shake, she kicked off her slippers, removed her stockings, then rolled her remaining petticoat waistband over onto itself. Its hem swung against her bare thighs, simulating her muslin skirts that she had left behind in Paris. They had probably been sold or turned into rags by now.

Vivianne splayed her stance. *First*. Stretched. *Second*. Extended an arm. *Third*. Raised it above her head. *Fourth*. Married the movement with her other arm. *Fifth*.

No music, no stage, no audience—none of it mattered as she leapt across the ballroom, spun, pushed herself to her toes before swaying into her own momentum. It was not a dance from Garnier, but a dance from before. A dance she had mastered while leaping in fields with her friends or spinning on her toes in the kitchen as butter and crepes sizzled on the stove, or by the road when she would move to a crowd's clapping rhythm hoping to earn a few coins to add to her family's meagre purse. The ball of her foot stuck firm to the wood as she elongated, then clasping her ankle, she raised a leg above her head. The bundle of tension that had gripped her muscles jerked free as she stuck a landing, was flung loose from her fingertips and rippled out into the still air as she thrust her arms into a new step.

Broad chest, wide arms, spinning body, the music of the village rang in her ears. She spun and inhaled, imagining a lungful of wheat, cut chaff, apple orchards, all of it combining into the scent of the last breath she took as she turned and screamed at her parents that they were wrong, that she would be a star, before she climbed into the carriage with a man who set her on the stage in the next town, and before the curtains had fallen, had sold her to the highest bidder.

Were her parents even alive? Was her mother still cooking in her kitchen with its dirt floor, did her father still cut chaff and pick apples with his neighbours in the lean times? Vivianne spun, her thighs tensing and relaxing. Against her closed eyes, the cacophony of her life pounded.

You will return dishonoured, Vivianne. You will put this family to shame.

Too broken-hearted to go home when abandoned on the streets of Paris, too embarrassed as a dressmaker, too self-righteous as a ballerina, would they accept her as a duchess? If she walked up the simple dirt path to the stone cottage and tapped on their door, would they wrap their arms around her and call her *notre fille* once more?

Or would they turn their backs?

Straighter shoulders, softer lips, a graceful pose, wider thighs, Vivianne spun until the heavy meat and potatoes from lunch churned in her stomach. Her ankle buckled as she swayed with fatigue. Without daily practice, she was already losing her skill, and she tumbled toward the floor. Readying herself for the familiar smack of wood against the straight line of her body, she tensed, waiting for the pain that had filled so many of her early days in the ballet corps, when Nicole had first shown her how to not just dance, but to dance like a Parisian ballerina. But before the wood slapped against her ribs and her cheek, firm hands caught her, and lifted her to her feet.

'You shouldn't be like this,' Arley chided. His hands lingered on her hips and stroked, his bodily warmth heating the skin beneath her thin chemise. 'Someone will see. Not all the staff are as loyal as Cecil.'

'I miss you.' Vivianne pulled him to her chest, but he remained stiff. She took hold of his arms and raised them into place to hold her like she had in the gardens. He resisted, but she pressed harder and forced his posture into compliance. She moved silently through the starting positions of dance. Waltz. Polka. Quadrille. 'Dance with me, Arley. Or has Monsieur West forgotten the steps he learnt in Paris?'

'We really shouldn't. We can't...'

Vivianne swept a foot behind her, then held her stance, waiting. Arley took a laboured breath, which turned into a conspiratorial smile, then he swooped to follow her lead, his feet as light as her own. She stretched, and he met her, she leapt, and he caught, she slowed, and he prowled. He kicked off his shoes and socks, then flung his coat and waistcoat aside before rolling up his sleeves.

'You cannot catch me, monsieur,' Vivianne teased, then fled, her arms flung behind as her legs spliced the air until she landed on her heel with a thump. She spun, beckoned, and teased into the movement.

'Just because I do not attend balls does not mean I cannot dance.' And with a leap that would have made Sarcay gasp, he vaulted into the air then scooped her into his arms, dragged her down his length, brushed a kiss over her lips, then stepped forward with an animalistic grace to counter her own. Hand braced in the small of her back, he craned her backwards. Vivianne surrendered into his possession. She brushed his hands from her waist and placed a lyrical distance between them. Arley grinned, then moved in his own musical pursuit.

No one had ever moved in sync with her before. As she skipped, he followed, as she slowed, he eased, captured her for just a moment, then released her into her steps. He caught her by the waist only to spin her free and then raced ahead so that she could follow and fly until he caught her in his arms.

Arley's eyes burned. He licked his lips as he pulled her against his chest. As she stepped backwards, he moved into the space she created, and when she turned in a half circle, he pulled her against his length and pinned her against him. Every supple movement of his body coursed against her. He loosened his collar, ran his palms over the flanks of her torso, before clawing his fingertips into her hips. He met her every step, followed her stretch, spun her by the waist and tipped her back into weightlessness.

Arley folded with her surrender, then pressed his face into her stomach, his breath spreading and racing through the cotton chemise as he exhaled. Lights blazing, burning skin, energy and strength radiated from him, and when he lifted her, she wrapped her legs around his waist, caught him by the shoulders, and inhaled him with a kiss.

'You feel dance,' she gasped. 'It's in you.'

With a firm arm around her waist, he cupped her neck as he braced her against him, swaying into the counter balance as he brought her lips to his. Hard, hungry kisses, breathless and demanding, Vivianne tasted him through her own puffs. He stepped back, half swung, and pressed her against the wall.

Arley kissed her neck, then tugged back her chemise to reveal a breast. Head craned, he licked before drawing her nipple into his mouth. Vivianne groaned rough with the pleasure of it. She had always been sensitive there, but with barely more than a bump to her cleavage, no man had paid her much attention. Arley squeezed her bottom to hold her in place and flicked his tongue over her again. He smelt like sandalwood, spice and silken soap. She hooked her ankles tighter as she tangled her fingers in his hair, his soft little curls wrapping around her fingers as she held him tight. Lips crashing into hers, all the elegance of his dance left him. He ran his palm up the length of her legs, then stroked between her thighs. They exchanged needy, open-mouthed kisses, and when he slid a finger inside her, she groaned against his mouth.

Vivianne buried her face against his neck and mewled at his delicate, deliberate strokes. He circled her clitoris with his finger while grinding his hardness against her legs. She bucked and gripped him tighter.

He felt so good, was so deft, and skilled. How had he learnt to touch a woman's body? Were they mistresses, or lovers? Married, or had he corrupted them? Had he been the sort of man who had lingered in hallways at the theatre and tempted young actresses to their downfall? Had he used his power to lure them to his bed with the unfaithful promise of becoming a duchess? He thrust inside her, faster, more frenetic, and her cry came out half strangled, one-part violent pleasure, the other questions and fear.

He pressed his lips to her ear and growled. 'Tell me I am your best.' He trailed kisses down her neck. 'Tell me Vivianne. Tell me I erase them.'

How could he erase them when he was one of them? How could she forget the men who had promised and taken, men he probably met with each day? She pressed her hands against his chest, unslung her feet from the small of his back until she stood on tiptoe. Caught between his body and the wall, she pushed with the supple strength of a lithe body made of little more than sinew, muscle and grace.

'No,' she spat. She swatted his hand from between her thighs. He withdrew and took a half-step back. 'How did you learn?'

'Learn?'

'How to touch. How to kiss. Men like you only learn a woman's body one way.'

He staggered as if she had struck him. The lust in his eyes turned black and broken, and his breath came in shallow gasps. 'Do you think I'm like them? Like the nobles who watch in the foyer?'

Eyes bruised with sadness, he implored her with a look. But she could not tell him what he wanted her to say. No lies. No pretence. He'd demanded it himself.

'You *are* them. Like it or no.'

He held her gaze for three steady breaths. He seemed to count each one in, then exhaled it between his teeth.

When he took a step towards her, Vivianne stepped back and bumped into the wall.

'I am not like them,' he said through clenched teeth. 'They watch. I will dance. I promise...' He raised his hands before himself in submission. Vivianne raised her hands to match, then pressed her palms against his, until she felt his warmth through her calloused bumps. He stepped backwards. Holding the press of their palms, she stepped forward. Another step back, and she followed again, and again, until they stood beneath the chandelier and its little shards of light cascaded around them.

Facing each other, he slid his hand across her body until his palm flexed against her waist. She mirrored his stance, so that they stood off centre from one another, joined at opposing hips. She took a hesitant step into their arc. He matched her distance.

'You want my honesty?' he asked.

She nodded. The story of her body, her intimate life, had always been exposed to the world, for their exaltation or condemnation. Why not his?

'I kept mistresses. An occasional affair. Physical meetings without substance. Some exchange of power, money or gain from them and me. But no innocents, I swear to you. And if I had gone to Paris as a duke, and not a monsieur, I would not have lingered in the foyer.'

Vivianne spun on her heel, changing the direction of their circling, moving counter to the clock. Their bodies brushed in the change, and his touch sent a prickling desire, all static and fire, through her, a trembling reminder of the unquenchable need that raced between them.

'You saw me.' His words were a statement, his tone a plea. 'Just me. When I am with you, I look to myself, and I am both a stranger, and familiar. Like I am reconnecting with an old friend now grown.' He caught her by the waist and turned into her, aligning their bodies. 'I will match your rhythm, Vivianne. I will follow your lead. I will dance with you, every day if you wish it. And I will never stop to watch.'

It wasn't the kiss of a brazen man, or even a certain one. Not the man from the hallway who issued orders. He kissed with hesitancy and trepidation.

'I cannot erase them. They are part of my story, and my story has happy and unhappy pages.' She ran her palm the length of his chest and intertwined her fingers behind his neck. 'But I never danced with the patrons. I have only ever danced with you.'

He inhaled her kiss, his chest swelling, his hold tightening. How could this man be so delicate when she folded back a few layers, when she herself was like granite beneath her façade?

She leant into his embrace, until he swept her from her feet and lowered them both to the floor. Arley grabbed at his coat, just within reach from where he had discarded it earlier and bunched it beneath his head. Vivianne straddled him, kissed him, then fumbled between her legs to find his trouser fastenings and flicked them open.

'A horizontal dance, *mon amour*?' She moved fast, working at the opening until she freed his cock, hard to aching in her palm. She guided him inside herself, their joining hidden beneath her petticoat. '*Mon Dieu*, I have missed you.'

Arley bucked into her body, slightly slipping against the floor, then held still. Eyes closed, his grunt spread into a low growl. Vivianne rolled her hips to settle lower so that he filled her, almost so deep it hurt. He scrabbled at her chemise, and she tugged it over her head. He pressed deeper, and she gasped at the sensation.

Arley gripped her a little tighter. She rocked in time with his movements, ignoring the bite in her knees where the wood rubbed as the pleasure he brought to her body pushed out discomfit. Vivianne leant forward, her palms flattened against the dancefloor beside his head. Arley licked a nipple, then grasped her hips and thrust with wild abandon.

'I don't care about your story. As long as you are mine, and only mine.' He cupped her neck and tugged her closer, bestowing greedy kisses on her mouth, her neck, her chest, nipping her skin just a little. 'Fucking you is like nothing else. I lose myself in you.'

'Not fucking. We dance.' She rose his length, pulsed over the tip of his cock until he rumbled with want, then thumped down. He grunted, his expression pained ecstasy and loss. Faster and more frenetic, they bumped against each other. Arley slid his hands beneath her skirt. Soft, lithe, he stroked her inner thighs with his thumb, before pushing into the space between them to rub her clitoris. Pleasure burst from the nimbleness of his fingers. Vivianne arched to give her gasp free voice as the thrumming beauty of the lost sensation of joining for fun, for desire, rattled and woke.

'Dancing, are we?' Faster his fingers moved and every part of her prickled in a racing surrender. 'Dance for me. Perform your solo.'

Vivianne suppressed a breath. She tried to push down the strumming, racing, tenderness from his fingers, from his body inside her, from the gentle ebb and the heady torrent that battered.

Arley pushed himself up to half sitting and almost too rough, grasped a fistful of her hair and wrenched her close for a kiss. 'If not for me, then with me. Let go, my love. Come undone. Let me catch you.'

He was the music of the orchestra, humming beneath her body, coursing through her limbs, guiding every motion and shaping every breath. His kiss set her chest to expansion, and she inhaled his sweat, his freshness, his aching. The intimacy of skin on skin set her body aflame, and Vivianne fell into the embrace, the burning and the ricochet of bliss. 'Mon amour,' she said as she clenched her thighs against his, and he grunted a reply into her neck, and with a nip of her earlobe, she tumbled into its beauty, warm and unfettered. Every place of their connection pounded like a bass drum, every racing breath was a melody through her veins. What sweet oblivion, to be bathed in the shattered shards of light cast by the chandelier with the man she loved beneath her body, and she let herself be carried away. Arley tightened his hold, the two of them tense and trembling as they shivered into their completion. Her name erupted from between his clenched teeth, and she arched into his hold as his name spilled from her lips. 'Arley, deeper. Arley, faster. Harder.'

Just one dance, just one partner, just one duke, for now, for always. Arley shuddered as he spent, his gasp a mirror to her own, and they stayed locked, trembling, exchanging huffs of air and feathers of kisses. He rolled back against the parquetry, and Vivianne collapsed against his chest. He brushed his fingers down her spine. Vivianne drew an invisible line between the men of her past and the man of her future. Just him, with his steady breaths and demanding mouth. Just him, forever.

'I'm not sure that particular dance has ever been done quite so brazenly in this room before,' he said, then kissed the top of her head. 'I love how you fit against me. Like you were carved for me. My petite ballerina.'

Vivianne turned her face up and kissed his jawline. He sighed his contentment against her chest.

'Arley?' she whispered into his neck.

'Hmmm?'

'I love you.'

The words felt different in English, felt somehow more defined, more formal. Three separate words, each little syllable moulded of itself, of no consequence alone, but when linked, they felt like a surrender.

'No *je t'aime*?' He chuckled. 'I love you too, Vivianne. It baffles me beyond reason, but I do.'

He shuffled uncomfortably, and as they separated and dressed, they filled the space between them with small talk and kisses.

'After we are married, do you think we could go home?' she asked, trying to hold the lightness of the moment.

'You want to see the estate?'

'*Non, non.*' She shook her head with a laugh. 'One day, yes, but I mean my home.'

He took up her hand and hid a kiss in her palm. 'Where is home?'

'*Bretagne.*' She stared at the frescos without seeing them, instead imagining the clear sky, and how it ran into the horizon of the sea and there was no way of telling where one ended and the other began. 'Brittany. Near the sea. I have always been too scared to return to my parents. Maybe they will forgive me if I have a husband. Even an English one,' she added with a deflecting laugh, before the sadness returned. 'I would just like to know if they are alive.'

'After Lords finishes sitting, we can go anywhere you like. Do you need help with your ribbon?' Vivianne turned, and he cinched the bow at her waist. 'Are you ready, for the company launch? Do you have everything in hand?'

'You don't trust I can do this?' She spun to face him, her words more an echo of her own doubts, but she saw the uncertainty in his eyes.

'I worry. There's a lot riding on this. More than the company. I've never realised until now, but men are judged by their wives.' He turned her to face him. 'I have a real chance this year to live up to my father's legacy. To achieve what he could not. I never had much time with him, and I suppose, I always thought I might make him proud, if I could do what he could not.'

'I understand,' she tugged at his coat lapels and closed them over, before fixing his buttons. 'I know what it is to have a dream.'

'I believe you can.' He smoothed her hair back from her forehead, before planting a kiss. 'You'll be my perfect duchess.'

As she left the ballroom, Vivianne gave it one last sweep. Tables along the wall, bright ribbons, French champagne and the chandeliers blazing. She would ask Cecil what music the English liked and find those who could play it well. She could do this. She would be the duchess he needed her to be.

Chapter Nineteen

The note had requested a meeting at the Hog and Thistle. Close to the docks, it smelt of the Thames, as if the ale had been brewed from its water. Winton sat in one of the central tables. A small cluster of empty tankards already dotted its surface.

He had the same cowlick of black hair as their father and the same grey eyes. Even when he leaned back in his chair and raised his tankard, he not only looked like the man who stared out from casual photographs and sketches, but lounged like him, tilted his head like him, grinned like him. And why wouldn't he be more like their father than Arley? He had been graced with the man's attention, and his mother had had his love.

Winton kicked out a chair.

Arley remained standing. 'I'm not giving you any more money.'

'Get out on the wrong side of the ducal bed?' Winton took another swig, then wiped the back of his mouth across his hand. 'Or has matrimony turned you sour.'

'I'm not married yet.'

Winton raised a brow. 'Not by vow. But in other ways, you are.' A darkness crept into his normally mischievous smile, adding a brutal twist to his expression. Charm was Winton's main currency, but today he was spending something more malicious. 'Frocked up in white and parading her about like she's the virgin Madonna, but really...' He laughed, his shoulders shaking. 'The entire time, you've been rutting a whore!'

'Ballerina.' Arley lowered himself into the chair. Winton laughed even louder. 'And courtesan,' he admitted through tight teeth. 'I don't care.'

'So magnanimous, after years of making me and my mother feel inferior. I only wish she was still alive to see it.'

'We were always second best to you.'

'He sent you to Eton while I had to settle for the local school. Your mother on that estate while we lived in near poverty.'

'A Hampstead cottage is not poverty.'

'And why?' Winton continued, ignoring Arley's sense. 'A turn of the blanket and you get to be duke. *Little* brother.'

'I have tried to help you with positions, advice and opportunities. You've squandered it all. Those, and what your mother left you.'

'You tried to control me. Keep me away from your precious town, and your career, like I might smudge your perfection.'

'You think it's all trips to the races and ballrooms?' The weight of the session was already fraying Arley's patience. He'd missed an important debate to come here, and he'd spend hours catching it up. His voice rose, and he couldn't tamp down the frustration. 'There's more to this damn title than what you see in the press. You have freedom. Choice. I can't give it to you, I can't just stop being a duke!' A few men at a nearby table turned. Arley extinguished his burning outburst with a forced swallow, and when he continued, it was with more restraint. 'Is it some debt you can't clear? How much?'

'Half,' Winton quipped.

'Half of what?'

The bell over the door clanged, bringing with it a sweep of cold air and river tang. Winton flicked a look over his shoulder before his lips turned at the corners. 'Everything. Agree, or I go to the press. I'll tell them who she is. Your attempt at the Exchequer and that ridiculous little company you have invested in, will both be destroyed.'

Arley was used to bluffing in the face of harsh truths. What else was Lords about, if not committed bluster in the face of a challenge? 'I could sue you for slander.'

Winton settled back into his chair, his posture as arrogant as his smile as he looked to the door. 'You can't sue if it's true.'

The protest on his lips died as Arley twisted in his seat. Algernon, as garish and flamboyant as he'd last seen him, strutted into the bar.

'Your grace!' Algernon boomed as he crossed the room, gesturing at the bar staff for a drink, before pulling up a chair at the table and settling into it. He extended his hand across the table to Winton. 'Algernon Pascoe. Any friend of West's is a friend of mine.'

Algernon rested his elbows on the table and raised both eyebrows in a caterpillar like dance. 'How'd things turn out with that ballerina, the pretty one? Fancy another adventure? Naples is fantastic at this time of year.'

Arley's chair clattered across the flagstones as he rose abruptly to his feet. Winton had always had freedom when Arley had none, and one minor slip, one breath of choice, and now he dared to taint it and level it at him like a sword. 'Nothing!' he shouted. 'Not even your allowance. You get *nothing*.'

'I'd think on that.' Winton's voice chased him to the door. 'You're not the only one with a scout in your pocket. You will not underestimate me again.'

Arley stomped over the marble portico and through the foyer of his club. He handed his gloves, hat and coat to a waiting attendant, before launching himself upstairs. He needed a table in the corner, a drink and some time to pluck apart the threat his half-brother had made.

As he slunk into his preferred seat, Hamish sat down opposite him. 'If that man suggests I have tea and not whiskey one more time, I will clip his ankles.'

'Were you in the house today?' Arley asked.

'*Observing*. Still observing, all my life, observing.' Hamish pulled a flask from inside his coat and took a swig, before tucking it away again. 'You never miss a debate.

Where were you?' He slumped back into his seat. 'What I'd give for an adventure.'

When Arley looked across the table to Hamish, both free of expectation and bound by its looming presence, he didn't know if he envied or pitied him. His youth had been free, but future responsibilities would likely weigh heavier because he knew the difference.

That lick of freedom... how delicious it had been. While Hamish chafed at the lack of trust and responsibility, Arley hated its consistency. That small week had opened just a shard of possibility, and he'd been drunk on liberty, Absinthe and Paris sunshine. Now, he was engaged to a ballerina with a complicated past that threatened to darken everything he'd worked for since the day Cecil had first called him *your grace*. Had Winton been waiting all this time for him to slip so he could exploit some opportunity? Like all of them—the press, his fellow politicians, the society gossips, all searching for a chink in his armour. For him to let his guard down. To care about others and show himself vulnerable.

Lawrence slumped into a seat at the table. His brandy glass knocked against the wood. 'Wilhelmina has banished me from the house. It's a sign she's close. Any day now.'

'What number is this?' Hamish asked.

'Ten,' Lawrence said without hesitation, and a broad, proud grin. He always counted the lost babe, no matter how many questions were asked. He seized his glass and took a swig. 'I think it's a girl.'

Phineas eased himself into the last vacant chair. Since when had Arley drawn so many people to him? It had all started that day last year. He'd had a well-ordered life, a plan, and routine. He was a duke and knew his place in the world. Now everything seemed to be unravelling.

'Ten,' Hamish said, then silently mouthed the word a few times, his eyebrows arching and frowning alternatively. 'Iris is reluctant to think about one. How on earth... ten? I was so lonely as a child. God, I'd love ten.'

An uncomfortable silence settled around the table, but whether it was for Hamish's confession, or Phineas's arrival, Arley didn't know. He tried to imagine his life with a string of following siblings. If he'd had a legitimate brother, would the fellow have despised him his luck as much as Winton did? Or, like Hamish, would he have revelled in the freedom, even if it came with a hefty amount of invisibility?

'The most incongruous character came into the bank today,' Phineas said as he leaned forward to pick up his glass. 'Wanted to open three bank accounts. Absolutely outrageous. Can you imagine the ruling margins required for such an extravagance?'

A different discomfort settled around the table as the threat of a potentially boring conversation loomed. Hamish moved first.

'I best head home. Iris will be wanting help. And Albert loves to talk about when we were younger. He thinks I'm my father.' He chuckled, then gave an awkward wave. 'Good evening, gents.'

Lawrence rose as soon as Hamish turned away. 'And I need to secure my bed for this evening. Hopefully the hotel has something available. It would be embarrassing if I have to reserve a room with the competition.'

Lawrence took one last sip, then followed Hamish out.

'Trust you to clear a table,' Arley said.

'Not everyone shares my passion for ledgers.' Phineas took a sip of whiskey. 'Your brother is causing issues.'

'Half-brother. How did you know?'

'It's my job to know. Do you want me to sort him for you?'

'Sounds a little extreme.'

'I'm not going to *exterminate* the man. What do you think I do?'

'I have no idea what you do. We are both happier that way.'

'I don't do *that*.' Phineas leaned back in his chair, his head tilted toward Arley, although his eyes darted at some action over his shoulder. 'What has he tried his hand at? Art? Investments? A stint in the dragoons?'

'Skipped out on service. Twice.'

'Perhaps it's time he learned to finish something he started?'

Arley spun his glass in his hand. 'Do you think I've made a mistake with Vivianne? Been too rash?'

'Are you asking me if becoming engaged to a woman you knew for a week was a hasty decision?' The words could have been sarcasm, but from Phineas, Arley could never be sure. 'Many a man in this room has been just as hasty, and for more mercenary reasons. Personally, I find marriage itself a ridiculous institution. You tie yourself to another for life. You change, they change. You both become different people, yet there you are. *Tethered*.'

'That's what I like best about her. I felt different. Like a whole new person I didn't know I could be. But what if she doesn't have what it takes to be a duchess? What if her history hurts my bid, or the company?'

'You don't have to marry her. She'd accept less. We could quietly announce a termination of the engagement, and she could move out to the estate. It's been done before.'

She'd wanted a garden. And a little cottage. He could give her both, and a washerwoman, and her own space. She could come up to the main house any time she wanted to dance. Perhaps it would be best. But how could he forget the sparkle in her eyes when they'd spoken of children, her delight as she stroked the fabric for her gown, and above all, the way she said *I love you*? She would accept less. Be a mistress and not a wife. But how could he? He didn't want her in a room across town, or away in a little cottage in Suffolk. He wanted her in his home, in his life, in his days.

And if he sent her away, the endless parade of daughters would only start up again. And he would not be a father to another Winton or be wed to a compliant woman while he loved another so completely.

'Everything was easier in France,' he mumbled into his glass.

'Everything usually is,' Phineas quipped. 'I can make some enquiries, about Winton. Find out what's driving him.'

Arley shook his head. 'He'll come back with some invoice for whatever it is he wants. He'll pipe down. He always does.'

The chatter of the room dipped. Arley looked to the entrance, where men were already gathering. 'Pemberton is here. Now's my chance to speak to him.' Arley put his glass down, stood, and rehearsed his argument for the Exchequer again in his mind.

As he stepped from the carriage and onto the portico of Number 10, Arley's bones ached like those of a man twice his age. Winton. Pemberton. He had a dozen thick folders of notes and reports clutched under his arm. And he still had to prepare some kind of speech for the launch tomorrow night. *Heavens.*

It wasn't the work itself, it was the people. Part of him always felt drained after too much interaction and he felt himself a little depleted until he could find some peace and restore his energy. He hadn't been on the water in days, and his body felt knotted.

Still, the conversation at the club had been promising. Pemberton hadn't promised his support, but he hadn't dismissed him. Unlike his uncle whom he had inherited the title from, Pemberton had become a stickler for tradition, and had congratulated Arley on his upcoming nuptials. 'More family minded men is what we need. Less of the old crowd, cavorting and carrying on. More even tempers. Solid values.'

In the foyer, Arley shook off his coat and passed it to Cecil, along with his hat. He shuffled through the mail. It contained the usual mass of invitations and introductions. Arley paused on one with French stamps in the corner. It was addressed to Vivianne.

Arley tapped the edge of the envelope against his finger as he strolled to the sitting room. Vivianne sat on the lounge with his mother, both of them with their heads slightly bent as they focused on small samplers of embroidery.

'I do not know why you suggested I practise sewing. I am very good at this,' Vivianne said with a slight smugness.

'You are too good. That is the problem. You should have enough skill to make a simple gift, but not be so talented that people think you might have spent an inordinate amount of time at stitching. And with your gloves on.'

'But I cannot feel the needle,' Vivianne protested.

'Gloves.'

'Good evening, duchesses,' Arley greeted them from the archway.

He didn't think his heart would ever tire of that moment when Vivianne saw him, and light bounded across her face, filled her eyes and ignited her smile. She went to push herself from her seat, but his mother's exasperated reminder of 'Gloves, Vivianne,' slowed her. She fumbled with the buttons at her wrist before she skipped across the room. Another cough. She slowed to a walk, then bobbed. 'Good evening, your grace.'

Her hair had been braided into an elaborate braid, and she wore a delicate turquoise and gold dress, with layers of ruffles and a cinched waist. When she emerged from her curtsy, her eyes sparkled with pride. She must have been practising. It was perfect.

'You have a letter.' He held it out and Vivianne gave a little squeal of delight. She turned it over and lifted the flap, before pulling out a thin sheet of vellum. Her lips moved a little as she read, and her smile broadened with each word.

'If I send her money for her ticket, Nicole will come. She will be here for our wedding!' Vivianne clutched the letter to her chest. 'I am so happy. I have missed her so much.'

'Nicole? From the ballet?' He leaned in closer and lowered his tone. 'The one who was in the wine bar the night we met? Who left with Algernon?'

'*Oui,*' Vivianne said as her eyes scanned the page again. 'I was so worried about her when her duke is not a duke at all. But she is well. She has a small part in the next opera. And not a duke, but an earl enjoys her company.' Vivianne giggled, then pressed her gloved hand to her lips. '*Désolée*, Nicole is so funny about these things. She likes the attention. How do I send her money for a ticket? Can your travel company arrange her voyage?'

'She can't come. Not for the wedding.' Arley shot a look over his shoulder. The archway was empty, but that didn't mean no one lingered in the hallway. 'And not after either. Her friendship is not appropriate.'

'But she is Nicole...' Vivianne folded the vellum over onto itself and slid it into her pocket. She placed a protective hand over her skirt. 'After the wedding, maybe we can also go to Paris?'

His head was throbbing, and he still had a mass of reports to read through. 'I thought you hated it there. Why would we go back?' he snapped.

'To see Nicole, of course.' She tapped her fingertips together in an off-beat tempo. 'She is my only friend for so long.'

Agitation gnawed at him. It had been too long a day. At one moment Winton seemed about to unravel everything from beneath him, the next, Vivianne acted like she was in collusion with him. She met his gaze, pinned him in it, and just as he was about to break away, she half closed her eyes and focused on the floor.

'The next few weeks are so important,' he said with a wash of guilt. 'Maybe after we can arrange something discrete.'

Fire flashed in her eyes, and her jaw clenched. He braced himself for her fury, or even a squall. She took a slow breath, swallowed hard, then nodded. 'Yes, your grace.' She bobbed a short curtsy and went to brush past him.

'No dancing, Vivianne. Not today.'

'Not even with the doors closed?' She smiled coyly. 'You could join me?'

'You can dance tomorrow, after the launch.'

'With you?' She smiled, and a little of her light returned.

He shook his head. 'I don't dance at balls, remember? I will make my speech, then retire, as I have too much work to do.' He planted a quick kiss on her cheek, and she swayed with the pressure like a leaf. 'But you will be there to represent me. And I know you will shine.'

Chapter Twenty

The woman reflected in the small glass squares of the ballroom window was a delightful stranger. Vivianne's hair had been styled with more finesse than she could manage herself, and the tips of it glinted with crystal beads that the maid had threaded through her strands. A light powder over her nose to try to conceal a few light childhood freckles made her skin glow. She'd decided on the yellow gown, with a modest neckline, short sleeves and a full, but not too ostentatious skirt. The silk shimmered bright as sunshine. But would the pink have been a better choice? Was yellow too brazen?

People, presence, persuasion.

It was too late to change now, as the first guests were already filing into the ballroom. Vivianne held a breath, closed her eyes, and tried to draw in the memory of standing in the foyer de la danse, and to feel the freedom of that moment after the patrons had gone, and to remember the contentment of her fellow dancers as they settled into one another's presence, no longer competitors vying for a new sponsor, but sisters of the stage.

She opened her eyes and caught her lone reflection in the glass. Her heart lurched into its hasty rhythm again.

Little prisms of crystal light, some flecked with rainbows, speckled the walls and blended into the dull gleam of the polished wooden floor. On the stage at the far end of the hall, a quartet played, the music humming between the odd moments of silence. A long line of trestle tables had been set up along one end of the room. Bright white cloths draped each one and coloured ribbons had been pinned to each corner. Blue, orange, green, lavender, Vivianne had tried to select a palette of joy and adventure. Attendants wearing a simple uniform of white pants and blue coats stood by each table, nervously holding out brochures to those who passed. Nobles, merchants, business owners, some lecturers from the university and even young students filled the room. What a strange metamorphosis this city was, where the old world mixed with the new, even though they detested it. Money changed so many things about people.

Young Elise, Iris's assistant who lived with her aunt in Number 7, greeted the guests. She handed each group a small booklet that summarised each tour, as an introduction to the company's offerings.

'May I see?' Vivianne asked. Elise passed her one. 'I like this picture of a cat riding in the balloon on the cover. This is everybody's Spencer, yes?'

'I drew him,' she said, beaming.

Vivianne opened the book. 'So people book these tours? And someone takes them on a holiday? Why do they not go by themselves?'

'Because a guide can help them find all the best places to go and helps them if they get into trouble or aren't sure what to do. And people might make friends along the way. Iris is always talking about the people she met when she travelled with her father. I'm hoping to lead a tour myself one day, when I'm older.'

Vivianne flipped through the pages in the booklet. *Explore Edinburgh. Venetian Vacation. Sicilian Sampler. The Mini-Grand Tour.*

'This is ours! With my list, that I helped Arley write. Notre Dame, Arc de Triomphe...' Vivianne ran her finger down the itinerary. No painter. No gardens. None of her restaurants.

'Iris changed some things,' Elise said. 'She was worried what people might think, especially if they haven't been abroad before.'

'What would people think that would be so terrible? About my painters, and the gardens?'

'The Mini Grand Tour is for students and young people, but it is their parents who will pay. They will want to know where their children are going. It just needed to be more specific, is all. And what people think can be terribly important, especially in London.' Elise spoke the last sentence with so much sadness that Vivianne felt the pain of her words. She coughed, then shifted her attention back to the door. 'Mr Worthington. Would you like a brochure?'

Arley had said it might be a challenge to convince them how to include her suggestions. But he had promised her he would. They had walked the city, talking and falling in love as she shared her thoughts with him. The food and wine in the Quartier Latin was as good as on the right bank, if you knew where to go, and the gardens so beautiful, and the labyrinth beneath the city a powerful reminder of the darkness they had endured, only to be reborn the city of light. They were the stories young people needed to hear.

Vivianne scanned the crowd for Arley, and when she spotted him, she made a direct line for him. He was speaking to an older man, both of them in almost identical evening dress and nodding enthusiastically. 'My father always wanted to hold the office, and I have always wanted to continue his legacy—'

'Arley, this is not my Paris.' She held out the booklet, open at the offending page. 'This is a list.'

Frustration creased his brow as he made his apologies, and the man left. 'Do you know who that was? You can't just interrupt me. I'm trying to garner support.'

'But you promised me my painter. You wanted my Paris.' She pushed the booklet against his chest. 'This is not it.'

He looked down but made no move to take the guide from her. 'I know what I said, but that was before. Things are different now. With the house sitting and the company launching, there are other points to consider. People are relying on us. We can't take any risks that might damage our reputation.'

'But—'

'We will talk later. I need to give my speech.' He leaned forward, as if about to kiss her cheek, then caught himself and pulled back. He made his way onto the stage at the far end of the room, and once he took up his place, he put on his glasses and shook out a sheet of paper. The gathering settled and quietened, and when he spoke, it was with his lion's voice, all stiff and commanding.

Vivianne pinned a smile as the words washed over her. That was one skill from Paris that was of some use—smiling—because so little of what she did and who she was had any place here. She could not dance. Could not bargain. Could not even sew as a duchess should. Applause filled the hall. Arley gave a short wave to the crowd, then moved behind the curtains as the quartet began to play. Couples moved onto the dance floor. She made a half turn for the door, meaning to follow Arley, but a man, tall, dark haired and full of charm, barred her way.

'May I have this dance?' He held out an expectant hand.

Something about the man's face, his eyes, and his amiable smile rang familiar, but she could not quite place the memory of where she had seen him. She knew his type of charisma though. It presented with a veneer of kindness but hid something more unpredictable beneath.

But she could not refuse a request to dance. Lorelei had warned her. He led her onto the floor, and together, they moved into a waltz.

'You are an excellent dancer, Miss Chevalier. I feel like I am flying.'

'*Merci*, sir. I did not catch your name?'

'Winton. Winton West.'

'West. Like Arley. Are you from his family?'

'I'm his brother.' Winton's hand clasped Vivianne's tight as she stumbled over her feet, and he slowed until together, they found the rhythm again. 'I gather he hasn't mentioned me.'

A little in the jawline, and maybe, the set of his eyes resembled Arley's, but more than that, he bore the most striking resemblance to the portraits in the hall. Thin lines curved his set mouth, and he had creases around his eyes that Arley didn't have, and just a few flecks of grey through his dark hair.

'You are his older brother? But how is he the du—'

'Bastard. Me, that is. Not Arley. My mother was our father's mistress. He married Lorelei for her breeding. Nothing less than a duke's daughter for a duke's wife. But Arley has definitely stepped away from expectation with you, hasn't he?' His hand shifted a little lower down her back as they moved through the triangle of steps.

Vivianne tried to pull her hand from his, but his fingers squeezed so tight that her bones pinched together. 'I am not that woman anymore, and you are not treating me as a lady should be treated. You will not even think of propositioning me.'

He laughed, his tone dark and malicious. 'Not a lady, though, are you? And save your flattery of yourself. After Arley and heavens knows who else in this hall has had you, I am not interested.' He pulled her a little closer to his chest, and his hand returned to her waist.

Fury burned in her, hot and raw, the sort that made her slap cheeks or throw perfume bottles at the heads of archdukes. Fury at this man for wielding her as a weapon, and for Arley who had not told her about his own brother, and whatever threat he had made. But then, she glimpsed Lorelei as she danced. She chatted with the man she spun the circle with, but Vivianne followed her stiff body and read the lies it told. She was trying to help, even though she did not want to be here. And Iris, with unmistakable dark pockets under her eyes, smiled proudly at her husband. Tonight was her triumph, although she could not claim it. Her own version of a spotlight on the stage. Vivianne could not deny another woman such a moment.

With a leaden breath, Vivianne pushed down her anger. Too many people relied on her now, and while she wanted to rage at Arley, and his secret half-brother, and shake Iris until she understood what she was missing, she couldn't. Not in a room full of people. Right now, the only thing she could do was dance.

People, presence, persuasion.

'What do you want?'

'I want my share. I want what's fair. And if I don't get it, I will shatter your lie. I've been waiting a long time for this. Through payment or the press, I am going to set things right.'

The song ended. Winton abandoned her on the dancefloor, and she slightly swayed with the rush of his departure. Vivianne pushed her way through the crowd.

Lorelei stepped in front of her. 'Where are you going?'

'I must speak with Arley. His brother—'

'Hush!' Lorelei looked over her shoulder. 'You cannot mention Winton. And you cannot leave a ball you are hosting. Everyone is watching.'

Vivianne was about to argue, when the man who had been speaking earlier with Arley addressed them both, introduced himself as Viscount Pemberton, then asked her to dance.

Why had Arley not told her about his brother, and his threat? How many watched her as she went about her day, also waiting for her to make some error? Not only Arley and Lorelei, or Mrs Crofts.

How many watched her, even now?

Her next dance was with a man named Jonah, then some earl, or was it a baron? She could not remember, but she smiled and stepped and held her stance through it all. Merchant, investor, politician. She held her pose. She smiled and chatted. She danced until her feet ached as much as her heart, until she did not want to dance another step. Not just that evening, but ever again in her life.

'Would you like the carriage, my lady?' Cecil asked as the last guest left.

Vivianne pushed past him and moved down the hallway. 'I am going to see Arley.'

'I think he has retired,' Cecil called.

'Then I shall wake him.'

Vivianne trudged past the line of disapproving portraits. Up the staircase with its polished handrail and along the hallway papered with flowers and gold leaf. She pushed open the door to the duchess's suite, crossed to the door that led into the bedchamber then shoved open the interconnecting door to the duke's room.

'You demanded my honesty. But you live on lies. Since we have met, it is all you have done.'

He sat hunched over a desk by the window, and as she spoke, he half rose from his seat. He removed his glasses and laid them aside. 'That was only because I had to know I could trust you—'

'Liar!' She sounded hoarse and shrill, old and angry. 'You cover me with lies. You cover your life with lies.'

'Is this the tour? I meant to tell you, but the session has been so busy—'

'I met your brother.'

Arley half choked on his next word before his expression turned from conciliation to anger. 'Half-brother, and he is not welcome in my house. I will not be dictated to by a man who is lazy, and irresponsible. Phineas has a tip off.'

'Your banker friend? Oh, but of course, he is not a banker.' Vivianne wrestled with her gloves and slapped them to the floor. 'More lies!'

'What did Winton say to you?' Arley demanded.

Vivianne bottled her rage with a held breath until it tempered into crisp, cold clarity. 'He called me a whore.'

'I will have him shipped off to finish his service with—'

'*Arretez*, Arley! I am a whore! I sold my body. On stage, and between sheets. Even now, I sell myself to you. I sell my history, my friendships, my dance, for food and a bed and a duke's company. Nothing has changed.'

'Everything has changed. I am going to marry you.'

'Send me back to Paris, or to your estate. Or even here in London, set me up in a small apartment. I can live quietly, and my terrible reputation will hurt no one.'

'You bloody will not!' He slammed his fist into the table. 'I don't care who you were. I only care who I am when I am with you. How you have given me the world simply by showing me how to see it. Everything, from a drop of rain to a dance step, is more radiant and dazzling because I share its miracle with you. You have worked so hard, and no one will tell me I cannot have you as my wife!'

'Free me from this insanity. Let me be who I am.'

Arley shoved his chair back so hard it toppled, and he crossed the short distance to her. She stepped back but did not lower her eyes from his outrage.

'Get into my bed,' he ordered.

'Make me your mistress.'

'No. I will not do what he did. I will not be a man of shadows and absences.' Arley raked his fingers through his hair, clenched his hands into fists, then shook himself free. He pressed his palm against his forehead, and when he spoke his voice was again that of a mouse, weighted with apprehension and heartbreak. 'Have I ever treated you as a courtesan?'

'The night we met,' she said, her voice hoarse from shouting.

He swore under his breath. 'After that. Have I ever tried to buy your body? To take anything from you that you did not want to give?'

Vivianne shook her head. Her anger shattered into fragments and anchored hard in her chest with a painful realisation. He was the only man she had ever given herself to. The only, *only* one. Even when she had tried to seduce him and place him in her debt, he had evened the balance between them.

'And I never will. I should have told you about Winton. I am still learning how to shoulder this weight with another and how to be a part of something beyond myself.' He gripped her chin, and brought his lips to hers, his kiss all force and eloquence. Even now, in his anger, he was roses and sunshine, softness and light. His fingers gripped as hard as steel while his tongue and lips were silk ribbons of desire. 'I will never treat you like that. Never.' Arley bent and scooped her up. Vivianne flung her arms around his neck, not sure if she sought respite from his ferocity or wanted to dive deeper into his torrent, his possession, and his certainty. His love, so jagged and untethered, promised to be terrifyingly constant. She clutched at his familiarity.

What else could she do? She could not return to Paris unless she wished to starve, and she did not dare go home. And even through his lies, when she pictured Arley's face, his smile, his half-bent form as they emerged from *les Catacombes*, as they tumbled in his bed while he made his promise of love, she knew she could not leave. His heart, his hearth and the safety he offered her were everything. She needed him.

He crossed the short distance to his bed, but with each step he felt less angry and determined. He bent his head and pressed his forehead to hers.

'Only a duchess can share a duke's bed.' His muscles bunched as he laid her on the covers. He curled the ribbon at her chest around his finger and slowly unravelled the bow. 'Even now, I feel so inadequate beside you. You, who are all sparkles and ferocity. Fragility and strength. You have been treated so badly, yet still your brightness persists.

You give so generously and take so little for yourself. But not tonight. Tonight, you will learn to be greedy. To think of no one but yourself. Tonight, you will give me nothing. You will only take.'

Arley tugged off his coat and dropped it to the floor. The side of the bed dipped as he eased himself beside her, and she rolled into him a little. With light fingers and a slightly awestruck expression, he brushed a loose curl from her cheek. 'Loosen your hair for me. Please.'

It took a long time to burrow out every pin, bead and hair comb. He patiently collected them in his palm, and their glass clacked as he dropped them onto the side table. He tickled his fingers through her hair. Tendrils of luscious delight slithered through her nerves and sent little bumps over her forearms, igniting in her stomach and shuddering over her thighs. A sigh, deep and wanting, puffed from her lips.

'I have not worshipped you as I should. From afar, yes, but when you have been near me, half stripped, and so sublime...' He pressed his fingers firm against her scalp, and she arched against the mattress as her skin prickled. 'Dear lord, you are magnificent. Roll over. I want to undress you.'

Earlier that evening, the maid had counted aloud each of her 56 buttons as she had fastened Vivianne into her dress, and Arley huffed and grumbled and eventually counted out 62. Vivianne, her head burrowed into her arms, giggled at his frustration and confusion.

'You are laughing at me,' he chastised. 'And I am so earnestly trying to be a worthy lover.'

'Let me help,' she laughed as she rolled from him.

'No.' He pushed her back against the mattress. 'I will figure this out. I will learn how to undress my wife.'

Vivianne settled over his pillows and relaxed into his comfort. His bed smelt like him, only concentrated—like a garden at the end of a summer day, when flower petals curled into their last display before they dropped, heavy with the scent of both languor and restlessness. If he took all night, what did it matter? His fingers stroked at a vulnerable patch of skin between her shoulder blades.

'I only know you as a puzzle.' He licked her exposure. 'Barely enjoying the entirety of you.' A ribbon hissed as he pulled it loose. He tugged her skirts over her legs. 'I will have all of you tonight.'

Vivianne pushed herself up and unthreaded her arms from her bodice. She exhaled as her corset loosened, and her petticoats were dragged from her body, and her chemise, her silks and every ribbon and trussed up bow was untied.

Arley hooked a finger over her stocking, at her thigh, and even before he'd removed it, his lips were on her skin. 'You are delicious,' he muttered as he kissed. 'My elixir.'

She rolled onto her back and reached for his shirt buttons.

'No.' He slapped her hand away. 'I told you. Tonight, you take.'

'I want you,' she said, stretching again.

'Do I need to restrain you? Teach you a new lesson?' He pulled his cravat loose and snapped it between his palms. The fabric cracked as it stiffened.

'Maybe you should,' she whispered, and raised her hands above her head.

He looped one wrist, then the other. She felt the slips of fabric tighten before her hands were pressed against the wooden bed frame. Straddling her, his weight spread across her thighs.

She tugged. His restraint held firm.

He smirked. 'I have you, Frenchie.'

'*Anglais*. You think you can conquer me? I will still defeat you.'

'You have not conquered us since 1066.'

'That is because you are not worth the effort.'

'I should be your servant, then. Your supplication.' Light glinted in his eyes, majestic and beautiful. He removed his white linen shirt and spun it above his head before casting it across the room. 'I surrender to you, Vivianne. You have all of me.'

His lips on hers quenched a thirst unknown to her, one she could not name, and too soon he snatched himself from her, before devouring her chin, then her nape, and the slight swell of her chest.

'Do you know what I love most about your breasts?' he asked, then licked his forefinger.

'You lie. You enjoy nothing. I am too small.'

'I do enjoy them. I adore them. Because when I do this.' He circled her nipple with his slick finger. Vivianne bucked into the sensation, then melted against the mattress. 'I surprise you. A woman who I would have thought impossible to surprise. And here you are.' His tongue flicked over his fingertip again. 'At my mercy.'

How stupid men were.

She'd been at his mercy since he removed his cravat pin in Paris.

His hot breath raced across her skin and its caress turned to an exquisite torture. Always too small for any man to fuss with, to even give more than a glance, let alone attention, Arley's reverence of her breasts slaked a hunger. She grasped her bonds and arched into him, both craving more but also enchanted by his languor. Lips pursed, his breath turned cool, before he pressed firm against her.

Vivianne, bent, watched him watching her, his sapphire eyes holding, and she tried to match his stare even as she marvelled at his tongue. His attentions were intensely detailed, like he meant to mark every bump and pore, and with a gasp, she collapsed against the pillows and revelled in the sensation. As his mouth worried at her, he pinched her other nipple, and the jolt was so magnificently thrilling she felt it burn, hot and heady and spread like a web over her skin.

'Touch me,' she moaned. Bodily, blissful, she rubbed her thighs against one another, desperate for some stimulation to break the throbbing, but all she could muster was an unsatisfying tremble.

'*Non, non, non*,' he mumbled against her, trailing his kisses over her chest, before taking her other nipple into his mouth. 'I will not be rushed.'

Sucking, then scraping, alternating his breath between warm and cool, he lifted her to the precipice of a crescendo, then snatched her back from the edge. Her entire body blazed as he laved, occasionally mouthing over her ribs, to her stomach, once even shuffling himself low enough to tease his tongue at her slit before he worked his way up her body again. Vivianne hooked one ankle around his waist and angled into him. The slightest brush of his body sparked a moan. Arley circled her nipple again, faster, his pace rapid and unrelenting. A hum vibrated in her, and as he pinched harder, then nipped her with his teeth, she came completely undone. Her hips thrust at air, all sensation concentrating on her breasts, before exploding like glitter and stardust.

'*Baise-moi*,' she cried, desperate for his frantic thrusting and wanting to feel him pound and draw his satisfaction from her body.

He shuffled lower and positioned himself between her thighs. Vivianne tugged at the ties, hating their restraint but also savouring his satisfied glint. 'I told you, you will be greedy. A glutton. You will think of no one but yourself.'

With the same alacrity that he had plied at her breasts, he slid his tongue between her folds, circled her clitoris, then drew it into his mouth with a murmured word. *Take, take, take.*

How often she had heard that word—take. *Take* it, *take* me, *take* my cock, and they all said it like it was a gift, but they gave her nothing, only stole, manipulated, and demanded everything from her and left broken promises. She lay stripped and restrained in surrender as Arley worked at her with ferocity. His fingers dug into her hips as he raised her cunt a little higher and licked deeper. *Take.* She was nothing but a mass of her own bliss, and she rejoiced in her own desperation to feel and enjoy. Grasping the ties, she jerked into the bond. She was nothing but his and with an agony of realisation that shot as white hot and bold as the fantastic sensations pulsing and blinding her, that for all her life, her remaining days, her body would be for him and no other. He would own her completely, he would tend her, he would make her a mother, he would make her a wife, would make her his, and never again would she have to ply herself for a chance at happiness.

'Fuck me with your tongue,' she demanded. Arley groaned, then followed her command. She widened into his soft penetration, hooked one foot over his shoulder and drew him as close as she could.

'Yes,' she cried as she thrust her hips. The ties bit as her body hummed. 'Join me. I want to feel you. I want you inside me.'

He circled, he devoured, he shook his head.

'I want to share this with you.' Dropping her voice to a low growl, she levelled him with her gaze, and he paused, his little pants of breath igniting her. 'Your grace. Fuck your duchess.'

His eyes half closed. He gave her an insincere lick, then roared and shoved off his trousers. One hand slammed into the mattress beside her while the other reached above her head and tugged her bonds free. She clasped his back and raised herself to him. His cock filled her, and wet with his attentions, all she could do was push her nails into the softness of his shoulder blades as he thrust. Hard, reckless and pounding, he grasped a kiss and tipped back to howl as he pushed himself deeper. Vivianne drank in the sight of him, exquisitely lost in his rapture. She wrapped her legs about his waist and crossed them at the ankle to draw him as deep as she could, and held him as tight as possible, mesmerised by every flicker of life and beauty between them. Everything, she'd give him everything—her body for his pleasure, her womb for his heirs, her heart for his fulfilment, her lips for his conversation and his kisses. The world had set her adrift and failed her. Arley would give her port and anchorage.

His weight pressed as he collapsed. 'Everything is so simple with you. You are my refuge. My sanctuary. The world buzzes, but with you, I find only stillness. I cannot say it enough. I love you, Vivianne. I love you with everything I have.'

He rolled off her and tucked her into his side. She fell into his slowing breaths. He took a long inhalation, then steadied into the rhythm she remembered from their few days of freedom in Paris and on the boat. She twisted in his arms and watched his face settle into sleep. She unwound his cravat from her wrist. Brushed her thumb over his eyebrows until his stupid grin curved his lips. She took a breath of him and held him tight, then exhaled into abandon.

Of all the emotions that had plagued her life—fear, desire, aspiration, despair, fury and passion, were any as terrifyingly beautiful as love? She felt it through every extremity, yet it existed only in him. Her heart pounded with its energy, but she knew each thump only felt joyous because she believed that when he swore his heart was hers, he was sincere. When he came home, her cheeks tugged at the sound of his foot on the step, even before she heard his voice, and her heart flipped at the confirmation of his voice in the entrance.

She'd been hungry. She'd been lit and observed from every angle. She'd flung her body into a song, and she'd ricocheted against fear and want. She crouched as shots fired overhead. She was strong, like he said, but also tired. So tired. She nuzzled against his chest. Her palm sought his heartbeat, then rested as she found it. His heart would form the beat of her new dance and his rhythm would calibrate her days.

Her eyes grew heavy. Tomorrow, she'd try again. She'd work harder to be perfect. She'd do better than before.

CHAPTER
TWENTY-ONE

Arley woke with a stiff cock and an empty bed.

Eyes still closed, he patted at the mattress, searching for Vivianne, but when he sat up and cast about the room, every piece of her was gone. Her clothes no longer strewn across the floor, and her pins had been collected from his bedside table. There wasn't even an imprint on his mattress to show that she had slept beside him.

In the foyer, Cecil passed him his mail, pre-sorted he assumed, as there were only two letters.

Pemberton. He knew he should take it up to his study and not open his mail in the entrance, but this morning he felt reckless. He snapped the paste seal open and drew out the heavy parchment.

'I don't believe it. He's giving me his support.'

'Sorry, your grace?' Cecil asked.

'Pemberton. For the exchequer.' He scanned the letter.

We need more family minded men. Men focused on domestic simplicity. Those with calm heads and quiet homes.

The years of attending debates, late nights, reading mountains of reports, joining committees and filing papers, they'd all come to this. Everything he'd worked for, what he'd wanted to achieve, was in his grasp. He'd done it.

No, that wasn't quite true. With Vivianne's help, he'd done it. Love and legacy. He'd have them both.

'What are they?' Arley asked. He hadn't at first noticed the box on the sideboard.

'Letters, requests, invitations. The usual.' Cecil poked his finger through them.

'Put them on my desk,' Arley said with a dismissive wave.

'They are addressed to Lady Vivianne.' Cecil neatened the pile. 'If I may be so bold, your grace, she is proving quite the success.'

'She's not a lady,' Arley said as he craned a little to peer into the front sitting room. 'What is going on in there?'

'It's Friday. The Society for the Promotion of Civic Morality and the Adherence to Proper Values has its weekly meeting. As you are patron, Lady—I mean, Miss Chevalier—thought it might be advantageous for them to meet here from now on, in the hope it might reflect well on her. Perhaps on both of you.'

He sidled into the hallway and angled himself off centre from the arch, as discreet as a duke could be. He'd never been to a society meeting and hadn't imagined them so well attended. Mrs Crofts held court at the front of the group. One hand waved through the air, like a conductor, and the members nodded in time with each swish of her wrist. He could not hear all her words but he caught enough. *Larrakins. Propriety. Morality.*

Arley searched the sea of pastel day dresses, perfect, pinned up hair, and straight backs. It was only when he scanned the room a second time that he found Vivianne.

She sat regal. A duchess exemplified, almost indistinguishable from the other society ladies. She wore pink, like so many of them, with a lace collar that tickled her chin, hair braided into submission and her gloved hands tucked neatly in her lap. He watched her for the longest time, but she remained focused on Mrs Crofts, and did not adjust her posture or even flick her eyes in his direction. Occasionally, she nodded. Mrs Crofts was complaining about children who fed ducks in the park and shouted when they climbed trees. Likely some of the Hempel brood.

She'd worked, she'd learned and with a relieved beat of his heart, he felt that perhaps they could weather whatever storm Winton threatened to hurl at them. No one would believe she had ever been anything but a perfect duchess. They could deny all of it, or better again, ignore any bad press and refuse to acknowledge its existence. Who would believe his complacent bride had been a fiery ballerina? He caught her eye and gave her a half smile. She frowned, then shook her head and turned her attention back to Mrs Crofts.

Arley moved to the centre of the archway. 'May I steal Miss Chevalier for a moment?' he called.

Mrs Crofts gave a half bow. 'Anything you need, your grace.'

Vivianne scrunched her skirts. She stood and walked across the room, her head high with her eyes fixed on the carpet. When she reached him, she dropped into her perfect curtsy.

'Your grace?'

'What did you say to Pemberton last night?'

'He asked about our engagement and our meeting. I told him in Paris. I tried to remember everything you said, in my history...' She wrung her hands. 'What has happened?'

'Nothing. Well, something. He's giving me his support. You must have made an impression on him.'

'That is good?' No smile, no light, she trembled like a leaf.

'Yes, it's good. It's what I've wanted for years. And Winton won't dare to—'

'Shush, Arley. They are listening.'

So drawn into his own enthusiasm, he who had spent his life aware of how others watched him, he did not notice the slight dip in conversation in the sitting room, or the stare of so many sets of eyes. Perhaps it was because they were all focused on Vivianne, and not him. One woman leaned over and spoke in her neighbour's ear from behind a gloved hand.

'Would you like me to make some excuse for you? We could take a turn around the park together?' he asked.

'Not in this dress. I will need to change. Perhaps later, after the meeting? It is very important I attend them, don't you think?' She bobbed again, and before he could grasp her hand and draw her back, she had returned to her place on the settee, her eyes once more focused on Mrs Crofts.

A quiet discomfort settled on his shoulders. She'd transformed from a woman who watched no name painters for fun and made love in a train carriage to one who wore colours so fragile she wouldn't dare to leave the house and who attended meetings for a society that equated joy with sin.

Because he'd asked it of her. Demanded it of her.

A visage of his days rolled out before him, into a long, regimented line, falling into place one after the other like soldiers on parade. They'd spend the season in town. The summer at the estate. He'd be appointed to committees, work longer days. Father children he'd barely know and return home each day to a wife who curtsied her hello instead of kissing him on the cheek or throwing her arms around him as she squealed his name.

Arley pulled at his cravat. His finger snagged on his pin, the same topaz gem he'd used to bargain for her time.

He twisted his signet on his finger.

She had become the perfect duchess. Completely proper.

And for the first time in his life, he wished he was not a duke.

'I think you're being overly dramatic,' Phineas said. 'You could just buy a chateau over the Channel and have another holiday. Say you don't want the appointment. Retire.'

Arley flicked through a few of the neglected envelopes on his desk. 'Winton will never stop holding her past over us, and over Spencer and Co. The requests for favours won't end, here or in the country. Every day, every season, there will be more letters, more demands. Vivianne will be lost in them.'

'Have you asked her what she wants?'

Arley shook his head. 'That's the problem, I never did. I just assumed. And now, she's already bent. Because of me.' His mother had been a demure violet for so much of her life, and it had frustrated him that she'd taken so long to stand up for herself, and for him. But how could she be anything else when her husband was a pompous duke? How could Vivianne be authentic to who she was, when he relied on her to bolster his reputation, and to stretch the distance between his shortcomings and his dreams?

He'd worked so hard to be like his father. And now he was. Winton had not gotten everything. The old duke had left him this legacy too, and the realisation curled coldly in his gut. 'I'll ask her, but not here. It will have to be away from all this.'

'I still think—'

'My father was thirty-seven when he became duke.' Arley raised his voice a little. He was tired of arguing with the only man in London who was prepared to argue with him. 'He held the title for nine years before he passed. His uncle held it for twelve. Before him, my great-great-grandfather, had it for just three. Do you know how long I've had this privilege?'

Phineas didn't react. He knew everything.

'Twenty-seven years. From three weeks before my sixth birthday until today.' He twisted the ring on his finger in a full circle. 'I think I've been a duke for long enough.'

CHAPTER TWENTY-TWO

'I don't think I've ever seen a more lovely bride. As fresh as a lily.' Mrs Crofts preened to Vivianne's reflection in the mirror. 'The society pages will love describing the detail of your gown. It really is beautiful.'

It was a little more ruffled than Vivianne would have liked. She had taken Mrs Crofts to her dress fitting and followed her advice for making choices on colour and cut. Since hosting her society meeting in the sitting room of Number 10, Mrs Crofts accompanied her most places. Lorelei had decided that after Vivianne's success at the company launch, she was no longer in need of lessons, and with Arley so preoccupied with parliament, she'd been lost in what to do with herself.

In the whirlwind of preparations over the past week, she had barely seen her future husband. But then, with his pending appointment to his new position, that was the type of life she needed to prepare herself for.

Mrs Crofts stroked Vivianne's veil. 'I do not have daughters of my own, and as your own mother is...' She paused, presumably to allow Vivianne time to fill in the missing information.

'Absent,' Vivianne said, ignoring the pang of not knowing.

Mrs Crofts simpered, then took a hard breath. 'In the absence of your mother, I feel it is my duty to inform you about life after you are married. What will happen and such.'

Vivianne frowned. 'After the ceremony? There is breakfast, and a celebration, in the ballroom at Number 10.'

'After that.'

'Speeches?' Vivianne asked.

'*After that*,' Mrs Crofts said between tight teeth.

'*Oh*. Do you mean in the bed chamber? Once Arley is my husband, he will expect me to...' Vivianne swallowed down a small bubble of laughter. 'Do things, perhaps?'

'Do nothing,' Mrs Crofts said with a confiding confidence. 'My advice is always to just lie there and pray he is efficient. Wiggle a little if you'd like him to hurry things along. But not too much. You don't want to encourage any more visits than necessary.'

'Wiggle. I will remember that.' Vivianne tried not to smile, before a sadness settled in her. Was this her future? Discussing prim and proper behaviour with Mrs Crofts?

No, Arley was her future.

His Grace, Arley West, Duke Osborne, future Chancellor of the Exchequer.

Who was already too busy to see her.

Vivianne jumped as a knock bounded through the quiet townhouse. She rose and made her way down the layers of stairs to the front door, then climbed into the carriage.

The maid fussed to drape her train across the floor so that it didn't crush. When the footmen slammed the door shut, a little of the hem snagged.

She should feel joy, or lightness or even fear and trepidation. Vivianne stared down the door.

She felt nothing.

'My niece is coming to town, and I was so hoping you might meet with her,' Mrs Crofts said from the opposite side of the carriage. 'And would you perhaps sponsor her, to debut at court next season?'

'I would be delighted,' Vivianne said with a fixed smile.

That was six requests this week.

Heavy droplets of rain flecked the window. Vivianne pressed her forehead to the cool glass as they rattled through the street. Mrs Crofts babbled and gushed as they drove past a park. Vivianne scanned the lawn, but saw no hint of an easel, or lumbering swans, or couples diving for protection. Did the English ever dance in the rain? Or were they all too proper?

'It's a lovely drive to the church. I can't believe that so many people are watching.' Mrs Crofts looked out at the people moving about the streets as they went about their day. Workers adjusted hessian sacks on their back, while a woman leant over to scrub at a young girls face with the gentle, guiding touch of a mother. Even though the girl flinched, the mother persisted. A boy shouted the day's headlines, and the now familiar tension clenched Vivianne's muscles. Was she reported on today? If so, what did they think? What did they say? The articles felt so different from a review of the ballet, when the journalist commented on the scenery, the singers and the conductor. Now, it was just her alone in the spotlight.

'There's quite a crowd outside the church. Surely they aren't all invited? Some of them look a little… rough.'

'They look like people. They are just doing their best.' Vivianne clasped her hand to her mouth. *Mon Dieu* how had she let her anger slip? No doubt she would now be discussed amongst the members of the society.

A jumble of conversation from outside distracted Mrs Crofts from her disapproval. The door opened. Not people, or guests—they were journalists, with notepads clasped in their hands as they pressed forward in a bunch.

'What will you do now?'

'What was your last conversation?'

'Why have you still come to the church?'

'Where is Arley?' Vivianne pushed open the carriage door and leaned out, one hand resting on the ledge. 'He said he would walk me down the aisle.'

'You haven't heard?' one man called. 'There's been a terrible accident, on the river. His Grace was rowing when a storm rolled in as the tide changed. The police think his boat tipped. All they found was his oar.'

'*Non, non, non,*' she cried. Vivianne grasped at the air. 'Not Arley. No!' She wanted to sink to the ground and sob, but what thrummed in her ears was not Arley, but Lorelei's last lesson. *Hold everything inside. If you show emotion, they will not sympathise. You will only give them more to feast on. Let them peck. Give them nothing.*

Arley's friend, the banker who wasn't, caught her hand. 'Breathe, Vivianne,' he rasped in her ear. 'Send Mrs Crofts away. I'll take you to the river. You need to see what has happened for yourself.'

Vivianne lurched from the carriage before it had stopped moving. Thunder cracked overhead, and heavy pellets of rain slashed her face and thwacked loud against her satin ruffles. She rushed to the side of London Bridge and leaned over the balustrade, scanning the murky grey green swirling water for a hint of his hand, his coat, anything. 'Arley!' she screamed into the torrent. 'Don't leave me. Don't—'

'Vivianne,' a low gruff voice came from the dark beside her. A slip of a finger, a pinkie, hooked around her own. 'Say nothing. Just look at the river.'

Vivianne stared into the water, then tilted her head and took a slow, steady breath. Roses, lilies, snowbells. The unmistakable scent of an English garden.

'Your banker friend said you were gone,' she said, scarce believing he was beside her. She was mad, beyond mad, full of grief and confusion. 'He said—'

'People believe what they will if you lead them on enough,' he said with a laugh. 'Phineas would know. I don't have long. Vivianne, I am dead.'

Her heart snagged. 'I have lost my mind. I am speaking with a dead man.'

'It's a pretence. Catch the lie, Vivianne, you are smarter than this!'

'This is ridiculous,' she said. 'Like a farce or a—'

'Rambunctious opera? Yes, it is. It had to be. I knew you would not have agreed if I asked you. You would have given me the world and denied yourself everything.' He squeezed her little finger then drew it against his side. 'You are not the woman I fell in love with. You have become the type of woman that drove me into your arms.' Vivianne gasped as his words cut like a dagger. 'That's my fault,' he said in a rush. 'I demanded so much of you. Demanded you change. But you should laugh. Dance. Be free to be yourself. But you never will be, as long as you are married to a duke. You will always be in the spotlight, and under more observation than even I can imagine.'

She chanced a look. He wore his flat cap from Paris, an old coat she hadn't seen before, and his bright blue eyes were wide with fear and worry and love.

'You are pretending to die?' she asked. 'Why?'

'There's only one way to stop being a duke,' he explained. 'It is a job one can never resign from. Right now, Duke Osborne is dead. But so is Monsieur West. Only one of them can be revived. The duke could slip down to the river bank and make a miraculous return. We can go to the church and make our vows. Or I can slip away and resurface somewhere else as Monsieur West. Vivianne Chevalier...' He turned towards her, just a little. 'Who do you want to spend the rest of your days with?'

One body held two men, as different as stone and lime.

His Grace, the duke.

Monsieur West, the poor man.

The gowns, the stability, warm beds, soft mattresses. Oh, they were so luscious. Hot tea and someone to fix her hair and press her frills. The help was so nice.

But the eyes, the whispers, the constant stab of anxiety about being watched and on display tore at her sanity. And forever living in the public eye, with no curtain to drop and give any peace. Not even trusting the members of one's own household. Keeping everyone at arm's length. Not being able to see Nicole.

Wearing gloves all the time.

She would have dealt with it all if he asked her. She would grit, and suffer, and his happiness would be hers, and the snatched moments with him would be her delight, because even now, her heart threatened to explode with her love for him. But this man, this man of *Londres* was a facsimile of the man who had danced in the rain and charged her for kisses.

'I miss Monsieur West so very much,' she whispered, her voice catching.

She wanted to draw his body against hers. To place her hand on his cheek, to fold him against her and to kiss his lips. But she couldn't, because all the world was already watching. She squeezed his pinkie. He squeezed back.

He gave a smile that even in the uneven light sent her heart into an allegro. 'It will be a trial. In every way. Listen to Phineas. You are so strong. And never, ever doubt me. I will find you.'

He freed his grip from hers, and the shadow that he had cast was replaced with the bright lights from a passing ferry.

She shielded her eyes, blinking, but did not catch a flash of his retreating form.

'I never have,' she whispered.

CHAPTER TWENTY-THREE

'Blast and sod it,' Arley mumbled under his breath as he slipped into the study. It would take some time to get used to this coat. Fumbling in the dark, he found a drawer in the armoire, and dropped the embossed ducal ring inside. He'd meant to leave it before the day's escapade but had forgotten. It had been affixed to him for so long, he barely registered its weight on his finger. And while he could have tossed it into the Thames, the final shred of his sense of duty would not allow him to be so careless. He rubbed at the dint it left on his finger.

'You could have killed your mother with a stunt like that.'

A lamp flared into life as Arley spun. 'I was going to tell you. Phineas has a letter.'

She raised a brow. 'I do not want a letter. I want to hear the words from my son.'

Eyes puffed, but not red. She'd ceased crying some time ago, then. Slumped in his father's chair, wearing her nightclothes and a thick dressing gown, she looked as fierce as the day she'd found her voice, all those years before.

'How did you guess?' he asked. He and Phineas had been so careful, their plan so meticulous. Had they made some mistake that would see the entire thing come undone?

'There is no way my son would have made such a mistake. You are too cautious. Too much like your father.'

'Perhaps I am really impetuous. Perhaps I am more like you.'

'I have only been impetuous once.' Her jaw tightened and her lips pressed. Dampness glinted in her eyes. 'I suppose you are.'

Arley dropped the ring into the drawer and moved away from the cabinet. He clutched at the sleeves of his slightly ill-fitting coat. In his mind, he'd prepared himself for her absence from his life, but now the separation loomed, he felt as torn as when he'd seen Vivianne as the perfect duchess.

'It's a little melodramatic,' she said finally. 'People might miss you.'

'Those who might miss me will be told the truth. Any others will miss the connection to the title. They will not miss me.'

She pushed herself from her chair and stood before him. Barely reaching his collarbone, her eyes weighed full of her incredible sharpness, and wit. 'She's lovely Arley, but are you certain she's worth it?'

'I don't know,' he said, and his uncertainty sunk in him. It hadn't been that long, not really, and here he was, turning his back on the only life he had known. But he also knew that to say it was all for Vivianne would be a lie, because he also wanted the escape for himself. Wanted to be free of expectation, to walk in the sun without the trim of his hat being reported on, to be invisible. For that scarce week where he had been a nobody of Paris, how he had loved it. He wanted to meet this man he could have been, and there was only one way to be truly free. 'I hope so. But if not, well... at least I will have tried. I wish it didn't have to be so final, but there's no other way to stop being a duke.'

She grasped him so tight, his chest hurt, and choking down a half cry, he gripped her in return. 'Your father would be terribly disappointed in you,' she said.

'Probably about time he was, isn't it?'

One last embrace, and Arley left, not turning back as he reached the study door and not pausing as he slunk through his house like the stranger he longed to be. He moved through the kitchen and to the side door where Phineas was waiting with a carriage borrowed from Dalton, its crest faded from storage and neglect. So focused on the door, he didn't notice the shadowy form by the carriage house until he was almost on top of it.

'Cecil. What in heavens?'

He wore a dark travelling suit, and half bent to pick up a case by his feet. 'I heard you and Mr Babbage the other night. Ready when you are, your grace,' he whispered.

'You can't come. It's risky enough that Mother and Tillman guessed before I am even out of the drive, let alone London.'

'Please, your grace. I serve the duke. I cannot in good conscious serve a man I know isn't. The line going back is so vague, it could be anyone.' He leaned forward, his voice low and full of consternation. 'What if it's an American?'

'You can't just leave,' Arley hissed. 'People will miss you.'

'I told the staff I was retiring, on the wishes of the future duchess. A terrible lie, but it raised barely a peep.' Cecil gave him a sad smile. 'No one will miss me.'

'I would have.' The admission rolled off his tongue with dangerous speed yet was propelled by truth. Beyond his mother, Cecil had been the one constant in his life. Perhaps, he didn't need to leave every thread of himself behind. 'Get in then. But you can't keep calling me your grace.'

Arley hauled himself into the carriage, then held out his hand to help Cecil climb in after him. He pulled the door shut.

'What do I call you then? You can't be Mr West. People may figure it out.'

The carriage bumped as Phineas climbed onto the driver's seat. A click of his tongue, and they moved forward with a jolt. Arley picked up a folder that had been left on the seat beside him and flicked it open, his eyes squinting in the faint glow of the street lamps. He shook his head and gave a half laugh. 'It seems Phineas has already picked a name for me. For both of us.'

CHAPTER TWENTY-FOUR

In the days that followed, Vivianne remained a fussed over, if slightly diminished, guest of Mrs Crofts. A week after the wedding that wasn't, the investigative officers declared that her beloved's body had likely been dragged under a passing boat, been caught up in the currents, and taken to sea with the retreating tide. Witnesses were found who gave jumbled accounts of a man in a skiff rowing easily along the river, and how they had lost sight of him as a storm rolled in. The discovery of a shoe, and a torn bit of cravat, seemed to settle the whole thing.

After all, why would he pretend? What type of man did not want to be a duke?

'What happens now?' Vivianne sat in the sitting room of Number 10 with Lorelei. Dressed in black travelling clothes, the duchess remained as steady as she had been throughout all their lessons together.

'Tillman will hire genealogists to comb the family tree and begin the search. A host of pretenders will come forward. There will be investigations. Eventually, the man with the strongest claim will petition parliament and become the next duke.'

'I meant for you. The estate has been your home for a long time. You will have to leave?'

'Tillman is my home.' Lorelei spoke the gentle words with her usual abruptness. 'I've always wanted to live by the sea. Perhaps, once all this is settled, that's what we'll do.' Outside, wheels crunched on the gravel. Lorelei rose and embraced Vivianne briefly, before she stepped back, blinking fast. 'Stupid tears. One should never show emotion to those below...' Lorelei caught herself, then captured Vivianne in her arms again. 'But I suppose I can make you my exception.'

Vivianne followed Lorelei to the door. Tillman handed his wife into the carriage and then climbed in after. The driver pushed the door shut. Lorelei leaned out as they drove away, her voice almost lost to the horse's jingle. 'Tell him I said he is allowed to be happy. He deserves to be.'

The carriage rolled down the drive, turned onto Honeysuckle Street, then disappeared from sight. Vivianne turned back to the entrance, then paused. No Arley. No Cecil. There was nothing inside Number 10 for her. She could have called for the carriage, but that was the transport of a lady, and she couldn't summon the desire to play the pretence anymore.

And her boots would not wear themselves into comfort if she did not walk them in.

It really was a pretty driveway and a lovely villa with a beautiful garden. A hint of a branch from an ancient oak gestured from behind the tall sandstone columns. But overall, it was too set back from the neighbours, too distant from the people, for her taste, really.

The groundsman open a side gate, and Vivianne stepped out onto the street.

'He left you an allowance, didn't he? Made some kind of provision in his will?'

Vivianne spun and knocked hard into the fence. Winton, his hair a mess, his chin unshaved, stepped from the shadows.

Vivianne shook her head. 'Why would he? We were to be married.'

'But you must have had something. How did you get your dresses? Your shoes, and everything?'

'He looked after me,' she said. 'Not always in the right way, but in the best way he could. I am sure Lorelei will not leave you destitute. She will still pay your allowance—'

Winton ran his fingers over his scalp before he cried out in anguish. 'I don't want an allowance, I want my bloody share!' He looked up at her. 'You're lying. I'll go to the papers, I'll give them what I know. I'll sell your story.'

Part of her tore at this man's frustration, but she also railed against it. It wasn't fair, but when was life? The poor of Paris, the dancers, the *grisettes*, nothing about their life was fair. They did the best they could with the cards dealt by fate, and his hand may not have been as lucky as Arley's, but it was better than most.

Vivianne stamped her foot as her familiar fury bubbled and brewed. 'I may not be a lady, but you will not speak to me that way. I was a *grisette*. I survived the siege. I ran the barricades. And after all that, I managed your *Londres*. Do your worst, Monsieur West. I am not ashamed of my past. Perhaps you need to settle your debts with your own.'

And having nowhere else to go, Vivianne crossed the street and ascended the short set of stairs to Number 5, to the sanctuary still offered by Mrs Crofts.

Four days after Lorelei returned to the country, Winton followed through with his threat, and with a shake of a headline, Vivianne was once again a dancer of the Palais Garnier. Invisible informants claimed to have known all along, to have been her manager and arranged the meeting with the duke. And every report seemed to forget why he had even been there at all, as if she had tempted him from across the Channel. There was no mention of Spencer & Co.

That same morning, Vivianne upended her breakfast into her chamber pot for the third day in a row. Sitting in the parlour, waiting for her society members to arrive for their weekly meeting, Mrs Crofts' conversation became shallow, and direct. Her once sympathetic gaze hardened.

'You must miss Paris,' she finally said.

'*Non*,' Vivianne replied.

'You don't have any friends there you'd like to visit?'

A knock sounded at the door, and Vivianne rose from her seat. 'Thank you for your hospitality, Mrs Crofts. I will always be grateful.' Vivianne took up her small traveling case she had left in the hall and made her way to the door. Outside, on the street, a hack was waiting.

Mrs Crofts, her black skirts swishing, rushed to follow. 'You're leaving? Is that all you are taking? What about your wardrobe? Your belongings?'

'They belong to a duchess, which I am not and will never be. Sell them if you like. You can use the funds for your society.'

Vivianne kept her expression schooled as Mrs Crofts visibly squirmed with the prospect of injecting a substantial amount of money into her cause but accepting it from a decidedly immoral source. Vivianne left the matron of morality to her deliberations and stepped out of the town house. By the door, the grey cat with the white tipped tail gave a small mew. She held out her hand, and he balanced on his hind legs to brush his head against her.

'It was lovely to meet you, Monsieur Spencer. Please look after Arley's friends for him. I know he will miss them very much.'

Phineas accompanied her to the French coast, then set her on her way to Nantes.

'What will happen if he's ever found out?' she asked as they said their goodbyes.

He shrugged. 'It's never been done before. Or if it has, no one has been found out. It could be viewed as treason.'

'He could be tried? And imprisoned? Or even...' She couldn't even say the word. Arley faking his death had been torturous enough. The prospect of him actually being lost would break her. 'We shouldn't have done this. Perhaps...'

'It's too late now,' Phineas snapped. 'The only thing for it is to make the best of it.'

During her years in the capital, Paris had been altered so thoroughly that some days she struggled to remember how it had looked to her seventeen-year-old self, so it was with surprise that Vivianne found the village of her childhood—the fence lines, the stone cottages, the dress of the women—almost unchanged. It seemed incongruous that so much of the world had been in flux, yet the open paddocks that had been her first dance stage were the same as when she had been a barefoot child in love with the feeling of taking a musically inspired step.

Vivianne took a shaking breath and rapped on the rough wooden door.

She had skin a little more weathered than in her memory, a little darker from working in the sun, and a few more heavy wrinkles lined her eyes, but the woman who answered the door was unmistakably her mother.

Vivianne itched to rush into her arms, but her mother took a step back. She scanned her, from her toes to her head, her eyes lingering on her stomach. Vivianne raised a protective hand and rested it on the slight bump.

'You are with child?'

Vivianne could only nod.

'Your husband?'

'I don't have one.'

'I told you this would happen.'

All her emotions swirled, and through her tears, her relief, her fear and her joy, Vivianne scratched out, 'Yes, Maman, you were right. Shall I go now?'

'Is that Vivianne?' her father called from deep in the house, before he emerged from the shadows. He shoved Maman aside and grasped Vivianne by the waist, before swirling her in a tight circle. 'Louisa, it is Vivianne! She has come home!'

'Maman does not want me back,' Vivianne howled. She cried so often with the baby.

'Still with the melodrama, always with the melodrama. I did not say I would not have you back,' Maman sniped. 'I only said that I was right.' And with a strangled cry, her mother wrapped her arms around her and Papa both. 'Oh, my child. How I have missed you.'

The new routine of work, where her toughened hands were an asset, and not a mark against her, fell into an easy pattern. She helped with the laundry, walked the cows through the paddock, and when no one was looking, she stretched onto her toes and spun a pirouette. The movement made her nauseous, but she did it anyway. She watched the road for Arley, never seeing him, but trusting he would come. In the evenings, she sat by the fire and with Maman, darned socks.

'You cannot stay unmarried,' her mother said. 'It is not proper.'

'I have no wish to wed just because I am with child,' Vivianne replied.

'There is a man in town. Tall. He has started a school.' Maman snipped at a loose thread.

'I am not marrying any man—'

'*English*.' Her mother rolled her eyes. 'Not very useful. He is no good in the fields and cannot cook for himself. His father does everything for him. Smart at some things, stupid with others. If you roll with him, then tell him the baby is his, he will believe you.'

'Pardon?'

'I said, you can marry him. He will give your baby a name.'

'*Non*... did you say he is English?'

'I said you cannot be fussy.'

It couldn't be anyone else, but the following day, as Vivianne sat in the kitchen, scuffing the dirt floor beneath her sabots as she waited for the knock at the door, her heart flipped between rapidity and cessation. They'd been apart more than they'd been together, the world had spun out from beneath them with more speed than she'd had stamina for. Impulsiveness had driven so much of her life and ended so badly.

What if this was the same?

What if it wasn't him?

She was so lost in her worries, she did not register the tap at the door.

'Your visitor!' Her mother clapped her hands before her face. 'Take him into the orchard,' she whispered hoarsely. 'No one will see you there.'

Framed in the doorway, the summer sun streaking behind him, his hand tapped the side of his brown coat. He stood tall and stiff, with the same dignified air of a duke, even though he wore a neat town suit and well-worn shoes. He held a bunch of hastily gathered wildflowers. His hair had grown a little long, and his chin had a slight stubble—the afternoon growth of a man who shaved himself.

'My name is Mr Knight. I'm new in town. I brought you these.' He held out the flowers. 'Would you like a walk?'

Vivianne didn't dare speak until they were away from the house, over the small rise and out of sight of the cottage.

'Mr Knight?'

Arley laughed. 'Phineas's idea of a joke, I assume. But I think I asked you to change enough for me. It seemed to fit. And you?' His eyes wandered her body, and unmistakably lingered over her stomach and the small bulge of her growing belly, so obvious against her petite frame. 'How many months?'

'Maybe four. He kicks sometimes.'

'He?'

'I think so.'

A glimmer of delight flashed in his eyes, and he tapped his fist against his side, spending energy he could not otherwise show. 'I did not expect it so soon.'

'We did little to avoid it.'

'I suppose we didn't. We were very improper.' Then he laughed, his tone both familiar and fresh. It was not the measured laugh of Arley the duke, or the exuberance of

Monsieur West, but a new lightness. It was the laughter of a man in control of his destiny, and with all the freedom and fear that came with it.

His stiffness melted with the sun's embrace. He told her of his escape and how he had been smuggled first south, then across the Channel in the hold of a merchant vessel, before landing in Nice. From there, he had made the slow journey around the coastline.

'I took up rooms in town with Cecil. I've been teaching. Latin and Greek. Not much interest in English.' He chuckled. 'I'm finally putting those lessons from Oxford to use. And teaching children—it's incredibly satisfying.'

She told him of her life in the spotlight, the article when she'd become unravelled and her departure from Mrs Crofts.

He raised her hand to his lips and kissed her palm. 'Do you regret it? You could have been a duchess.'

'No, I couldn't.' She leant into his soft linen and slid her hands beneath his coat to gather about his waist, enjoying the awkward push of her stomach against him. She stroked at the centre line of his back and tugged his shirt tail from his trousers.

'Are you trying to seduce me?' he asked.

'I am. I need a father for my baby, and my mother says that if I bed the silly Englishman, he will believe me when I tell him the child is his and he will marry me.'

'So, everyone will think my child is not mine? Blood, and legacy, will mean nothing?'

'*Oui*. And they will think you a fool for being so easily manipulated.'

'What a fall from grace this is.' He laughed, then ran his hands down her back and nuzzled into her neck. He found her mouth and stole a kiss. 'Seduce me, country wench, then lie to me. I cannot wait to make you my wife.'

CHAPTER
TWENTY-FIVE

Meanwhile, back on Honeysuckle Street...

'He's not dead. He's happy. It says so, right here, in his letter. That's how I know. Because he wrote to us. From an undisclosed location. How else would I know?' Phineas pushed the note into the centre of the table.

It was the first meeting of Spencer and Co since the wedding that wasn't. Since Arley had pushed his skiff into the river and Phineas had taken the carriage out past the docks and thrown his oar in the water. Since the world had made a fuss for a moment, then sunk back into itself. Since with a disturbing accuracy, Arley's prediction that almost no one would miss him had been proved correct.

'It's incredibly irresponsible,' Lawrence said, his voice filling with his familiar stubbornness that he so often directed at Phineas. That he himself took pains to coax from the man. Lawrence leant across the table and snatched the note up, then read aloud.

Phineas has, I hoped, told you enough. I am sorry, my fellow board members and neighbours, to have deceived you. So much of my life has been one of pretence and putting on a show. Some days I could scarce remember where the reality ended, and the façade began.

Until I learnt that it is not the lies that matter, but who we tell them to. And I will live a life of lies so that those I love can be their honest selves.

I spent so much of my life watching you all. Your lives, your loves, your squabbles. Always an onlooker. Until that day last year when Hamish forced me to attend that meeting in the front parlour of Number 4, and it opened a new world. Camaraderie. Friendship. Frustration. What it means to be a neighbour. And while I did not at the time feel it for myself, I believed completely in Iris's sincerity when she said that travel was not only about discovering new places but discovering oneself.

I am finally ready to embark on my own adventure.

Sincerely,

A.

Lawrence pushed the note across the table, all his indignation gone. 'He fell in love.'

'With her mind,' said Elise.

'And her anger,' said Hamish.

'And her passion,' said Rosanna.

'And with life.' Phineas swallowed and blinked away a mist across his eyes. He would not cry. He never did. He took up the note and walked to the fireplace, then struck a match against the stone and leaned into the cold hearth. He held the flame against the corner of the letter until it caught, and the paper curled, then he dropped it into the grate as little yellow flames licked and ate the last shred of evidence. The A, with its small flourish, was the last drop of ink to be consumed.

The closest thing he'd had to a friend, gone.

'We should have stood by him,' Iris said, her voice only audible because of the depth of silence in the room. 'By both of them. As you all stood by me. Never again. From this point on, no matter the onslaught, we stand together.' Iris tapped the table with her pen. She turned to Elise. 'How many bookings do we have?'

Elise riffled through her papers. 'Some tours are selling well, others slow. The mini-grand tour is not quite half booked.'

'That's our point of difference. Our flagship. Less than half is not enough to break even. We'll have failed before we've begun.' Spencer nudged at Iris's leg, and she leant down and scratched his head. He arched and purred into her hand. 'A painter by the side of the Seine. Dancing in the gardens. Experiences to ignite a ready mind,' she mumbled under her breath. 'Elise, make a note. We will need to call the printer to have new brochures made. Let us find a way to put Miss Chevalier's Paris onto our tour.'

EPILOGUE

Two years later

Arley hoisted his son over his head and set him to rest on his shoulders. Addi gripped his knees against Arley's neck and scrunched a handful of hair in his palm. '*Papa. Papillion.*'

'Butterfly,' Arley said as the two of them watched its haphazard path through the air.

Addi tapped his cheek. '*Non, Papa. Papillion.*'

The boy would argue with him over anything.

He was entirely too much like his mother.

Arley balanced the canvas bag of bread and fruit on his hip and lay a steadying hand over Addi's feet as they walked down the street. The boy was getting stronger, and only gripped tight if they took a corner a little too fast. He had good balance and a sound posture. Arley was certain he'd be a good rower. Vivianne insisted he was made for the stage. Addi spent his days hitting things with sticks. Who of them would be correct about his destiny? Only time would tell.

After easing their way into their life together, they'd settled in Vannes. It was a town big enough that they could disappear into a type of anonymity, but small enough that the news and conversation of the outside did not penetrate to any great depth. And the double storied townhouses with their bright yellow, red and blue painted facades had reminded him a little of the row of identical townhouses, each with a different coloured door.

Town was busy today, full of the hubbub of early summer. Each year, more artists came to stay. Already some had set up their easels along the promenades looking over the sea, even though mostly, like the writers, they spent much of their time in the cafés talking about politics, philosophy, and how the world needed to change.

Arley braced an arm over Addi's legs as they jogged over the narrow road towards home. Addi squealed with joy and leaned over to tighten his hold against Arley's chin. Even now, the small, quaint, everyday moments of snatched delight caught him and squeezed his chest. He didn't think anyone had hoisted him on his shoulders to run across a road or walk through town. The lack of memory had no bitter bite to it though, because living it all for the first time with Addi, and with Vivianne, somehow made those moments sweeter.

While he'd left behind the life of a duke, there was no point adopting the life of a pauper. He'd brought enough capital in a mix of francs, expensive silks that were easily carried and sold, and small buttons and trinkets, so that he could gradually sell them off and build up enough savings to buy their own little place. Once settled and he was vaguely accepted as a member of the community, Arley had purchased a townhouse with three levels. One level with the studio, schoolroom and kitchen, the next level where they lived, and the top level where they slept. On hot evenings, they'd open the windows and the sea air, fresh and without a breath of soot, would rush in. Four bedrooms in a village this size was an impressive luxury. One for him and Vivianne, one for Cecil, one for the boys and one for the girls that would fill their life.

Although not as many children as Lawrence and Wilhelmenia had.

He didn't think so, anyway.

Arley ducked under the doorway into their home. He placed the bag on the stand by the door, before sticking his head into the small studio where Vivianne taught dance. She wore a slightly longer skirt these days, although the sight of her still flipped his insides. She clapped her hands to address the small ragtag group of mostly girls, and a few boys, who came to her to learn not only ballet, but any dance steps they desired.

'Do not be late next week, children. My friend Nicole is coming to show you how she twirls. She is a prima ballerina of the Palais Garnier. She will help you practise your positions at the bar.'

Vivianne skipped across the room, as light-footed as her departing charges, and kissed his cheek. 'You have a visitor.'

'Not a parent, is it?' he said with a groan. 'There is only so much I can teach their children if their children will not listen.'

'It is a parent, but not one that will give you grief.' She held out her arms, and Addi fell into her embrace with a gurgled laugh. 'Not that type of grief, anyway. They are in the kitchen. Cecil is making them tea.'

'Tea?' No one in the village drank tea, except for Cecil. They had to get it in for him each month, and it was ridiculously expensive.

Arley moved through the studio, into the narrow hallway, then pushed open the door to the little kitchen that faced into the small yard. Crisp and green, and full of tumbling boxes of vegetables and flowers, Vivianne and her mother had nurtured the courtyard until it flourished. A light breeze moved the leaves and twitched the curtains.

Arley took off his coat and batted at a patch of dust that had come off Addi's shoe. He had learnt it was best not to acknowledge the parents who came like this too early. It was better to make them wait a little.

With an apologetic mumble, Cecil appeared at his side and grasped the coat from his hands. 'I'll take this to the laundry for you, your grace. I mean, son. I mean...'

'It will be fine. It's only dust.' In odd moments, Cecil faltered into the rhythm of their former life. Arley did too. Arley would pass Cecil his hat, Cecil would sort the mail into nonsensical piles, or Arley would tap his cup when he wanted a refill of coffee. Then Vivianne would tease them, and they'd laugh, and settle into their seats. But today Cecil did not relent, and with a firm tug, half wrenched the coat from Arley's hands.

'It's no bother, your grace. I mean...' And with a shake of his head, Cecil fled the room.

'Hallo Arley. What type of crops do they plant through here? The soil seems dry. Do they hand hoe, or have tractors made their way—'

'Tillman. Now is not the time for farm talk.'

They must have come straight from however they had travelled, and possibly not even stopped into their accommodations to change, as his mother wore a dark blue dress with dust around its hems. The colours of a woman coming out of mourning. Shock, surprise, elation and guilt thumped at his chest as he was struck full with the realisation of the weight she must have carried for him.

'Mother, I'm so sorry. I never meant—'

She held up a silencing palm. 'The people in this village think Cecil is your father. And that your son is another man's child that you were tricked into believing is yours.'

He tried to hold the moment with seriousness, to explain what they had become and why but after so long away, with his duke voice long buried, it was too hard to muster, and instead he laughed. 'I am apparently very gullible when it comes to a pretty face.'

The door creaked open, and with a tumble of laughter, tears and little cries, the pretty face that had turned his world flittered into the room. Vivianne, still wearing her ballet costume, bent and rocked Lorelei in her arms until his mother, at first stiff, relented and returned the hug. Tillman tapped her awkwardly with a farmer's reserve, and Cecil sidled through the door. Vivianne took the kettle and lit the stove, chatting the entire time until she drew all of them into conversation.

Addi walked the room with his uneasy gait. He toddled around Arley, then with a curious trepidation, he walked to Lorelei and placed his little sticky hand on her knee. The chatter of the room lulled, as Arley's mother met his son.

'This is Addi.'

'He looks so much like you when you were this age.' His mother scooped him up and drew him onto her lap. Addi inspected her face, then poked at her cheek. He leaned back against her chest, instantly at ease. Lorelei blinked fast, and when she spoke, her voice cracked. 'Children know so much without knowing.'

'You aren't crying, are you.? It seems most improper to show emotion with others below your station.' A grin tugged at his lips, while Tillman tipped back his head and laughed. His mother pinned him, her face like thunder, before she too smirked. Addi tucked himself against her side, and she kissed him lightly on the top of his hair.

'I was always so busy when you were like this,' she finally whispered. 'So lost. And by the time I found myself, you were a man grown and didn't need me.'

'I did need you—'

'Not this type of need. It's different.' She stroked at a loose curl on the top of Addi's head. His eyes half closed, then his lashes brushed his soft cheeks as he relaxed into slumber. She shuffled in her seat to easier bear his weight, then cleared her throat. When she spoke, her vulnerability was gone, and she resumed the demeanour of a duchess. 'My husband and I have decided to spend our twilight years abroad. We tire of England. Too much rain. We have purchased a small cottage just out of town.'

'Just a cottage?' Arley asked.

'Fine then, a modest chateau. As a fellow *Anglais* abroad, we'd love to get to know you better. Come for tea. Bring your wife. Addi can play on the lawn.'

It still amazed Arley how quickly the conversation in a rough kitchen settled into comfort compared to the luxury of a parlour or formal sitting room. How Cecil easily took up the place at the stove watching the water boil so that Vivianne could pull down cups as she answered Tillman's questions about her vegetables and the rainfall. And how when Addi drooled over his mother's elbow, she simply tisked, and asked him for help, instead of excusing herself to change. Arley pulled his handkerchief from his pocket and leant over.

'The new duke?' he asked.

'Is settling in.' She shuffled Addi in his seat so that his head rested more firmly against her chest. She grasped her mug with a free hand. 'I am on strict orders to tell you no more than that. It will do you no good to know more than a teacher in a little French village should know.'

She was right of course. But he couldn't resist one last question.

'How is Phineas?'

She eyed him for a long breath. 'He's happy.'

'Happy? If you don't want to tell me, then don't, but there is no need to lie.'

She only smiled and raised her mug to her lips.

Over potatoes, onion soup, fresh bread and warm red wine, they gathered around the table. No one spoke of the past, and no one breathed a word about the future.

They only sat together in the profundity of now. Cecil made a terrible joke, and only Tillman laughed, their heavy clay goblets collided over and again, and the scrape of wooden spoons on mismatched plates filled the rare silences. Eventually, mother and Tillman left, both of them giggling as they bumbled their way down the path and into the street in search of the inn they had booked for the night. Cecil hoisted Addi onto his shoulder and pressed the back of his hand over his yawning mouth. 'I'll tuck him in, your grace,' he murmured as he made for the stairs. 'And I might sleep late tomorrow.'

Arley rubbed his heavy eyes. Vivianne took up his hand.

'*Non, non, non*, Monsieur. You are not escaping.' She raised his hand above her head and spun beneath his arm. 'Tonight, you will dance with me. Let us stretch the magic. We are in no rush to remember the world.'

She led, and he followed. Out the kitchen door, into the garden and beneath the full glow of the moon. She placed her hands on his shoulder, and he clasped her waist.

'I had a realisation today,' he said as they swayed into one another.

'*Oui*? What was it?'

'You only showed me five places in Paris. Garnier, Vendôme, your painter, *les Catacombes* and Luxembourg Gardens. You owe me two more.'

'You stole a kiss. You were a dreadful thief.'

'You stole from me first.' He nipped her ear. 'One, then. You owe me one more place.'

Vivianne leaned into him. She pressed the length of her body against him, and even now, he sighed into her gentle strength, her delicate ferocity, and her fragile robustness. She lay her palm against his cheek and scratched her work worn thumb over his lips. 'I could take you to heaven. Would that settle our debt?'

Arley grasped her, tipped her back into the dance, let her squeal wash over him then scooped her into his arms. She clung to his neck and kissed his lips, his ears and his cheeks.

'Heaven will get us half way there,' he said. 'First stop—a humble man's bed.'

THE END

Historical Note

A few years ago, I came across the story of Prince Czetwertinski, also known as Mr Jules. Prince Czetwertinski was a member of one of the oldest families in Russian Poland. Under an alias, he served with the Turkish Army in the Russo-Turkish War (1877-1878) and fought with distinction at Plevna. At the Battle of Pelischat, his horse (a magnificent black stallion that only he could ride) was shot out from under him. In the ensuing annexations of territory, his property near Odessa was confiscated. Finding himself without any type of long-term income, Czetwertinski did the logical thing—he begged, borrowed and pulled together all his savings, amounting to about £3000, went to Monte Carlo and within 3 days lost the lot.

From here, he became a sailor, and eventually came to Australia, where under the alias of Mr Jules, he taught French to the children of families on outback stations and later worked at Xavier College in Melbourne. His extraordinary exploits took him through Queensland, Sydney, from big wins at the Flemington races through to near starvation. He returned to Europe to resume his duties as a prince but could not manage the cost, and so eventually returned to Australia. Again using his alias, he set up a school in a little place called Wagga Wagga, where he was extremely successful and well respected. He never revealed his true identity. It was only after he caught pneumonia and died that his story became known to the people of the town where he lived. He is buried in the Wagga Wagga cemetery.

I found it impossible to shake the story, and the multiple facets to it. Of a world of extraordinary connection where people traversed the globe like never before, but also a disconnected world where it was possible to simply drawing a line and start over with a new identity. Of the upheaval of the old ruling classes in Europe, and the rise of the middle and lower classes that changed the power base and prestige of the aristocracy. And while Prince Czetwertinski/Mr Jules seems to have made his choices for financial reasons, I wanted to explore the idea of a noble who gave up everything to become a nobody for love, and in a historical romance, who better to give it all away than a duke.

I've always been more fascinated by the 'in-between' periods of history rather than the great moments themselves. Arley and Vivianne walk through a Paris on the cusp of a new era, at the dawn of *Belle Epoque* (the beautiful age). The scaffolding that marks the city is a combination of building works being completed as part of Haussman's colossal urban design project, as begun under Napoleon III, and rebuilding parts of the city that had been destroyed during the Siege of Paris and later during the brief but bloody Commune government and the following suppression. I did my best to find if a street or location was completed or still under construction at the time Vivianne and Arley were walking along it. Apologies for any errors.

Sous (as making up a French livre) stopped being used as an official currency in 1794 (Year II) during the Republic following the first French Revolution. French currency has its own long and tumultuous history that I won't go into detail on here, except to say that by 1876, the official currency of France was the Franc, but the word *sous* remained in common use. In a similar way to how in Australia we still use old idioms invoking pennies and pounds, even though dollars and cents have been the official currency since 1966, the word *sous* was (and still is) used as a colloquialism, particularly when describing hard circumstances and poverty. It seemed obvious to me that Vivianne would use *sous* as naturally as she talks about millimetres.

Given its busyness as a port, I was surprised to learn when researching the history of rowing that the Thames was used by sportsmen and amateurs in the late nineteenth century. Before clubs formed, many rowers made arrangements with publicans and warehouse owners to store their boats and lease a room to change in before and after a jaunt on the water. For many years, the Lambeth launch, directly across from the houses of parliament, was used as a launching spot, along with other access points. By 1876 when we see Arley rowing on the Thames, many clubs were formalising their memberships and building clubrooms further along the river, in quieter (and more affluent) areas like Mortlake and Richmond. The Ilex Rowing Club was active from 1846 until about 1880 and rarely engaged in formal competitions. The prerequisite for membership was being a graduate of Oxford or Cambridge.

Honeysuckle Street is not, and to the best of my knowledge, has never been a real street in London. It is drawn from the rhythm of life of the time in which I write. Modern townhouses that cater to the burgeoning middle classes line one side of the street, while older houses line the other. Dukes and earls live alongside merchants, traders, and other members of the upper crust. It is a street depicting a world in limbo, constantly changing and evolving.

A Song and a Snowflake

Before Vivianne and Arley came to Honeysuckle Street, there was Charlise and Sinclair...

A woman seeking redemption at the end of a church aisle...

Beautiful songbird Charlise Hartright is ruined.

Introverted, shy and grieving her mother's loss, she would do anything to restore the family name, even commit to a loveless match, if it means her beloved sister Elise will have a chance at finding her own happiness.

A man out to make his own name...

Sinclair McIntyre has travelled halfway across the world to pursue of his own destiny. Tired of being in the shadow of his older brothers, he is determined to do things his own way to become an independent, self-made man.

A future laid out before each of them...

But with a song

And a snowflake

Everything will change.

A Song and a Snowflake is a story of chance meeting, the power of connection and sisterly love. It tells the story

ALIVIA FLEUR

of the scandal caused by Elise's older sister, and how Elise came to live with her aunt on Honeysuckle Street. Sign up to my newsletter An Old Fashioned Quickie to receive your FREE copy.

Undercover with the Heiress

Rosanna Hempel has the world at her feet.

She is a darling of London society. She has a father who is training her to take over the family empire. And she has the eye of a charming young man who will make her a lady.

What more could a young woman want? Her life is perfection.

Until she is compromised in the park, and the man who promised her everything flees, and the only person willing to help her is none other than her father's nemesis, Phineas Babbage.

Phineas Babbage has no interest in a wife.

In a family.

In living another 5 minutes more on Honeysuckle Street.

He has plans to tie up loose ends, flee this wretched city and start anew. Until, in a moment of weakness, he finds himself pledged to none other than Rosanna Hempel, and she becomes both his salvation and his condemnation.

With her help, he can find the truth about what happened to the woman he loved.

Yet her help makes him want to scream at the sky.

Her ferocity makes his skin tingle. Her obtuseness is a delectable challenge.

Rosanna cannot stand the sight of the beige man next door who is obsessed with margins.

Until he is gone, and then he is all she can think of.

Can the two of them find some common ground? Can they set aside their differences for long enough to solve the mystery, annul their sham marriage, and get on with their own separate lives?

Because that's what they both want.

Obviously.

Undercover with the Heiress is *book 3 in the* Tales from Honeysuckle Street *series. All books in the series are loosely connected standalone reads. With a guaranteed HEA,* Undercover with the Heiress *is a story of love lost, family and redemption. It features HOT open door intimacy. It includes strong language and sexy times.*

This novel contains themes of loss and death that some audiences may find confronting.

Releasing November 2024.

Acnowledgements

Thank you, dear reader, for the time you have spent reading my stories. As I am at the end of another book baby—my second big book, and my eighth idea that I have taken from spark to publication, I really feel that in this story, something has shifted in my outlook. At the end of this, I feel more confident about myself, my vision for this ragtag bundle of characters, and of the stories I want to bring into the world. And that is in no small part due to the kindness and encouragement of my beautiful readers. Thank you, all of you. To those who read, to those who review, to those who picked up a freebie or a discount, to those who wrote to me with your own stories of love, art, travel and especially to those who sent me photos of your chickens. I adore chatting with you all. It is your quiet DMs and emails that sustain me more than any other accolade. Reading has always been an intimate part of my life, and to share my words and find they resonate with you means the world to me.

Thank you to my long-suffering editor Gabby, who somehow helped me piece together this thing here, and to offer a guiding hand even though I am rubbish at speech tags.

To the fabulous Louise Mayberry who beta read whatever that thing was that I sent her and cheered me on despite its incoherence, and to everything else in between.

To Rachel, thank you for being a tireless sounding board even when I'm so wound up, I make myself stupid. The award for best pep talk of 2023 goes to you—I've got a screen shot saved of it and pull it up on crappy days. You're a rock star.

To Alexandra, for checking my French. I claim any errors as my own. And thank you for being a wonderfully kind and encouraging supporter of indie histroms. You're a treasure to so many of us. Thank you for taking a chance on my little Tryst and for taking the time to say hello.

To the beautiful, incredibly funny and gobsmackingly talented authors I hang out with in the Society of Smut and Scandal. Thank you for your support of me, but also of each other. Being a part of a community as we fumble through our stories (or I fumble, some of you are hella organised) is a delight. I love travelling space and time with you all.

As always, to Mr Fleur. Thank you for always finding something to get at Bunnings when I need to get out of the house for just a little bit. You are my everything.

And to the skin dogs. Stay weird.

About Alivia

Hi! My name is Alivia, and I write steamy romance for history lovers.

I started writing romance in 2022. At first I wanted to write short stories, but then my characters kept turning up with copious amounts of back story, demanding I help them solve their problems! In April, 2023, I published my first novel, *A Beginner's Guide to Scandal,* the first in my series, Tales from Honeysuckle Street.

My novella, *The Portrait Sitting*, is a Romance Writers of Australia RUBY award winning story.

I live on a farm a long way from anywhere interesting, with my husband, our three dogs, and a charismatic chicken named Persephone.

You can learn more about me, my stories and upcoming releases at aliviafleur.com

www.ingramcontent.com/pod-product-compliance
Lightning Source LLC
Chambersburg PA
CBHW030655260626
47157CB00007B/2655